Trapped in Time:
Book 1 in The Carrington's Trilogy

Written by Sarah Eaton

[Other titles, written by the author;]

Book 2 in The Carrington's Trilogy is called Captured in Time.

Book 3 in The Carrington's Trilogy is called Released in Time.

Dedicated to my family,

- Thank you for your support.

Love you always.

<Published by Sarah Eaton>

<In 2014>

[Style = Copyright]

Copyright © <2014> by <Sarah Eaton>

First Printing: <2014> <Australia>

ISBN <978-0-9941626-0-1>

<Sarah Eaton >
<4/4 Allara Ave,>
<Palm Beach>, <QLD> <4221><Australia>

www.facebook.com/profile.php?id=100007098812148

Ordering Information:
Special discounts are available on quantity purchases by corporations, associations, educators, and others. For details, contact the publisher at the above listed address.

U.S. trade bookstores and wholesalers: Please contact < Sarah Eaton>< Tel (Intl 061)07 5520 2332 or email <saraheatonauthor@gmail.com>.

Chapter 1

"Nat, where've Chris and Ben got to now, in their exotic world travels?" my best friend Trish tidies her things, into her small tan, leather rucksack, slinging it, hard, over her shoulder of her black leather motorcycle jacket making it slap. She was putting her long blonde hair into a bunch. Getting ready to leave her desk, where she works as a secretary, in the lawyer's office, where we both work. *She's always very keen on news of Chris, my only and younger brother; they went out for 2 years, after they left school, 4 years ago I think she still lusts after his body,*

"Last time I heard through mum, they were still pub crawling round Ireland. That must have been, 2 weeks ago now. They've almost certainly moved on to the English ones by now. Chris and Ben are having an absolute ball!" I quickly cleared my legal files off my fairly new, black melamine computer desk. I'd put my desk in such a way, making it seem like I had my own office, even though I shared with Trish Townsend and one other secretary Donna Smee. *I think sometimes, I just wanted to, close all the doors and end it all. I'm glad that I have someone to talk to, I suppose,* with tear filled eyes, I put the files into my grey filing cabinets, noisily sliding them shut. I brushed my long wavy blonde hair, in the large, oval, mirror on the wall. Put some of my favorite 'Berry Kiss' lipstick on, my pale face and checked my mascara was OK. I checked my black dress; I'd been wearing all day, looked OK my new black handbag I just bought at lunchtime. I glanced eagerly at the seemingly slow hands, on the black wall clock in our room moving towards 5pm. I was so excited, seeing my sister Rosie, for drinks at 5.15pm. We have been trying to catch up, in person for a few weeks now. Rosie Hungerford changed her name to Tilbury. a year ago, marrying her high school sweetheart Sebastian. Then 5 months ago, they bought a hugely successful, detective agency, now called Tilbury Detective's, I'm supposed to meet Rosie outside the prestigious red brick offices of Rumble and Smith' Lawyers in the High St where I've worked for over 4, mostly happy years. I flew through reception, out the open stained glass front door. I breathe in the warmness of the spring air, which I love. I jumped eagerly, down the wide stone step onto the slightly busy sidewalk. Thud! I knocked down a girl with joggers and grey track pants on. Who gave me the evil eye, as she picks her skinny body up from the dry bur hard sidewalk. Her blonde hair tied into a bun, in her twenties. Turning, I mouth 'Sorry': to her, and luckily she runs off. *What an ass, it's so embarrassing.* Looking up, elderly Charles Rumble, my boss is knocking on his office window, asking if I'm Ok .*Shit.*

"Just like you, you are so clumsy Nat, that's set me up, with something to tell the others, at the pub tonight" Trish couldn't stop herself from laughing.

"Have a good weekend Trish, text me and we'll go out tomorrow if you like.

"Don't have anything planned as yet." Still trying to control her giggles, putting her red helmet on, she jumped onto her beloved black Ducati Monster and loudly, roared off into the distance, leaving me still waving.*bye.* I smiled. My iphone rings, Rosie's picture comes up.

Uh oh "Hi Nat, You're not going to believe this. I'm so sorry we've got a rush job, that's literally just come in. Sebastian has begged me to help him. I'll only be a couple of hours at the very most. Do you still want to meet me at Moo Moo Café, or leave it altogether for tonight?"

"I haven't seen much of you, since you married Sebastian. I'll wait at Moo Moo Café. Please just, try to get there as soon as you can Rosie." My excitement waned slightly, as I slid my skinny body, into my old dark green Saab convertible. I drove as slowly as I could, alone. *Shit! She'd better not be too long.*

Moo Moo Café is almost brand new, café and restaurant, that we'd yet to christen, tonight's the night Wow*!* Through the quiet, electric glass entry doors, inside its bright, modern, sleek, design, allures and invites me in. Going towards the long black marble bar, beautiful clear glass block walls, hanging like starry pictures behind the bar.. It's getting full of people, who've come, obviously by their attire, straight from work. I'll remember this place for next time, we all go out.

"What would you like?" The young, sexy, tanned barman asks, as I perch, on the hard, silver, round barstool, attached to the white marble floor.

"Sweet red wine pleases, what house red do you have?"He put a taster in a glass, I sip it and nod and he fills a new glass. *mmm sweet nectar.*

"Are there any more tables anywhere?, these are all full," glancing around at the chattering throng, enthralled in their lively conversation with one another.

"Normal Friday night, it will clear out a bit soon, people going home, after work pop in here for one drink." He assures me. *I'll find a table then. I* sipped my wine, gazing at the true beauty and color of the place. Sparkling like new, with the bright blue halogen down lights, dancing like blue rain from the ceiling. *I love it.* Turning my barstool, so I could put glass on the counter, Someone *fuck* touched my shoulder, and up my full wine glass slowly left my hand, into the air the glass caught by the agile young barman with a silly grin on his face. And red wine landed, in the barwoman's, now ugly, dark red, streaked, blonde hair.

"Shit" she was toweling herself down, with a bar runner saying 'Moo Moo Café.

'Sorry,' I mouthed to her, and turned to face the perpetrator.

"Wow, sorry, didn't mean to surprise you like that" a slow, deep, sexy, man's voice came from behind me.

"Just wanted to know if you'd mind if I sit on the seat next to you?" A dark suited man approached me. I moved my gaze up about to tell him about Rosie *oh my – Wow, fuck me,* beautiful, gorgeous, glinting baby blue eyes, staring at me. Thick, shoulder length dark brown sun kissed hair. I was out for the count.

"Yes… of… course" I stuttered, smiling. *Rosie won't be here for hours.*

"Bourbon please, and whatever the young lady would like to replace the one she just threw away?' He had an accent, of some kind; he smiled, and was oozing confidence and so self assured. The barman smiled and poured his bourbon.

"I'm Marcus, would you like another wine? His voice was dark, erotic and tempting me, to think in ways, I haven't for years *Get a grip Nat.*

"Yes, same red again please, I looked at the grinning, barman. I'm Natalie" Our eyes met, and I could barely, release myself, like some powerful force of nature, holding them there.

"Have you been to Moo Moo before?" His gaze on me continued, bearing deep into my soul.

"My sister Rosie and I were going to come here, when it first opened last year but she, was too busy, running a new Detective Agency business they just bought. She is coming much later tonight." My eyes still glued to his, taking in his incredibly sexy, manly, aura and hint of aftershave.

"Look, if it's ok with you Natalie, a table's come free, we can sit there instead?'

Nodding, I stand, and eagerly follow his well built, taller than, my medium build, muscled beautiful, sexy body, to the low glass table and bright orange sofa next to it. He took my drink, *possibly to make sure it gets there*, and puts it on the table. He moves out of the way, so I can sit on the comfortable low sofa, and then slides in beside me. *I can't say a word, what the fuck is happening to me.* He takes his well cut black jacket off, and puts it beside him. His open neck, white linen shirt, revealing his toned, slightly tanned, dark brown hairy body beneath. *Oh shit, he's so close to me. I can smell him, I'm unusually dumb struck.* Electric thrills run through my horny sex-starved body, as his knee accidentally touches mine. He smiles at me, as I sip my wine.

"Do you live around here?" His blue eyes attached to mine again.

"Yes, not far from here. I share an apartment with a friend that I've known for years, Andy."

"Is he your boyfriend?" He gazed at me, as I put my drink, on the table.

"No, nothing like that, he and I have been friends and flat mates for 2 years. *I think of the slob that Andy is sometimes,* He's just not my type. I don't have a boyfriend, at the moment. What about you, do you live and work around here?"My hopefulness was perhaps too obvious as I sipped my drink.

"I live mainly in L.A but sometimes around this area too. My family business owns some shops that I, mainly run now, my parents are only working it part time" He was obviously proud of them. *I want to bear your children.*

"Are you married, any kids?" *This is what I really want to know, get straight to the point Nat. He wasn't wearing any wedding ring on his long slender sexy slightly hairy fingers. He's in his early thirties.*

"Neither, *my pussy is red hot, not sure if I do want to get married or have kids.*" *I can do that. Just want sex with you, right now, no kids, great, just you and me.* His sexy slightly tanned, hand gently stroked, the rim, of his glass, sipping briskly some bourbon.

"Are you here on business today Marcus." *Saying his name sounds like he belongs to me and we're on a date - I fucking, wish.*

"I've been here all week, doing some business with local suppliers, I didn't realize it was going to turn into pleasure, at the end of It all" He smiles, as he turns, towards me, my insides melt, and I smile back.

"Would you like another wine or something else?" He rises

"Let me pay, this time please." He declines.

"Could I have a mineral water with ice please Marcus?" He nods and smiles at me as he stands, leaving his sexy, aftershave for me to smell and gape at his sexy, tall, well proportioned, lean body. In his well cut black pants, and sexy see through white linen shirt, and shiny black shoes.

Nipping to the ladies, I redo my lipstick, blush and powder, in the huge wall mirror dimly lit by globes, all around it. Feeling like a star, as I do it. My face is flushed, *Simply can't believe my luck, Marcus is truly a man of my dreams.* Glancing at my watch, it's 6.35pm. *Rosie will be here anytime now. Shit, bugger.* I felt disappointed, as I took a last look at my face. .I swung sexily through the ladies door, because that's how I felt. .Marcus is back at our table. He has a small light beer and my mineral water already on the table. *He's oozing man smell, I love it.*

"Thanks again Marcus. I'm very grateful."

"It's my pleasure Natalie." He clinks glasses with mine, and leans his other arm on the back of the sofa behind me. *Oh my god!*

"I have to drive back to L.A, after this one" H*e really is going soon, please ask me out Marcus, please.*

"What type of work do you do, Natalie?' He picks his beer up and drinks a few gulps of it, nearly finishing it. *Fuck, how can*

I make you stay longer, I want to lick, your body, your cock, have you fuck me all night, Marcus.

"I'm a Paralegal. I do lots of legal document work. I work in a lawyer's office here in town." I am proud of my ongoing achievements. He nods.

"What time is your sister getting here?" He picks up his jacket and puts it back on. I glance at my gold, watch my Mum gave me last Christmas, it's nearly 7pm

"Anytime now" An unexpected sigh, leaves my body as I spot my sister Rosie's short slightly rounded body coming in through the electric glass doors, seeing me makes her way towards us.

"Leave you alone, for two hours, and you find yourself a man" She gazes at Marcus,

"Marcus, this is my younger sister Rosie." He takes her hand to shake.

"Pleasure to meet you, but I really must go now." He gazes, at me and I'm sad now he is going. Standing he puts his strong, sexy hand on my shoulder and keeps it there. Strong thrills run though me like, hot, steamy, orgasmic sex.

"Thanks for being such lovely company tonight. It's been great I feel so relaxed around you. Have a great night with Rosie. Goodnight Rosie" He nods his head, and releases his grip on me. *Please turn round and ask me out, right now. I have such an insatiable, urge, to hold on to you, and have sex with you like we are soul mates.* He walks with a quiet confidence, of a person in charge. Outside, I clearly see him through the clear glass floor to ceiling walls. He pushes the remote on his keys, and gets into a bright red sexy low to the ground car, pretty sure it's a Ferrari Italia, and my brother sings their praises. Marcus roars off. *Shit he's very very rich.*

"Earth to Natalie, earth to Natalie. He was super gorgeous, where did you find him?" Rosie takes his place on the double sofa. *Oh shit he really has gone.* I sipped my mineral water, clutching hold of it like it was a beautiful present from him. Then I went over every little thing that happened, in the last two most wonderful; thrilling hours of my life, that went so quickly. *I feel like a part of me is missing I missed his company that was clear. But he has gone now; I can't hear him turning his car around coming back to me. I must get used to that.*

Rosie orders red wine and a Dr Pepper, and looks around for the menu and brings it to the table.

"I'm so sorry about tonight, I really am. I did think you'd be here all alone, so I did text you earlier, but got no reply" She sipped her drink.

"Sorry, I didn't hear my phone go off" I bring out my iphone, from my handbag. Sorry must have been otherwise engaged." A wicked grin, releases itself on my face, causing me to remember Marcus's presence here. .

"You like him, don't you?" She smiles.

"Yes, I do" I admit. *I haven't felt sexual feelings for anyone, ever, like I have for you Marcus.*

"Shall we eat now? Let's see the menu, just bar snacks.

"I'll have a chicken salad" I'm famished and getting a little drunk I realize.

"I'll go and order and pay, I owe you that Nat, no discussion. as she heads off to the bar. My strong willed sister, it's great to see her again, I've missed her. My thoughts go back to Mr. Perfect. *Marcus I think I've fallen for you so deeply. I wish you'd asked me out, perhaps he'll come back later, I'll stay here, as long as I can. Just keep, remembering, your beautiful, sexy, blue eyes. I love the way your hair gently skimmed, your erotic transparent white linen shirt, moving against your skin, as you did. Your hard, muscled chest, rising and falling as you breathe.* Rosie sets our drinks on the table, the noise disrupts my erotica.

"How's Sebastian?" I'm amused at my random thoughts.

"Working all the hours, our business is open plus more. I just want him to slow down, but he does enjoy, being the

Detective." I imagine Sebastian's small frame with a huge Sherlock Holmes hat on his ginger brown hair and big grey raincoat holding a spy glass makes me smile.

"He's working all the hours, before I stop working next year." She looks at her belly.

"Oh my god, you're pregnant?" I'm so surprised.

"Yes, due in February. Sebastian is so happy and, into everything baby.

"What about you, happy about it?" I hug her, briefly.

"At first, I was so shocked. I was taking the pill still, and just took some meds for a pain I had. Dr Ramsin thinks the meds made the pill ineffective. I'm so happy, now about my baby." She recalls.

"Boy or girl?"

"I can find out soon, but I prefer not to. Sebastian wants to know. Just want my baby to be healthy." She rubs her tummy.

"You're going to be a great Mum"

"Hope so" She beams a bright smile.

"Ladies your food" The waiter puts, huge modern square white plates on the glass table, then places our, cutlery wrapped in a red paper napkin, next to them.

"Well congratulations, to you both, sorry 3 of you. I'm still shocked. And we clink glasses. Have you told mum and Al yet?"

"Yes last week we went over to West Hollywood, have dinner with them, and told them. They were both so happy and thrilled for us." I remember, mum and my step dad Al Wheeler, getting together about 5 years ago now. My mum had led a pretty lonely, existence when we all moved out. Mum hadn't looked at anyone since my dad died in a car accident, when I was 15, and Rosie was 11, Chris was10. I felt pleased that mum fell in love and married Al, who is a writer of many novels. He is so kind to mum and all of us.

"I'm glad you went to see them, are they both ok?

"Yes both very happy, and in love. Al has just finished another novel, so they are going to his publishers in L.A for its release, next week.." Rosie loved him as a dad, like I did, proud of his achievements. As we finished our food, we said our goodbyes. I was truly glad I'd decided to wait for Rosie tonight. Learning all about my new niece or nephew has been awesome. And I hadn't forgotten my erotic encounter earlier

with my sex god. *I have to see Marcus again; he's my way out of my problems, I know he is.*

Chapter 2

A week later, Marcus still has made no contact with me. The last 7 days and nights have been like hell. On the Saturday morning after seeing Marcus, was my first sleepless night. I came to, pulling my heavy tiger skin quilt off me making me even hotter. All night, I'd been thinking of all the ways, Marcus and I could have mind fucking sex. I was totally worn out just thinking about it. *If Marcus came to the door right now, I'd have a mind blowing orgasm, just looking at him, not like me at all.* Grabbing the wooden bed post for support, my feet landed on the cold, white tiled floor. *Ouch, that hurts.* I'd kicked my alarm clock radio, on to the floor somehow, it was blinking at me. I went to the thick, dark blue curtains and peered outside. It was daylight, I closed them again to keep the bright light out. Felt like 99, not 29, I was so worn out. Slowly opening my white wooden bedroom door, I glanced at the clock on the microwave. 11.15am *Wow perhaps I did get some sleep after all.* The white lounge room of our rented apartment was quite huge. I lay, gently, on my huge comfortable flowered sofa.

"Andy, are you here?"

"Wow! Sleeping beauty has woken up did you get drunk?" Andy's blue eyed short black haired head, bounced quickly, upside down in front of mine. He moved his tall, thin, body towards the kitchen. He was wearing blue jeans and a plain, white T shirt,

"No, I was driving. Just lack of sleep, over man" I yawn.

"You have a boyfriend, are sure you're ready?" He sounded quite shocked and concerned at the same time. *Maybe the fact that I haven't been on a proper date, since I was attacked almost 2 years ago. Just not being ready and putting men off*

completely, without any explanation to them.

"Make me a coffee and I'll tell you everything" I moved slowly towards the black melamine breakfast bar. After I recounted all of the disasters and joys, of yesterday, I sipped my favorite blue Kombi mug that he gave me, as I talked.

"I'll make you a late breakfast? What would you like, you had a crap day." He was a good friend.

"Just a couple of whole meal toast and peanut butter please Andy, thanks for that"

"So now what, are you going to do? You think you'll see Marcus again?" He put the 2 slices of bread into our red toaster.

"Oh I hope so." I was feeling much better now. I sat and finished my toast and coffee. I put my stuff in the dishwasher. I smiled at him, as I went to my bedroom to get changed and get up.

I sat on our balcony off the lounge room, with my laptop and wireless broadband. I'd made just me, another coffee, as Andy was off to work soon. I waited for it to start up, thinking about sex god again *he was just the best looking man that I'd ever come across. Titillating my senses, thinking of him made me feel so fucking, horny, I felt wet already, no man's ever, done that to me, before or after my attack. Certainly, I seemed ready to move forward and see myself having a relationship with Marcus only, and Marcus alone. He made me feel so erotic and sexy, just him. I have to find him.* I typed 'Marcus Los Angeles'' into Google, thinking this is gonna be a tough one. I didn't even have his surname. As expected hundreds of thousands of results that meant nothing. *This is like finding a straw in a haystack.* Andy appeared in his black pants, and white short sleeved bar work shirt.

"I'm off now, working 2-10 tonight if you want to go out"

"I may pop in, if I go out with Trish, we haven't decided anything yet though. Have a good night, Andy see you later." I got back to my search results, 2 hours passed of looking at other people, nothing on my sex god. Even if I knew his surname, he's almost certainly silent anyway. Then I did a business search for his store. "Stores in L.A' again, thousands of results L.A to choose from, I didn't even know what the store sold" I gave up having spent the last 4 hours searching for him online. It was starting to get dark. I watched the setting sun, behind the many other towers in front of it, *stunning.* Trish sent me a text.

"Hopefully you've got over knocking people over by now. Want to come out tonight still?" I smiled.

"Sorry Trish, I" just not feeling very sociable right now. I'll get you up to speed, on Monday."I spent some time online again, seeing if I'd missed something. Then curled up on the sofa, with my quilt on top of me, watching TV until I fell asleep. Not even hearing Andy come in, at 10.30pm, with a female.

On Sunday lunchtime, I drove slowly, past Moo Moo Café, just in case he was there. I ended up at Rosie and Sebastian's House. Rosie was the only person who'd seen him, and felt I could talk to about Marcus. Their house was a white, older style brick built bungalow and on waterfront. Luckily, they'd bought their home before prices went up, for waterfronts in the area. Otherwise they just couldn't have bought their house now. I rang their doorbell, hoping they were in. Sebastian came to the door. He was wearing his blue jeans and white t shirt. I thought immediately of him in his Sherlock Holmes outfit and smiled.

"Nat, how are you?" He was surprised to see me.

"Hi Sebastian congratulations on your exciting, baby news!"
He hugged me.

"Thanks Nat, I'm really excited about our little surprise." He
stepped aside and opened the black front door.

"Is Rosie in?

"Yes sorry, go through, she's in the kitchen I think?" I walked
though their white painted open plan lounge room with a very
large comfortable green sofa, to the kitchen ends. Rosie was
wearing black leggings and a very large pale blue t shirt. She
looked like a mum-to-be. Her shoulder length brown hair tied
up in a ponytail. She spotted me.

"Hi Nat, what a lovely surprise, twice in one week." She
grinned.

"Hello Rosie, We hugged each other tightly.

"Coffee or tea?" Rosie turned on her stainless steel kettle.
They'd done their kitchen up after they married, with money
they were given, at the wedding. It was stainless steel
appliances set beautifully in a modern black shiny, cupboards.
It looked lovely, I hadn't seen it fully finished. I ran my hands
along the gorgeous, smooth, grey marble slab workbench, with
round edges. "Your kitchen looks stunning now it's finished.
Coffee please, Rosie." She got two latte colored mugs out of
the storage cupboards up high.

"Thanks, we like it now it's all over too." She gave me my drink.

"It's a lovely day outside, you happy drinking out there?" I nodded. We went through the kitchen, into a white painted laundry area then through the fully glazed back door with a cat flap in.

"Where's Tilly?" Remembering, their silver colored, Persian cat.

"Probably out for a walk, she always comes home for dinner. She's getting quite fat now, Sebastian keeps feeding her extras. She looked at me with slight annoyance. The vet wants us to put her on a diet now." Her eyes roll. As we walk down the stone step, over a terracotta tiled patio with silver metal chairs, table and a barbeque on it. The garden is mostly lawn, with just a few flowerpots, on the patio. We walked on the terracotta stone steps, laced in the lawn, towards the pergola. Into the beautifully made, wooden pergola, with its black tin roof.. The wooden floor roughly sanded and tinted mahogany. We sat on the wooden bench and table, right on the water's edge. The river was on Main River, and moving quite fast. "This is so lovely out here, you must sit here all day, staring at the river, now it's warmer?"

"Not as often as I'd like to, maybe when I'm at home all the time I will. I wished I had visited them more often, as I sat there in the peacefulness.

"We'll have to get the fence done, before baby arrives. I am so looking forward to it now; Sebastian has his list I've given him, of things to complete before baby. She sighs. What brings you, Nat?" She looks concerned. I remember why I came in the first place.

"I can't get sex god Marcus from Moo Moo Café, out of my head. I even searched the internet, to try and find him. I waited until they were open and went Past Moo Moo Café, on the way here, to see if he'd come back. I haven't eaten or slept since I met him. I just want to see him again, to get to know him better he seems to be getting me, over my attack. It's only Marcus Rosie; he is the only one who's made me feel like a woman again. I need to find him" tears flow down my cheeks.

"You ok? You're totally in love, alright." She holds my hand over the table. Rosie has always been so, understanding when it came to my love life. Truth was, she'd found her soul mate at school, and lived with then married him. So not really up to date on the romance, and dating scene.

"He may turn up during the week, its only Sunday. Call you at work maybe. Does he know where you work?"

"I said I worked in a lawyers in town here, didn't give any names. Damn, perhaps I should have, and dug much deeper, for more information,, including his surname. At least I would know what store it is that he owns. If it's under his name of course, I was smitten, by his hot body, Rosie, not with getting facts." I sob, and Rosie gives me a clean tissue, from her pocket, and I wipe my nose and eyes noticing my mascara, is smudged too. Rosie, takes the tissue, and wets it with her tongue, and then she wipes, my face clean.

"I know, just settle into the week, and watch what happens, Nat. If it's meant to be, it will." Rosie finishes her coffee, putting her china mug on the wooden table.

"I know, I'm being too impatient. Marcus had a startlingly major effect on me. No one comes close. I wanted to get to know him, be his girlfriend. He's different, so self assured, sexy, so good looking, I could marry him. I've never felt so connected to anyone like that before Rosie. Certainly not since, you know. I know he's got money, but I didn't know that until he left, getting into his Ferrari. So it wasn't the money. He's sexy, and we got on well, I thought. Then, after all the sexy innuendo he didn't ask me out or for my number, perhaps because he lives in L.A. I don't know the answer, Rosie. You're right; I'll see how it all pans out, this week. I'll give you your Sunday back now, thanks again Rosie."
"Hugging her, I grabbed our mugs and we walked back up the path through the house I said goodbye to them both. I got in my car and drove home.

On Monday at work, I hoped the call from Marcus would come. I got Trish up to speed, and she knows how little I date and why. And it's been like that all week. So now it's Friday again, I asked Trish on Wednesday if she'd come with me to

Moo Moo Café, tonight and she said yes. I'm so excited. I put on my red lipstick, and checked my short sexy red dress, looked ok in the car mirror. I saw Trish pull up next to me, on her Ducati. Taking her shiny helmet off and locking it to her bike. It had been another lovely clear sky, spring day. I love it when it's aromatic and warm. I close my convertible top and lock it down. Gliding through the automatic glass doors again, I made my way to the bar with Trish in her black camisole top and black jeans. It was again, quite full of people after work. I had a quick look round, not seeing him. Then sat on a different barstool than before, with Trish.

"It's great in here, really chic. She sat on her barstool and twirled it. Glad you bought me here, normally go to the pub, this is so modern" The barman recognized me.

"What would you like red wine to spill, over the barmaid again? He joked. Martha's not working tonight, so you'll have to throw it over me." He laughed.

"Hi, yes the same red wine please the house one. Promise to keep it to myself tonight Adam" I joked back at him, looking at his badge, cheeky so and so. He gave me a taster, I nodded and he filled my glass.

"And for you?" He looked at Trish, who was a bit taken back by him, despite her own, cheeky outlook on life.

"I'll have a glass of the same wine please, so I can throw it all over you." She smiled.

"Coming up" He poured her taster first. She nods; she took her glass lifting it higher, looked like she was going to throw it at him.

"Just be nice to my friend," She lowered and took a sip of her wine. Adam smiled.

"Always." He grinned, at Trish. I gaped at her, with my do you fancy him face. She looked away at the bar, shaking her head. I looked around the place, men in suits and casual attire strewn around. Some people were standing, others sitting on the orange sofas. *None of them was Marcus. Marcus had a presence about him, a self assurance so strong. Marcus's body was lean muscled over 6 feet high. His body was like touching electric eels, not that I've touched one. The intensity of his stare controlled me, held me in his power. Oh, I really want to see you again Marcus.*

"He's not here at the moment," I sighed.

"We have all night, let's just stay as long as we can" Trish grabs my arm, and points at a sofa and table that comes free. As we walk to a different table. *I remember Marcus and I doing exactly the same, watching his sexy body smelling his aftershave as I sat breathing every bit of him in. I remember him revealing his white linen shirt and sexy hairy chest under his jacket.* I put my wine on the table, after sipping it.

"I can't believe that we are in here looking for a man for you. It's been a long time coming, I'm glad it has though." Trish whispered in my ear.

"You have no idea, how happy I am about it." I smiled.

"Tell me what I'm looking for, so I'm looking at the right men." She glanced around.

"Over 6 feet, shoulder length dark brown hair, and gorgeous sexy blue eyes. And he was wearing an expensive, black, two piece suit and white linen shirt under." I grinned.

"Sounds just my type, she joked. How old you reckon?"

"Definitely in his 30's, early 30's I think. He's also got a very muscled lean body, he must workout" I kept looking, around, in case he came in.

"Makes your nightly beach walks seem like nothing" She joked.

"I do have a gym in our apartment." I remember going to when we first moved in there 2 years ago, just after the attack. I'd wanted to get my body strong, to be able to fight off anyone I needed to. I haven't been there for age's now." tears well up as I remember.

"You've been so brave Nat; now let's find Mr. Right for you. Can you see him yet?

She puts her arm round me.

"No, I've been looking all the time. I'll pay for your dinner, have you looked at the menu yet?"

"I'm so happy to come here, you know that and I'm paying."

What do you want? I'll go and get it, more wine?" She picked up our glasses.

"Thanks Trish, I'll have the same wine and Spaghetti Bolognaise with garlic bread.

You're so kind, I'm so glad you went out with Chris, and became my BFF." I hugged her arm.

"We've been through a lot, I'll agree with you there" Smiling she went to the bar, with the menu.

I took the opportunity to go to the ladies. I remembered coming in here last time. I redid my lipstick. I looked at my slightly flushed face in the mirror, put on some face powder. I ran my hands through my loose hair. There were a group of young women all talking excitedly together sitting on the marble bench top. I pushed the exit door, and sat down at our table. I looked at the clock, it was 7pm already. This time last week Marcus was just leaving. *I can't believe that I won't see him again.* He's still not here, I looked around, as I came out.

"Thanks Trish, as I took my glass. It would have been good if you'd married Chris, you'd have been my sister in law. Do you still think about him in that way" I had a suspicion that she did.

"Sometimes, I think about where we'd be now. We were so young, just left school" She recalls

"But in love?"

"Yes, I thought so, anyway."

"And you had 2 years going out together. I thought Chris was in love at the time too."

"Probably, but we both wanted to do other things as well. Look at him and Ben now, travelling around the world having fun. I wanted to get a job, which I did and focus on that. He wanted to have fun, travelling around America first, then the world."

"If he came back right now, all grown up, would you get together?" I quizzed.

"Maybe, if he really wanted to settle down with me. It would get me out of having to live at Mum and Dad's" She joked.

"How are they both?"

"Interfering, but I love them still. I thought, Chris and I were going to start living together and move out, 2 years is a long time to spend with someone you love. But I'm still here. Guess I'm looking for Mr. Right too." We cleared a space as our food arrived. I haven't heard Trish talk like that about my brother ever, so it's nice to confirm my suspicions. We ate our food quietly.

"Thanks for buying this Trish, much appreciated." It tasted delicious, I was so hungry.

"You're welcome. She shoved a mouth of lettuce in.

"You'll find Marcus somehow; he must have seen how lovely you are. Perhaps next week at work. He does know you work in a lawyer's office, he could ring round asking. Don't give up hope Nat. He's obviously had an effect on you; you may have had a similar one on him."

"Well, I think as it's after, 8.30pm now, he's not going to be here now. Thanks for coming anyway Trish, I really appreciate it"

"No probs, I wouldn't have missed it for the world."

"I'll get you another drink?" I jumped up.

"Yes just a coke please Nat Thanks" I took our glasses. I felt full on my spaghetti bolognaise, as I moved slowly to the bar.

"What would you like?" Adam smiled.

"2 cokes please Adam." He grabbed the glasses, and then he filled and returned them to me, smiling at him. After my attack I became quite shy with men, whereas before I was life and soul of the party, always getting invited out to liven things up. But now, I don't know what their after, so I don't go out as much. The only men around me like Andy I've known for years. But with Marcus, he is different, please call me somehow.

Standing I let Trish come back in, from the ladies. The soft orange sofa is very comfortable.

"What about those lights on the ladies mirrors, aren't they great fun?

"Yes, I remember the time I was here with Marcus; I felt like such a star with lights around my face " We talked about work and life for an hour or more. Then not seeing Marcus at all, we said our goodbyes. And I went home: alone.

Chapter 3

Monday morning I'm back at work. No sign of Marcus all weekend. *I give up.* On Saturday, I'd waited outside Moo Moo Café in my car, for hours. Just in case. On Sunday, the same tragic wait at Moo Moo's for someone who didn't turn up. I was just sorting out my desk getting ready to start a new day.

"Trish, Donna I'm getting coffee, want anything?"

"Nat, you look knackered, have you slept at all? Trish looked concerned.

"Not for a long time, I yawned, but still so tired"

"If you're going to get a drink, I'll have my usual coffee, one sweetener please."Trish said as she, looked up from typing on her computer.

"Donna want coffee?" I smiled at her, as she finishes her phone conversation.

"Yes, 2 sugars please" Donna puts the phone down.

The office kitchen is a small white room, with, only enough space, to make drinks, and a very tiny grey bench top I picked up the old white kettle, and filled it from the old silver taps. I get my office, Kombi mug, Trish's Ducati mug and Donnas pink flower mug out of the plastic drainer, fill them with coffee. Hunger pains; have taken over my trim body, as I realize I've missed breakfast again. I look at the big white enamel, cookie jar. Grab a couple of milk chocolate digestives, my favorites. As I nibble on a biscuit, the kettle boils. Making the drinks, I bring them slowly on a silver tray I found on top of the fridge. Up the mezzanine, nearly there *fuck, I don't believe it shit.* The whole, tray upturns as I sit on the last step, picking up the cups. There are, people coming to my rescue, from all directions. My boss, Mr. John Smith, helps me up, holding his strong surfers arm.

"Wow you're on fire this morning, It's not even 9.30am Natalie." He hands me a hopefully clean handkerchief out of his black jacket, of his suit.

"Thanks Mr. Smith" I wipe the stains off my smart black skirt. Then when he's gone off the wall, stairs, and the carpet. Trish grabs the tray of mostly empty cups, and orders me back to my office.

"I'll sort it out Nat, you are so tired. Why don't you take a day off, and get some sleep?"

"If I could be sure to get some sleep, I would" A half smile, was all she could drag from me.

Slumping into my desk chair I answer the office phone, and get into my day. As much as unrequited lovesick teenager can. An hour later, my iphone rang, Rosie's picture came up. *What's she want, hope it's not bad news.*

"Rosie, Hi everything ok?' I was worried, about the baby.

"Nat, I'm so excited. I can't calm down" She giggled.

"Rosie, what's so funny?" *At least it's not bad news.*

"A man called Marcus Carrington, phoned and spoke to Sebastian about half an hour ago.. He told me that Marcus was looking for a young lady he'd met on Friday a week ago, at Moo Moo Café. He only had her first name, Natalie to give him." *Oh my god,* I slumped back in my chair, big smile on my face.

"That's him Rosie, Marcus Carrington, he's looking for me" I grinned.

"It's definitely you right, I can tell Sebastian?" She was clearly happy.

"Yes, it's definitely me, I'm the mystery woman, and he's looking for."

"I'll call you back, once Sebastian's spoken to him, see what he says, ok?"

"Ok, Rosie thanks so much." I put my iphone on my desk top.

"Is that him, looking for you?" Trish came over and sat on my desk, her mouth open.

"Yes, he called 30 minutes ago, to their detective agency to find me. I remember telling him that they had an agency, it's so great. I wonder if he realizes, it's my sister's. Wow, I'm so excited." My grin was permanently attached.

"What's happening now?" Trish put her arms around me.

"I'm just waiting for Sebastian to call him back. Rosie will call me as soon as she can."

"I guess this is why you've so upset, all last week. Donna smiled he must be wonderful Nat, taking your heart." She came out with, some old fashioned things sometimes, and a heart of gold.

"Yes, the only, man I want to be with, Donna."

"Glad I still love Glen, and got my two kids. I'd hate to go through all that dating again. I wish you all the best, Nat. You truly deserve it." She hugged my arm.

"Thanks Donna, he's the only man I want to be with too, hope he feels the same way."

With that my iphone rang. We all jumped.

Rosie's photo came up.

"Hi Rosie, what's happening?"

"Sebastian is so glad it's you, Nat. He said that Marcus wants to take you to dinner tonight. If that's ok with you, he'll pick you up at your place. Is it ok to give him your address?"

"Yes, of course, what time? " I was so excited.

"I'll let you know, soon. This is like a fairy story Nat, I'm really happy for you, I know how much you want this."

"Just get back to me soon Rosie." I ended the call; put the phone on my desk.

"Well?" Trish couldn't get any closer.

"He's taking me out tonight, for dinner. He's picking me up at my place." I couldn't feel any better than I did right then. I took a sip of my cold coffee ew *yuk*. A long 20 minutes later, my iphone rang, it was Rosie.

"Well Sebastian has given your address to Marcus, and he'll pick you up at 7.30pm tonight. Are you happy?"

"Couldn't get any happier, I'm kind of shocked at the moment still. Everything is moving so quickly. I'll let it all sink in

soon. Have to and buy a dress for tonight at lunch break.
Thanks Rosie so much."

"I'm going to dinner tonight, with the man of my dreams.
He's picking me up at 7.30pm. Please could you help me find
something new to wear, at lunch Trish?" She hugged me
again.

"Yes, of course. I'm so happy for you Nat. Better get on with
some work now" she sat at her desk, and started typing.
Donna was on the phone, and giving me the thumbs up. My
office phone rang; I dealt with the client's problem with a big,
smile on my face, which stayed with me until lunchtime.

We came out of the office for lunch, Trish beside me. Careful
to look both ways, as I eagerly came out.

"I've never seen you so happy" Trish checks her phone, for
messages, and puts it in her backpack.

"What if I'm not the person he's looking for? How
embarrassing that would be?"

"It's you Nat, Just a shock to the system. What do you want to
buy for tonight?"

"I'd like to find a sexy, black off the shoulder dress. I walked into a fashion boutique, called "Butterfly" just down the road. Or something tied around my neck, and strapless.. With a nice new pair of black heals. Inside the shop was packed with fashion clothes, lined along the side walls and a big display of handbags, in the middle. I looked through the dresses set to the back of the shop. I spotted the most beautiful black satin, off the shoulder dress.

"Does that come in a UK 8, they always fit so nicely?" I went towards the assistant.

"Yes, here you are." The blonde young assistant handed to me, and pointed to the changing area.

"You can change in there, if you want to try it on?" She smiled

It fitted perfectly, and despite being a week's wages, I bought it.

"I hadn't got a really good quality dress that I could wear tonight. He was so worth it." I looked at Trish, and got out my credit card.

"Now shoes, where's the nearest shop, Trish? We only have 20 minutes left of lunch." I grabbed my bagged dress, and wandered onto the sidewalk.

"I think "Tremlows" in West St is closest." Trish looked at her watch.

Less than 5 minutes later, we were in the boutique shoe shop. It only had a smaller selection. Then, the mall shops, but much closer. Looking around Trish points at a pair.

"I prefer something that my toes poke through to show my nail varnish." We looked at several pairs, I tried a couple on. The elderly assistant was not really able to help. Then I spied a pair in the window display, and the assistant got them for me.

"These are a UK8 they fit perfectly; normally I take a UK 9." They felt so good, as I walked around the store. I put my new dress up against me. Trish nods.

"Perfect, I'll buy them, please." I put my old shoes back on, went to pay.

As we stop off at our usual deli, to get sandwiches and coffee, whilst were waiting for them, I can't get the now permanent grin off my face.

"There you are, and we'll have, some of what you've got, that makes you so happy" the deli man as he, hands the sandwich bag to me. Trish looks at her watch.

"We only have 10 minutes, want to sit in the park and eat them? I nod, walking to the park across from the office. Sitting on the bench, I get my and Trish's sandwiches out. I sip my coffee slowly, because it's very, hot.

"This has been a day of firsts for you, Nat. Your sexy, new dress, which cost a fortune. Don't think you normally spend more than $40 on a dress. Am I right?" I nodded.

"Then, you got heals, I haven't seen you wear heals, normally flats, right?" I nodded, with my silly grin munching on my whole meal tuna salad sandwich.

"I hope you get to meet him Trish, he's worth every cent."

"I keep wondering how your date, is going to go tonight. I hope you keep on seeing him, because I'd like to meet the man who's, got you past all your shit." She smiled.

We finish off our food, sipping our drinks. My iphone rings, Rosie's picture comes up.

"Hi Nat, did you buy anything for tonight?"

"Hi Rosie, Yes I got a beautiful black satin dress, and new black shoes."

"Sounds great, have a lovely time won't you. Have you told Mum yet?"

"I will have an awesome time, thanks Rosie. No I'll leave Mum until the wedding.

I joked. I'll tell her, when I know he's more than just a date for tonight."

"I get ya. Got to go now, Sebastian is hollering." The call ended.

We grabbed the last of our drinks, bringing them into the office. Luckily I was quite busy, which made the time go quicker. At 5.00 pm, I jumped up, eager to go. Trish gave me a good luck hug. And Donna wished me well. As I went through reception, Megan our receptionist wished me well for tonight. *How did she know?* Driving home, I made sure my dress and shoes were with me. I grinned wickedly, at was about to happen. Stopping at the lights, I imagined Marcus

was here, with me now, on the floor, lifting my skirt up, then, peeling my sexy panties, off, giving my clit a gentle lick with his tongue, then sucking my pussy, dry, watching me come, and getting off himself on it. Thrills went through my horny body, at the thought of it.

Andy had the day off, I straddled his runners coming through the door, nearly falling down. *Shit not again.* He looked up from the sofa, where he was, munching a big bag of potato chips, little yellow, and bits all over the floor. *Yuk*

"Sorry, meant to move those!"

"It's ok Andy, guess what happened today?" I sit next to him on the arm of the sofa.

"Obviously something good, because you're smiling. I haven't seen that since, did he call your office?" He munches on a chip. He's got his blue jeans and a black T shirt on, absolutely covered with bits of chips. Smiling, I go to the bathroom and run a bath and go back to get my bags.

"Yes Marcus Carrington, his name is, and he's picking me up here at 7.30pm, to go to dinner with him."

"Wow, that's awesome Nat, He's coming here to pick you up?" He was half watching English, Football on the TV.

"Yes, I'll be in the bathroom getting ready." Laying out my new dress in my bed, in my room, I grabbed a Pepsi out of the fridge, and back to my half filled bath. I dropped my work clothes in the washing machine. I admired my naked lean body, *I hope he likes what he sees. I felt so special, Marcus Carrington, what a beautiful name. Natalie Carrington, that sounds good, but he's not into marriage. Marcus was looking for me.* I remembered his sexy body hair, coming loose around his white linen shirt as he took his jacket off. *This man is mine tonight.* My nipples hardened, just at the thought of him, as I sat in the warmth of my bubble bath, it smelt of roses, I put my forefinger, on my aching, clit, moving so slowly, thinking of my Marcus's naked taut, erotic body. I touched my breast with my other hand. I closed my eyes, focusing on sex god, my sex god now. I was floating on a cloud, feeling it build then I felt my orgasm fill my whole body, waves of pulsing orgasmic pleasure. I kept it going; still touching in slow circles of pleasure my body comes back to normal. *wow, it's been so long., Marcus makes me feel so erotic.*

Putting the towel around me, I go to my room to get dressed. Andy's watching something on TV. Locking my door, I open the bottom drawer, in my vanity unit, get out my pink vibrator. I turn it on, and change the batteries for new ones. *I'm still feeling so fucking horny.* Lying down on my bed, I pushed my quilt on to one side. I move the vibrator, into my vagina; *I'm so wet, already.* I imagined Marcus's hard cock, being the vibrator, closing my eyes. I move the vibrator slowly in and out, pulsing my pleasure zone. I feel the other tip on my clit, holding it to make the orgasm last as long as possible. I stay enjoying the erotic pulses as they vibrate through my body. *Oh Marcus, I will have sex tonight with you.* I lay there for a while, until he last erotic sensations, have pulsed through my body.

I get dressed, with my make up on, and dry my hair. Looking at my alarm clock, it's 6.30pm already. I paint my toes and hands, with a new color, "Red Crimson" I bought and haven't used yet. I walk back into the lounge room.

"Wow, look at you, got a hot date tonight?" Andy moved over, to give me space.

"I'll chill out, until Marcus comes"

"Is he really going to come here tonight?" He said with a wicked grin on his cheeky face.

"I do hope so Andy, he's .the one for me, I'm so sure he is. Just want to be with him."

"Longest relationship I ever had was a month. I like to have sex on a regular basis; I couldn't go without it, like you do."

"I see the women you bring back sometimes; they are nice, but gone the next morning. I couldn't have sex like that. I want a relationship too much Andy. Doesn't it get to you sometimes? You are 35, aren't you wanting kids, or a family at some point?"

"Happy the way things are Nat, different partners every night if I want each have different ways of having sex, I then use what I've learnt on my next fuck."

"Ewe, too much information." I stared at the TV; it had one of Andy's favorites on, I looked at my iphone, 7.00pm. *He'll be here soon.* I picked up my new shoes, and put them on to wear them in. they felt so comfortable. I got my new black handbag; put my iphone back in it, together with my lipstick and perfume I had on.

"I do admire you finding Marcus, after your attack Nat, I really do. You know that if I'd been there at the time. I would be on a murder charge now, and in prison. I hope you find happiness, really I do. I know you don't really talk about it, but I'm here if you do, you know that." He patted my arm.

"Thanks Andy, I know you are, but I'm not ready to start opening it all up again. I tend to ignore it, hoping it will go away. But it doesn't, I get teary I will tell you though if I can one day, promise."

"Don't get your lovely make up ruined." he gave me a tissue. I went to the bathroom mirror, and dabbed the corners of my eyes.

"Got there just in time," My make up looked fine. Looking at the microwave clock, as I came out, 7.15pm. I was getting a little nervous now, last visit to the toilet.

"I'm so excited Andy, I hope I don't mess it up."

"You are going to have a great time, Nat, and if you have sex, that's a bonus too."

"Andy, you truly have a one track mind."

"Thank you, kind madam." He was kind of good looking in his own way. I wasn't surprised that he managed to pull, almost every time he went to work at the bar. I was not attracted to him, knew all his bad points I suppose. He's a good friend   though, known him for a couple of years now. . Only bloke that's been that close in my life. I trust him totally. I glance at my iphone, 7.25pm. *Oh my got any minute now. I felt wet again,* I like this feeling of anticipation, and being ready for sex with Marcus, I couldn't deny it, happy and excited, and a little nervous still, waiting for him.

"Buzz" went the entry phone.

Chapter 4

Marcus stares deeply into my eager green eyes, with his twinkling baby blues. He kisses my cheek, electric thrills run, through my longing body.

"Hi Natalie, He whispers in my ear, looking beautiful as ever." He stares at my tight body hugging new dress. Andy pops his head around the door.

"Hi Marcus, is it? I'm Andy Nat's flat mate, just wanted to say look after her, please, she deserves it." He shakes Marcus's outstretched hand firmly.

"With my life, I can assure you of that, Andy." He took his hand away, smiling gloriously at me. He was wearing, a dark blue jacket, and tight, black Armani jeans, black shoes, and his white cotton shirt, with the neck unbuttoned showing his tantalizing slightly tanned lean body beneath. *I can feel myself, wet already; oh my how am I going to ever get over, feeling so hot around you.* Marcus took my hand, thrills ran like electricity through me. He smelt of delicious sexy after shave, and body wash, with a hint of fresh mint.

"Goodbye Andy." I grinned at him as he shut the door.

"Have a great time, both of you, See you later Nat." He gave me the thumbs up, and closed the door, but I wasn't looking.

"Marcus walked me down the well lit, light grey hall, into the lift, just around the corner, still holding my hand firmly. As we waited for the lift to come, he smiled at me. I felt like the whole world revolved around me and Marcus, in some clear bubble no one else could see. In the empty old brown painted lift, I pressed ground.

"I really love what you're wearing, is it new?" He stared at me, squeezing my hand.

"Thanks, I bought them all today, at lunchtime." I push my long hair, over my shoulder, with my free hand. I shyly looked away, it took a couple of minutes, to descend the 12 floors. I was struck speechless again.

As we came out of the lift into the, open slightly shabby reception area, that smelt of dust.. He took his hand off, to open the glass, reception door. I could see on the street, a black Bentley Limo, the older, sandy haired driver seeing him, getting out and opening the doors for us.

"Thanks Barker." As we settle ourselves inside the luxurious inside, Barker goes to drive off. He grabbed my hand and he traced with his fingers, *it felt so erotic, I was hungry for him, right there and then*, His hands had masculinity to them, hardness.

"When I phoned that Detective agency to find you, I didn't realize it was your sister's business. I remember you said they had a business, but it's still under the last owner's name in the directory. How easy was it for them to find you? I'm pleased that I found you. What about you, Natalie?" The Limo is all black buttoned leather inside, with a electric privacy screen that was up. It has a drinks cabinet. *Very classy.*

"I am so glad you decided to find me Marcus, I was really hoping you would do. Call me Nat please." *I love you, I'm wet all the time I think about you, I want to have you fuck me as soon as possible in this Limo.* The car starts to move, smoothly away.

"We are going just down the road, to a restaurant in a hotel. I hope you like it? It's only a short drive. I wanted to spend as much time as I could, with you tonight."

"That 's great, I'd love spending as much time as I can with you tonight." I smiled at him.

"That's what I'd hoped you'd say." He released me as he saw where we were.

The Bentley stops under the huge white covered area, the Plaza Hotel. It had five stars on the sign outside. Marcus grabbed my hand and smiled his beautiful sexy smile, to me as Barker opened his door. We were greeted by the concierge.

"Good evening Mr. Carrington, Madam, well today I hope?"

"Yes very well thanks, Carlton. We have a dinner reservation at 7.45pm." Carlton beckons us through to what appears to be a, private lift to the side. We get inside alone, Marcus presses a button.. We take a couple of minutes again to get to the restaurant floor. *I love this beautiful place, it's so classy. Normally out of my price range, not even been in here before.* As the lift gets to where we are going I take hold of Marcus's hand, as he smiles, offering it to me, and walk down a wide and short corridor, mainly painted off white color. The floors are all white marble, I can see, gazing at the large, modern flower paintings on the walls.

We reach The "Seaview Restaurant" which is a revolving restaurant, doing American and European food, I can see by the mounted menu. We are greeted by the Restaurant manager. *Wow look at the view, it's amazing, at lit up at night.*

"Evening again Mr. Carrington, Madam, (he looks at me) it's good to see you again"

"Hello Max." Following him to a medium rectangular table in the edge with one of the best views I'm sure, which could seat 4 people, but just 2 settings facing each other. It was nicely decorated with white candle in a semi translucent glass holder, and a small fresh white, single flower in each small black glass vase, white tablecloth.. I look around; we're the only one's there. The restaurant is quite huge, fit at least 300 people in it, and is my guess. It's very modern inside, which I liked, with a black and white theme, very classy again. Against the white walls are modern artworks, this time huge, abstract ones with a mainly monotone theme to them. The whole place was done beautifully. The waiter holds out my black chair out for me

"Thank you, how come there's nobody else in here?" I gaze at him sexily taking off his jacket, arm by sexy, arm and putting it over the back of his chair. Revealing his muscular arms under his shirt. *Feeling so fucking horny again.*

"Because I asked them to just put us in here until 9pm. If we want to stay until then" He picked up the menu, and gave me one.

"Did you pay for the whole restaurant, until 9pm then?"

"My family business owns the hotel and restaurant, that's why." He smiles at me. I was a little shocked, I knew he was rich, but I'll have to get used to it. I looked at the A La Carte Menu; there were no prices on it. *I suppose he got free..*

The waiter came to take our order, on his notepad. Marcus looks at me.

"I'd love the grilled Barramundi, with salad please." I looked at the waiter.

"Sir" He looked Marcus.

"Medium rare T-Bone steak, with vegetables Diane sauce," He looked at me.

"What would you like to drink Nat red wine to pour over someone?" He grinned.

The waiter looked bemused.

"Yes I do, want a sweet red wine please, to drink please." I glared at him humorously. *We even had our own private joke already.* The waiter took the menus. He looked at Marcus.

"Bourbon for me"

"Right Nat, I want to know everything about you, tell all. This is now officially our 2nd date after all." he grabbed my hand across the table; my whole body went into electric shocks.

"Well, I'm 29, a Paralegal in Rumble and Smith Lawyers, in the town centre. What do you want to know? "He looked deeply into my eyes; *I could sit here forever staring at his sexy body as he moves. But I have to relax, I'm too uptight, haven't been dating for so long, I'd forgotten how to, I'm acting so shy with him -why?.*

"You must know that I don't normally do this, chasing you and dating stuff. It's just not me, Nat. There's something about you, I tried to stay away, for a week, but kept thinking about you." Our drink's arrived. I took a sip of my wine, delicious, I nodded and the waiter filled my glass. Marcus's voice was dark and dangerous, when he spoke, it was so dam sexy.

"I felt the same way Marcus, I just had to see you again and talk to you, find out more about you, and believe it or not that's not what I normally do either." *I can't tell him about all the tears, and stalking outside Moo Moo's. The hunger for his body, not yet.* Marcus's hair flopped in front of his face, covering his right eye. He pushed it over his head in a very sexy way. *Does he know how gorgeous he is?*

"Do your parents live near you?" He sipped his drink.

"My dad Stephen died when I was 15, in a car accident. My mum bought us all up alone really. She found Al after Rosie and I left home, he's a great person, we all think of him as our dad now. They've been together for years now. Married 5 years ago,, they live in a beautiful large acreage home in West Hollywood now"

"You've got Rosie I met, any others?"

"Yes my baby brother, Chris he's 22 now. And backpacking around the world at the moment, with a friend of his."

"What about your family?"

"Mum and Dad live in San Diego, no brothers or sisters."

"Do you get to see them often?"

"Yes, probably about twice a month, it really depends where I am work wise as to when I get to see them; I like my space, that's why I agreed to run the business from the L.A. office."

"What about you, see you mum and Al regularly?"

"I try to see them, the usual birthdays, etc. I suppose I go down every few weeks too, I speak to mum more much more often."

"When you left me at Moo Moo's, you had a Ferrari Italia, is that right, because my brother raved on about them when they came out."

"Yes, it's mine; I do love sexy cars, and this one I was on a year waiting list for mine. I went to Italy to order it, and get the specs I wanted. I truly love it, it's fast too."

"So you're in to fast expensive cars then, you have the Bentley too, anymore?"

"Yes of course, at my L.A. home, I have a Porsche 911, Do you like sports cars then?"

"Yes I do, I only have a Saab convertible, not as fast as your cars though."

"I'll have to let you see my Porsche, sometime, if you want to?"

"I would, please." I was quite excited, to be seeing more of him and his exotic cars

Our food arrived, and my hand was released, I put my large white napkin on my lap. In front of me was a headed barramundi, which I've never had at a restaurant before., *Ugh I felt slightly sick just looking at it, looking at me.* As I cut the head and tail off with my silver knife, which was amazingly sharp, and put it to one side, with a napkin covering it.. The fish is sublime, the best I've ever tasted though. Marcus is still eating his steak.

'How's your food? Mine is delicious." He finished his mouthful.

"The chef has done well tonight, it's good." He finishes off his bourbon, catching the waiters eye, with his empty glass. The waiter picks it up.

"More bourbon sir? More wine madam?" I finish off the dregs in my cut glass and hand it to him.

"Yes, more of the same wine please, it's delicious."

"So what type of business do you have, Marcus. When I saw you last time, I thought you owned a store in L.A... But you own The Plaza Hotel too?"

"We have a family business, that I mainly run now, as mum and dad are semi retired. Have you heard of "Carrington's" the large department stores all round America, and around the world?"

"Yes I have, that's yours? That's a huge empire." *Wow that's such a huge, American icon, how could I not have heard of it. It must be making megabucks.*

"Wow, you must have good managers, to be just you at the top?" I was in awe.

"Yes, we have the best, I totally trust them to get on and do their jobs and they seem to."

"Do you get to travel to the stores overseas? I've always wanted to travel to London and even New York.

"Yes, sometimes I do a few times a year. We are just, sorting out a new store that we've just found space to build a store on, in Paris, so I'll be off there some time in the future.." He was clearly proud of his business achievements, but not in a over the top way. I finished the last delicious mouthful of food, bringing my napkin onto my plate, as the waiter took it from me. I stared at Marcus eating, his food so slowly, devouring each mouthful. I let him finish, it was a good show to watch. His thin white shirt that I love so much. Wonder if he knows it turns me on, perhaps he has 20 of them, because he can. He certainly looks so hot in it, gazing at him is making me wet, ready for steamy erotic sex anytime now *Marcus my boyfriend*. He gazes at me as he chews his last mouthful. The waiter takes his huge white plate from him. He sips his bourbon. I gaze at the changing view outside; it's now overlooking the mountains, in the hinterland. The night sky is clear, with stars visible, from inside the restaurant.

"Thank you for bringing me up here, it's so pretty."

"Yes one of my favorites, day or night. Sometimes a thunderstorm is amazing to watch, as it streaks across the sky. We have 360 degree views, which is awesome. How long have you worked at Rumble and Smith?" He takes my hand across the table, leaving my wine hand free. Thrills pulse though me, as he does.

"I started there when I was 25, so I've been there for 4 years now. It's a good place to work, my friend Trish works there too, so sometimes, we don't get much work done. Trish used to go out with my brother Chris for a couple of years, we thought they would get married, but they were young, only 18 at the time, just out of school." I was starting to relax; now I could feel it.

"So Trish, is your best friend?"

"Yes, she's the one who gets all the gossip. She's been a good friend to me, especially over the last few years. She's always there, for me. What about you, do you have lots of friends?"

"I have a few, mainly outside of my business, or I wouldn't be able to be the boss so easily. I used to play rugby in my early and mid 20's, but I gave it up, couldn't keep up the commitment factor, as the business grew. So now I just have my own gym, which means I can fit it in according to my daily schedule. They always have gyms In the places I stay in any way now, so it fits me perfectly. I'm not frantic if I miss it though. Do you play any sports, not that you need to?" He beams at me.

"I just like walking along the beach, or the footpath near it. I love being near the sea, It's fascinating to me. I used to cycle, but haven't for a while now. I did go to the gym in our building a last year now, to build up my body, which I did. I haven't been back there for months now."

"What about Andy, your flat mate? Have you had any romantic flings with him, he's in his thirties, isn't he?"

"No, I shake my head vigorously, we are just flat mates. I don't see him as anyone romantic, *ugh I thought of Andy and me with kids flash, through my head ugh* I've known him for almost a couple of years now, I know all his disgusting habits, definitely not my type is Andy, a good friend at times though." He laughs at my repulsion of Andy that way. It sounds so good to hear him chuckling; it was the first time, and it felt blissful to listen to.

"I presume you are single, with no wife and kids at home, But I just have to make sure?"

"No lurking girlfriends or wife or kids at home, just me. Dating isn't the way I operate normally, as I said to you before "

"So do you have sex at all then?" I was a little bemused, as to, what am I doing here.

"Of course, but it's just fucking, no relationships, that's the way I have liked it to be, He looks into my eyes. So the dating with you right now is a first for me. You have to understand, that you are different somehow, I feel different when I'm near you. I haven't felt that ever, in My 32 years. That's why I'm here with only you Nat." My knees went all wobbly, I smiled at him, and grabbed his other hand, holding him gently. *Wow is that what I want though, I could try to change him.*

The waiter appeared, with the menu.

"Would you like any dessert Nat? I took the menu, and Marcus his.

"I'll have a look, and see." Looking through the dessert menu, I saw lots of different ones that I liked, had to choose one, difficultly for a pudding lover extraordinaire.

"I'll have the sticky pecan pie, with cream please." I gave the menu back. Marcus looked at the pudding list.

"Nat, would you like a coffee now, or another drink, "

"Yes a cappuccino, now would be lovely please, thanks' Marcus."

"Good, I'll have a long black too, and a carrot cake, no cream with it, thanks." The waiter took his menu.

"Thank you." Marcus's hand held mine deliriously again, giving me a quick thrill.

"You don't smoke, do you?"

"No, I don't, I used to when I was a kid just out of school though, got through a few a day. I gave it up, because it didn't taste great any more, especially in the mornings. So no I don't" I shook my head.

I hope he wants to meet with me after this, I'd be gutted if he didn't. He smells so wonderful; my senses had become used to his I could gaze at him all night, but at some point tonight, this was going to end. I can't bear the thought of that, delicious odor of expensive cologne, and him, I took another breath of him, before he went to the gents, I stood up to go to the ladies, which were halfway down, on the right, he'd pointed out. Swinging the black door, I entered a huge, bathroom, which had a lady attendant for anything I wanted. *Wow I've never had one of those before.* She smiled at me. Smiling back, I did what I'd come to do, and went to the very modern white, basins, with nothing underneath. I moved the tap around, it didn't work. The lady came over, to me.

"It's got sensors on it, you just put your hand under here." She put her hand under and it worked, and went off when she took her hand away.

"Wow, that's a good tap, Thank you for helping me."

"Pleasure, hope you're having a good night?" She enquired.

"Yes I am, but you must be a bit bored, with just me in the restaurant at the moment?"

"I love to read, she pulled out her Fifty Shades Freed book.

"I love those ones to your nearly at the end, so I won't spoil it for you." I dried my hands in the dryer. And nodded as I reapplied my lipstick, and checked my hair. *He said so many lovely things to me tonight; it feels like he's going to want to see me again, oh I really hope so, I'd be so gutted of he didn't. Especially after what he's just said to me.*

Coming back through the ladies, I could see Marcus at the table; he got up and pulled my chair back for me to sit on.

"Thanks." Our desserts and coffee had arrived; I got a sweetener out of the sugar bowl, and stirred my plain black cup, with my silver spoon. I saw Marcus didn't add any sugar to his long black.

"This looks so yum." I picked up my silver spoon and fork, and started eating little bit at a time, to make it last longer, I love puddings, especially sweet ones. I saw Marcus watch me as I ate.

"Do you love sweet things like lots of women?" He grinned.

"Of course, I can eat anything I want, and always stay the same size, have been able to all my life. Which is a good thing really" I took another small bite. His finger reached across and gently took a bit of my cream that was at the corner of my mouth. *It felt so dam sexy* Thanks."

"My pleasure Nat, it really is." *Who said Mondays were bad, this one is the best for a long time. I still can't believe I'm his first date, I wonder if he uses prostitutes, he must do, yuk but they would clean themselves, before he used them surely. Perhaps He doesn't use them, I hope not. I want him all to myself.* I looked at the modern black clock on the restaurant wall, not too far away, it said 8.50pm. *Oh why does It have to end, I want him tonight, my appetite for him is huge.* I could hear people coming up to the outside of the restaurant, as it neared 9.00pm. We finished our delicious desserts, and coffee's.

"We can still stay here after; 9pm if that's what you're thinking Nat." He looked at the crowd gathering at the doorway.

"I just don't want tonight to end, I think.'

"Nor me, look I really would like to make this evening last longer. But unfortunately, I have to be back in L.A. tonight. Would you like to come and see my home now?"

"But won't it take an hour there and hour back at least won't it?" M*ore time to stare at his gorgeous athletic body.*

"Oh, just leave it to me, would you like to go, tonight?"

"Of course I would." He got on his phone and made a couple of calls. I was thrilled, and got ready for our journey.

Chapter 5

As we left the revolving restaurant, holding hands I felt thrills running through my entire body. I stared at Marcus, as he pushed the private lift button. *My boyfriend my sexy, athletic Marcus,* thought I'd dreamed and gone to heaven. Luckily, I'd just had time to re do my makeup, in the ladies, before we left. The lady assistant, called Sue, had wished me luck, she said that she hadn't seen Mr. Carrington, as happy as he was tonight ever. She'd been working here in different positions, for 6 years, and always would have heard if he had a date, "You're special to him." She'd said. As the lift comes quickly, Marcus pulls me gently inside, and pushes the button.

"This is a private lift for just me and my family, so no one else will come in." He pulled me into his arms, pressing his lips upon mine gently, pushing his tongue deliciously, touching tenderly inside me, his kiss went on forever, and then a loud ping, as the lift doors opened. Marcus moved apart, still keeping his arm around my shoulders,

"Goodnight Mr. Carrington, Madam." He nodded to the concierge, who opened the glass door for us. Barker had the Bentley, door open for us as I climb in I thank him. Marcus talks to him, and he gets on the phone talking to someone. Marcus climbs in through the open large side door of the Limo, and sits closely to me. Barker, is off the phone now, and starts to drive off slowly. Electric thrills are pulsing within me, as Marcus grabs my hand.

"Thanks, again for coming out tonight with me, for saying yes." He put his jacket that he'd taken off next to him. Just his muscles are making me hot and sweaty, in all the right places.

"It's been an awesome day for me; I wouldn't have missed this for the world." He lifted my hand to his face and kissed it, gently. I'm *smitten; he totally has my love in that one gentle moment.* We gaze at each other, as Barker drives on, both oblivious to our surroundings. The lights outside of the hotels, restaurants and general nightlife, speeding gently past, the darkened partition between Barker and us brings a silence where I can only hear the beat of my heart in. Then he moves his head gently towards mine, and I close my eyes as he kissed me passionately, he holds the back of my head as he does. I feel heat rising in my body, moving me to a place that I'd never been before. His soft lips caress mine, as his arms go tightly around my small waist. He smells of body wash, and expensive aftershave. His lips release me, as I feel the car slow down. A speakerphone calls.

"We're here now, Sir." Is all he says? *That wasn't far; perhaps he lives closer to me than I thought.* I moved my gaze from Marcus to the outside.

I read a sign "Long Beach" we're at the airport.

As Barker opened the door, I looked quizzically at Marcus. He had a huge grin on his face, and didn't say a word, as we went through security, very quickly, too quickly for my understanding of the local, and indeed any domestic airports I'd been in. Not that there'd been many, a few trips over the years to local places. We entered a side gate and walked through the narrow terminal, Marcus still saying nothing, he stopped to kiss me passionately again, then took my hand, and carried on walking. There was a mainly glass corridor exit that we took. Outside was a black helicopter, we were heading towards.

"This is my baby." We halted at the steps, of the still helicopter.

"You fly this, really?" I was in awe of him again. "Yes, she's very special to me, I bought her new last year, she's so lovely, I love, flying her." He opened the side door that said

1 –Trapped in Time of The Carrington's Trilogy

229ZZLK on it in big white letters. As I stepped up into the helicopter he made sure my seatbelt was on. I had some headphones too if I wanted them, I was getting so excited now.

"I haven't been in a helicopter before, I'm so looking forward to this, thanks for not telling, it's made it even more thrilling for me."Marcus fiddled with buttons, and switches. He put his headphones on.

"Tower 229ZZLK, requesting take off confirm, over?" He finished with the buttons, and put his belt on. He started up the engine and the propellers started to move slowly first, then very fast.

"Flight 229ZLK confirmed over." Then it spattered directions at him. It was dark and the lights began to disappear, or get smaller as we went higher. *I was totally thrilled still, such an exhilarating way to go, I hope we get to use this more, I love it.* Marcus totally loved this too, I could tell. He looked across at me.

"You OK?"

"I think I've found my favorite mode of transport, this is beyond good." I laughed at my previously being scared of heights; it felt so safe in there. He grinned at me.

"It's mine too, I think, unfortunately it doesn't take long to get to places. But such fun." We went on, he looked so damn sexy my boyfriend, sitting there piloting his helicopter, an awesome sight. We went on for about 10 minutes more, moving over a more bushy area; I could see acreages on allotments, all of varying sizes, only seeing them from the night lights, glowing in the dark.

"Nearly there, just a few more minutes"

"How long does the flight, take in full?"

"15 minutes, roughly, so not the time, you're expecting eh?"

"Any time spent with you works for me." *I couldn't believe I just said that out loud.*

He gazed at me adoringly, and then pointed down to a big black H on the ground.

"We're here." The helicopter moved across towards and over it, smoothly going straight down, he was a good pilot, I could tell. We landed smoothly, and he did his post flight checking, turning the motor off as the rotors came slowly to a halt. Now turning to the outside view, it's mainly grassed lawn that I could see around us. But behind in the shadows, I could see a huge double storey house, it was softly lit from the ground. Someone was coming towards us, a tallish heavy built man in a dark suit.

Marcus got out, and the man in his 50's came around to let me out, with a slight smile on his face.

"Welcome, Miss." His voice was slightly English tone to it, as if he'd been in America for many years now.

"Nat, this is one of my security team Smith." He nods his head at me, and closed the door, staying with the helicopter. As we walked towards his, huge dimly lit, white, I think it was, colonial style home. It had huge big white columns, outside. Walking down the beautifully manicured borders, we got to the black tar of the drive. As we moved towards the big double fronted black door at the front of the house, I could see, the climbing roses, making an arch, over the doorway. "Here we are." He ushered me in.

Inside was a massive entrance hall, with closed mahogany timber doors leading off from all around. There were white marble tiles on the floors.

"It's so big, and beautiful, you live here on your own?" I couldn't believe it, when I thought back to Andy and me living in such a small space in comparison.

"Yes I do love lots of space." As he finished, a short cuddly lady in her fifties, with a frilly flowered apron on, came out of the kitchen, a surprised smile on her face.

"Oh, I didn't think you'd be back yet." She touched Marcus's arm with a motherly tenderness. She had an Irish accent that was quite strong. He looked at me.

"This is Claire Grogan, my cook and housekeeper"

"This is Natalie" He grinned at Claire.

"Hi." was all I could come out with, I was a bit shy, I never expected him to have staff, I was feeling overwhelmed.

"Do you want something to eat? "She still looked at me.

"We have just eaten thanks Claire, just going to get us a drink, in the lounge room. I'll let you know if we need anything.""Ok" she was so friendly and wanting to please him. We walked off to a white, double door into a huge lounge room, with a large piano in the corner, facing a picture window, with white pleated curtains on it. It had a traditional look and feel about it, not what I'd expected from him, from what I did know, which wasn't much I was beginning to realize.

"I love your colors; in here did you do it yourself?'

"No I used Gina, our color consultant, at the store. I'm useless with that sort of stuff I'm more into running the stores, and leave this to Gina. Do you like it, I'm not sure if It's me, but it goes with the house I think. Marcus moved swiftly towards the bar.

"What would you like to drink, Nat?" I moved towards him, and it was fully stocked.

"Got any pilsner beers?"

"Of course, in a bottle or glass?"

"Bottle please." He handed me a Carlton Pilsner bottle, with the top off. He got himself a Pepsi in a bottle. Putting our drinks on the coffee table, he sat with me on the huge cream sofa, that went with the rest of the room. It squished right down, it was so comfortable, and he sat so close to me, our legs touching, along their length, making me feel warm inside. He put his arm around me, and twisted me towards his sexy body. Moving my lips to his, he kissed me, long and hard, his taste divinely left on me forever. Moans came from me as I realized how horny, he was making me. *Fuck me, fuck me right now on the floor; I was, so ready for your body.* As we pulled apart, a silent sigh came from within my erotic depths..

"I'd like to go for a walk in the garden, show you around?" *Aw, fuck me here please.*

"Love to."

I grabbed the fingers, of his outstretched hand as he pulled me up. We walked hand in hand to a side, double patio door, as he pushed the cream curtains aside, and opened the doors wide. As we stepped out onto the terracotta paved area, we walked down through the garden, on the pavers in the lawn.

"You know, that I've never done any of this dating stuff before. I'm getting to like it with you." He took my hand and kissed it gently.

"I could see Mrs. Grogan's face when she saw me here, totally gave you away I'm afraid. Although I still can't understand it, I only know dating, doing it this way."

"Well that's the way it is for me, perhaps maybe, I can tell you why one day, but I'll need time for that one." He moves onto the steps, leading gently downwards

"You can tell me anything, you know that Marcus."

"I hope I can release my demons one day, maybe if you're still around and want me still by then." I looked at his face, he was covering something, well, something so fucking frightening, I knew the signs, I did it myself on a daily basis. It was quite dark around here, not well lit at all.

"I'm here for you, anytime you want to tell me." As we got to the clearing at the end of the steps, I could see the most magnificent lake, with an old fashioned large wooden boatshed next to the water, with metal rails allowing the boat access easily, going into The still darkened water..

"Wow its beautiful." the lake was massive.

We moved to the unlocked door at the side, going inside, it smelt of old rotten wood. In the middle was a small pale grey yacht, with its sail rolled down, two jet skies, and a small black bow rider style motor boat, all above the water, all looking new. The boats had fishing and diving gear in them, from what I could see. We walked over to the side, where a comfortable sitting area, with a newish red leather sofa, chairs had been put n so they had a good view of the lake. In the side area was a toilet area, and a small kitchen, with black cupboards, and a stainless steel fridge, microwave and sink.

"This is more me." He looked at me, and sat with me on the sofa, with him so wonderfully, close again, breathing in his man smell, with a hint of aftershave. Touching my legs with his, and keeping his body there, making me feel so hot and so fucking, erotic. He kissed me, his tongue, pressing the back reaches of my mouth, oh that feels hard, and yet, so good. My back arched into the sofa, he was quite heavy, with his muscled body, but didn't seem to realize it. Trapping me, the weight was starting to hurt, I tried moving him to the side, but he didn't shift.

"Please, Marcus, you're too heavy, could you lift off a bit?" But he didn't seem to hear me, his baby blues were, in a trance, as he dry humped, and pushed into me, hard, over and over, I felt bruised.

"Sorry, I told you, I have sex, show me."

 I sat my slim body, gently, on top of him. Still feeling, a little battered, I slid, off him, moving my hands, slowly and sexily, undoing his zipper Pulling his jeans off, onto the floor, then pulling at his Calvin Klein black silk boxers He gave me a condom out of his pocket, to put on, before I slid them off. I opened my legs wide, moving my wet fanny, onto his erection, sliding, deeper, and deeper into me, his eager eyes on me. He felt good inside me, in a new and satisfying way, as I rolled slowly, then quicker, back and forth. Moans from within me, as the tension, of last week melted away. He came within me, filling my closed eyes with erotic fantasy. The sex was good, but quick but I wasn't expecting to come during penetration, I'd always said I had in past relationships, nothing to change there, as I moaned a rehearsed climax. As I rolled over to, the side of him he kissed me again passionately, his tongue getting used to all the delicious parts in his mouth.

"Did I really hurt you?"

"It's all good now." *Must remember to call the doctor and get back on the pill.*

"That's how I have sex, always in charge. I'm sorry Nat." He kissed my lips tenderly. We cuddled up on the sofa for a few minutes, and then he got up and put the used condom in the bathroom bin. He stopped as he came back into the kitchen and perused the cupboard.

"I have a kettle, to make coffee here, if you'd like some, it's instant though. Or a tea, I think I've got tea, no I haven't just coffee? So would you like one? I'm going to have coffee." He filled the black kettle, and put it on.

"Yes, coffee please Marcus, I've got sweeteners if you don't have them." I got them out of my handbag, which I'd dropped by the door as I came in earlier, as I walked over I noticed how large the place was inside.

"I'll get Claire to put a proper coffee machine and some sweeteners here for you if you decide to comeback sometime." I handed him my sweeteners. He poured milk and stirred mine, his was black. He handed me my plain black mug, and I put it down beside me on the floor. This area was very much a man's area, with his likes showing a through a bit more, no niceties or womanly touches in here as yet.

"Here you are." He handed my mug to me.

"Thanks Marcus." I put it on the floor next to me and sat on the sofa with Marcus.

"Do you use all these boats?"

"Sometimes, nut not as much as I could, I like being on the water, and under, but I suppose this place is a little neglected since it was built last year. Been at work and travelling for work takes up most of my free time I suppose. Do you like the water?"

"More a dry land person I suppose, no one, I know has a boat, or wanted one. I guess I'd like to have a go one day." We sip our coffees; I wanted him to put his arm around me, but he didn't. I wanted all these, relationship things, from him, if he obviously, didn't know how.

"So you like my helicopter ride then?"

"Loved it so much, we are going back in it tonight aren't we?"

"Yes we'll have to make a move after our coffee; I'll show you around a bit more."

"That would be great, Marcus thanks."

Stretching our legs out so they touched each other, felt so good, not one thing, could ruin this feeling of wanting, that I felt for him. I just want to be as close as I can for as long as possible. I gulped my coffee down.

"So how many boyfriends have you had Nat?" He put his cup on the floor, next to him.

"Well at school none, more interested in my schoolwork. After came, Matt at around 22, lasted a year or less. Then Craig, at about 24 didn't last long, just a few months. Then Simon just after, lasted about three years. Then no-one since really"

"So were you stuck on this Simon, that why you haven't dated since?"

"No not at all, it was him that ended it, I was changing, and moving on, and he couldn't keep up." *I can't tell you about my attack, it changed me totally. Simon was a simple person who wanted a simple life, and I was fucked up - Big Time.*

"What about you, you don't do relationships, so how many have you had sex with?"

"You don't want to know, Nat it started early that's all I'll say. You just don't want to know." He looked slightly sad, not the confident, man I was getting to know.

"But you haven't bought anyone back here or at your work, so it would seem from the staff's faces. Is that right?".

"Yes, I only use one place, so it's all away from prying eyes." He finished off his coffee.

"And where's that?"

"At my penthouse:, in the Plaza."

"But won't the staff see?"

"No it's all timed to perfection."

"Finished?" He put his hand out, changing the subject quickly.

"Yes, thanks" I give my mug to him. He grabbed it, putting it in the sink unwashed.

"Ok it's time to move on." He walked to the boathouse door, with me following him behind, something had shifted in him, he didn't want to talk about his sex life, but I wanted to know everything, well almost everything. He held the door open for me, and I grabbed his hand as we walked up the concrete steps. We walked in silence up to the lawn. He had something on his mind right now, that's for sure. It was slightly dewy on the grass, so I made sure I was on the stepping stones.

"You ok?"

"Just not sure if I can do this relationship thing, Nat, I hurt you tonight, and you have no idea what you're in for." He stopped halfway across the grass, turning he kissed me passionately. I felt his tongue reaching for the deep chasm as far as it could go. It was a hard kiss, not loving. But I just wanted him to kiss me, so it didn't matter too much to me. When we stopped, I really wanted to reassure him, he's mine.

"I really want to be with you Marcus. I don't care what I have to do, to be your sex partner, just yours though, I just want to be with you. I don't give a damn about, how many lovers you had, or what your number is. That's all in the past; I just want to be with you now." He kissed me more slowly, our tongues entwined, his arms wrapped very tightly around my body. He released me after a few minutes.

"I hope you are right Nat." We walked inside to the open lounge room door, hands held tightly together.

"I know that I won't be the one leaving you, Marcus. So unless you leave me then we'll be ok."

As we came in through the lounge, he stopped and looked me in the eyes, a little confused.

"No-one's ever said that to me, you'll just have to guide me with this. Even though like being with you, I've never had anyone, get this close, like being here at my home. You'll have to just tell me if I'm out of line, Nat., because I just don't know how it's supposed to go, in a relationship." He held his hands up, lost in the moment. I caressed his chin, which had, slightly dark bristles showing through.

"I'll let you know" I kissed him on the cheek.

As we walked back towards the kitchen, I checked my iphone for messages, none, it was almost 11pm,

"I'll just get a snack, for the journey. Do you want anything?" He walked with my hand in his to the kitchen, *Claire had gone to bed I think.* He opened the huge stainless steel fridge door, and looked around, grabbed a cold Pepsi, and a bag of plain chips.

"The same as you've got, cheese and onion, chips through please, if you have them?"

"Of course we have all varieties in here." He threw the bag at me, and pretended to throw the can, and I pretended to catch it. We took them and went out the kitchen in the hall.

"Bye Mrs. Grogan, if you're up?" I waved. Then out of thin air.

""Bye Nat, hope you had a good time tonight, and that he treated you well? Love to see you back again." Still no body arrived. Then she came out of a side door, her apron off. She hugged me, like my mother did.

"See you in the morning Claire, go to bed, I'll be back in about an hour."

"Ok, see you later then, thanks. Have a great flight back both of you."

As we got to the open front door, we walked hand in hand across the driveway, and along the path, to where I could see the helicopter sitting there I was getting so excited about flying back. *What did he mean about not wanting to tell me about his sex life?*

Chapter 6

Barker opens the door of the Limo, with a slight grin on his face. I remember the excitement of the flight here, with Marcus, he'd not really discussed as much as I wanted to, but I know he had to concentrate on flying. He was a really good flyer, I felt safe with him. I'd spent my time mainly looking at the beautiful specs of light that were cars, moving swiftly like ants, on a dark night, carrying some delicious delicacy on their backs. It was an amazing sight, something I hoped to see more of. As we landed, I felt a little sorry, it was such a sensory overload, being in a little glass fishbowl, secretly, gazing at people from, high above.

"Thanks, Barker." Marcus took his jacket off and threw it on the limo seat next to me his sexy cum aroma, I breathed in,. He sat next to me, as close as he could. I could smell us; I smiled, knowing I wanted him again, and soon.

"Well I think we made the evening last as long as we could, what you think? Did you enjoy yourself?"

"What's not to enjoy. I loved every single minute of it Marcus, I think you know that." I smiled a wicked grin at him. He kissed me with a passion, our tongues entwining in ecstasy. His hand moved to mine holding me as tightly as he could from his seat. Warmth moved into my pleasure zone, making me want him right here and now. The car stopped, and Barker came to open the door, Marcus and I still entwined.. He looked away, clearly embarrassed. As we moved into the elevator of my building, we held hands tightly. We were alone.

"I want to see you tomorrow, do you?"

"Of course I do, yes."

"I want you to come to see my penthouse, at the Plaza. Is that ok? With dinner at 6.30pm first of course?"

"Yes I do." *Oh shit, that's where he said he has sex which the millions of women do I really want to see that place? It's a big part of him, I think. I hope I'm doing the right thing by going.* The lift door pings open. As we walk hand in hand, back to the apartment, I wonder if Andy's back if he went out. I get my keys, ready, so I don't disturb him if he's asleep. Marcus leans in gently; and kisses me slowly, breathing him in for the last time tonight, *My boyfriend Marcus* he releases me, gently. Putting my keys in the door, and moving inside I wave goodnight.

"Night, see you tomorrow." He waves, and I watch go. Inside I hear movement, he's awake. I turn my keys.

"It's 11.45pm, you dirty stop out. He shouts, as I open the door, hope you had an awesome time." I then recount, almost all of it, highlighting the helicopter trip, missing out the sex. Andy's really happy for me.

"I'm so glad, he's" the one", he seems ok, from what I've seen of him, you have my approval." He laughed, we mess around for a while, and then I have a shower, sadly, washing his aroma, off me, and put myself to bed in the early hours of the morning. Dreaming about what a wonderful time I had, and looking forward to tomorrow, no today now. How much we'd done in a few short hours, it's amazing being with him, full on excitement. I drift off.

I sip my coffee, with a big childish grin.

"Well, what happened I'm waiting?" Trish was excited, eager for all the information she could get out of me.

"We went to the Plaza, which he owns for dinner, and it was so lovely. We left there and went, by helicopter to his home in L.A."

"Wow, Nat, did he fly you there?" She grinned.

"Yes he did, he's so good at it." *Erotic thoughts of Marcus flying, with me sucking him off,* fly through my head.

"Did you have sex?" She whispered. *I won't tell her, he's mine to remember, just me.*

"A lady never tells." I glared at her *it was too personal, for me.*

"Your grin is giving you away Nat, wow you did. He definitely may be "the, one" like you said, I'm really happy for you: she put her arm around my shoulder.

What's his house like?" She sipped from her Ducati mug.

"It's big, colonial style, with big round columns out the front. It's on about twenty acres I think." "Sounds so lovely, lots of privacy, right Nat?." She winked at me.

"Yes, apart from Claire, the housekeeper, and Barton the driver, and Smith, the security guy, yes lots of privacy." there was a hint of sarcasm in my voice..

"But you did have sex, though? Please tell, I won't ask any details, it you don't want to tell me." She whispered in my ear.

"Yes, in the boathouse, it was beautiful." I whisper, Trish jumps up and down like an excited child.

"Wow a boathouse too. Let's get back to work." We leave the tiny kitchen, mugs in hand, heading back to our office.

"You must have had a great time on your date, Nat with a smile like that?" Donna, is already in there, and smiled at me.

"Yes, he's perfect,, thanks Donna, we had an awesome time."

"So when are you seeing him next?" Trish clasps her mug.

"Tonight of course, he's taking me out to dinner again, at 6.30pm." an erotic grin, as I think of where I'm going with him tonight. *Wonder if we'll have sex in his sex-emporium, wouldn't mind if we did, just got to try and get those millions of other sex slaves, he'd literally had up there, in his penthouse, out of my head.* I sip the last dregs of my coffee, as my computer fires up. I'm a bit behind this morning, for some reason. My iphone rings, it's Rosie.

"Well tell all, did you have a good time?"

I told Rosie, I had a wonderful time and that he's a really nice person I re counted the trip in the helicopter, and left out the sex.

"I have to get on with some work now, Rosie. Talk soon, I'm seeing him again tonight. How's the bump?"

"Great thanks see ya."

I open up my personal emails, I've got one from Marcus Carrington, I remember we'd swapped all our personal stuff in the boatshed last night. *Including body, fluids mmm*

From: Marcus Carrington

To: Natalie Hungerford

Subject: Dinner Tonight.

Hope you're feeling good Nat?

Marcus

Marcus Carrington

CEO, Carrington Store's Worldwide.

From Natalie Hungerford

To Marcus Carrington

Subject: Dinner Tonight.

Good thanks for asking, looking forward to tonight.

Nat x

From: Marcus Carrington

To: Natalie Hungerford

Subject: Dinner Tonight

Me too, I'll pick you up a bit earlier, say 6.15pm is that ok?

Marcus

Marcus Carrington

CEO, Carrington Store's Worldwide.

From Natalie Hungerford

To Marcus Carrington

Subject: Dinner Tonight

That's fine, see you later.

Nat x

From: Marcus Carrington

To: Natalie Hungerford

Subject: Dinner Tonight.

Got to go to a meeting right now, see you later.

Marcus

Marcus Carrington

CEO, Carrington Store's Worldwide.

I get on, at last with my morning's work, remembering to call my Dr, to make an appointment on Friday, to get on the pill again.   My phone rang, and I felt relieved to focus of something other than Marcus. The morning went quite quickly,

"Do you want to get something for lunch, with me, I might sit in a café for lunch, if You want to," Trish had her red bag on her shoulder, next to me.

"Yes, "The Deli", has great coffee and sandwiches, I'd like to sit outside on this beautiful sunny day too." We walked slowly down the stairs, onto the office steps along to "The Deli."

"Hi, can I get a whole meal cheese and tomato toasted sandwich, please, with a cappuccino, to go." Once I'd collected my order, I waited for Trish, at the sunniest spot outside, I could find, A few minutes later Trish sat down, opposite me.

"I'm so excited about tonight, Trish; last night was such fun, such a rush for me. It's the first time in a helicopter, and you know me and heights, I just loved the whole trip." I sipped my take away cup of delicious coffee.

"You're in love with the pilot, I believe. It's the only thing I can think of."

"No, not love I'm smitten, yes. I've only been on two dates with him Trish, it can't be love yet." *Who was I kidding!* I couldn't eat my entire toasted sandwich. I sipped my coffee, visions of Marcus in his sexy white linen shirt, revealing, his dark chest hair, flash through my head, *I hope to get him naked tonight, this is my plan, for tonight sexual pleasure, in his penthouse..*

"Well that's what it looks like, from someone who hasn't met him yet, and knowing you the way I do." She finished off her, tuna salad sandwich, putting the plate to one side of the clean, white table. After lunch, we headed back to the office. Just as I reached reception, I was handed a bunch of cellophane wrapped, flowers, with a typed card.

"For you the delivery guy said."

"Thanks Megan." I took them off her and went upstairs, to the kitchen, for water. I took the card out, it was typed

"To Nat,

Thanks for last night.

From Marcus"

They were a mixed, colorful, bright, display. Putting them in the sink, I got a large vase to put them in, added water, to take them home later. I felt on top of the world *perhaps he's in love too, but he doesn't do relationships, this is a relationship thing to do, I'm confused, but happy, so happy .*I sent him an email.

From Natalie Hungerford

To Marcus Carrington

Subject: Flowers

Thank you for my beautiful flowers; they were such a lovely surprise see you later.

Nat x

I had a busy, afternoon, which was a good thing, because it distracted me, from my erotic thoughts of Marcus, romping erotically round his king size, bed in his penthouse. At 5pm, desk's cleared, and I've collected my flowers from the kitchen, *they are beautiful, he has taste, I'll give him that.* Trish walked out to my car, with me.

"Do I need to say, have fun? I know you will." She put her arm round me.

"Not really, I will, but thanks. Ride safely." Trish got on her motorbike and roared away, waving one hand in the air. I put my flowers, into the passenger seat, and drove home.

Andy was at work, when I got there, so I might see him when he gets back later .I put my flowers in a vase; I didn't get flowers often, so finding one was a challenge I arranged them, as best I could, in a large glass storage jar, which was the closest I could find. They looked beautiful, despite the slightly flared look. It was nearly 5.30pm, I'd better get a move on. I peeled off my clothes as I went to the bathroom, slinging them on a chair; the shower was old and took a while to get to my perfect, which is quite hot. Once I shaved my public area with my razor, I thought of Marcus, I put my finger over my clit, rubbing gently as if he were doing it, closing my eyes and imagining, his face close to my clit, as he rubbed harder and harder. I came an exquisite orgasm, pulsing through me, I kept it going, circling for as long as my body would let me. *I haven't done this for years; he's bought me back to life down there, he's so exciting, so erotic, so mine.* I got out and changed into a black skirt, and white camisole top, that I'd planned to wear. I sat in front of the bathroom mirror, and put on my favorite shade of nail varnish, "Hot Chocolate.". First my feet, as I lifted my foot up, I kicked the bottle, flinging it high in the air. The nail varnish went all over the mirror; it also bounced back, onto my white top. *Oh shit, why now.* Cleaning it off with nail varnish remover only smeared it, making it much worse. *Not sure it will come off.* I threw it under the tap, *my favorite camisole.* I threw it in the bin in the corner, hitting the wall instead, leaving a brown smear, *yuk.* I went to get a new red camisole top, *this will do.* Carefully, I painted my hand nails only, there wasn't much left of "Hot Chocolate." My makeup took less time, thank goodness. *Stop stressing out Nat, you have been out with him before..* My hair I left loose, hanging, sexily round my shoulders. *You are looking good girlfriend.* I looked in the mirror. I found my black, low court shoes, to cover my naked toenails. My iphone said 6.15pm, just in time. I waited, in the kitchen.

"Buzz" the doorbell. I put my new black bag over my shoulder, checked my iphone was in its pocket, and opened the door.

He was dressed in different black jeans, with a pale blue linen shirt, open at the neck, *Yum* and a dark blue single breasted, quality jacket over. He looked gorgeous, as ever.

"You look beautiful, Nat."

"Thank you, you look hot too."

"Do I?, he looked at his attire, not really sure what to wear on a date."

"You'll do fine." I smiled and he kissed me passionately, our tongues entwining once again. He had a different smell to him; his body wash was, fresh and outdoorsy. He took my hand and electric currents ran up my arms, as we touched. We walked to the lift, and waited.

"Thanks, for the flowers, hope you got my email."

"That's OK; it's something men do in relationships, Martha, told me. So that's what I did." I look him in the eye.

"Who's Martha?"

"Are you jealous?"

"Who is she?"

"You are, she's my assistant, in the office."

"Oh OK sorry."

"She's seen how different I've been, in the last couple of days, and put two and two together. I don't find her attractive, if that's what you want to hear. This is one of the reasons; I don't do relationships, very well. All of this emotional stuff."

"No course I'm not jealous." *I have to get used to him being around other women, Let it go Nat, or you'll destroy this perfect bliss, that I want so much.* The lift came, It had a couple in their 50's already in there, so we got in the opposite side, holding hands in silence, all the way down, I know I wanted to kiss him, but put it off. As we came out into the foyer, Marcus let the couple go out first, we walked to the front door, Barker saw us, he opened it.

"Evening Miss"

"Good evening Barker good to see you again." We got into the opened door of the Bentley. Marcus sat next to me.

"We're going to somewhere different tonight, hope you like it?"

"I'm sure I will, do you own it too?"

"Yes actually, it's part of our family business." A few minutes later, the car pulls up outside, an Indian restaurant, right opposite the sea.

"Hope you like Indian food, like I do?" He helped me from the car.

"Actually, I love it, my favorite." As we walk from the car, the views were stunning but on entering the restaurant you see the sea through a huge glass picture window, there were just seats in the window for 2 people. All other tables were cleared.

"You've got this place until, what time tonight?" I grinned at him.

"All night, if we want, they'll shut when we go. You're getting to know how I work, Nat." a cheeky grin appeared for a second.

"And this only our third date. I know you so well."

"Well you will after tonight." His face like stone again. He moves towards the counter.

"Hello Mr. Carrington, Miss. come with me please" The Indian manager, who had the name Deepak' on his badge, walked us to the table in the picture window, pulled the chairs back for us. I was given a colorful menu, but I knew what I wanted. I checked they had it though. Resting my menu on the table, the waiter came to take our drinks and food order.

"Claret for me, please, and then chicken tikka Marsala, with jasmine rice please." He took the menu.

"Med chicken Curry, with white rice please, and some naan with the drinks. And a bourbon please" his menu was taken. Marcus took my hand, thrills pulsed through me. We looked at the view.

"I know why you bought this place; it's such a wow, for customers."

"Yes, only bought this place four months ago, the owner was looking to sell, and I wanted to buy. Deepak is one of the original staff, promoted to manager. It's has huge profits, not that you're interested in that." He took his bourbon which had been place on the table. I sipped the taster, the waiter bought and nodded, as he poured the rest into my glass. I sipped it, I could drink this one all day. I nibbled the warm naan bread from the weaved basket on the table the waiter left with the drinks. Marcus put his legs against mine under the table, a warm rush, like we were connected, went through me.

"We are still going to your penthouse, tonight aren't we?"

"Yes, after this." He sat up, moving his body away from mine. *Weird.* Our food arrived, and we ate in virtual silence, it was as delicious as the view. I sipped my wine, and watched Marcus eat his food, there's something not quite OK with him tonight, he seems a little tense.

"Are you OK?"

"Yes." He had another mouthful, and stared at the view. *Oh, well I have asked him, I'm sure it's just showing me where he has had sex, with his millions of adoring women, but I'm with him now, so he can stop feeling like that, I'll tell him later.* As we finished our dinners, I didn't want anything else to eat, or drink. In the ladies, I adjusted my makeup, and perfume. As I came out, Marcus was already to go, he nodded to Deepak, and took my hand, Barker holding the outside, door, then the limo door,

In the Limo, it was deadly silence again from Marcus, no hand holding in the car. We drove for about 10 minutes down the road, then stopping outside the Plaza Hotel. Benson, opened the doors, then Carlton, greeted us, but Marcus just nodded and walked to the private lift in silence. Waiting, felt like an eternity. As we got in, I grabbed his hand, trying to get him to speak to me, *I'll leave it, we are here now, well almost, and he'll be better once I've seen the place.* The lift door opens, onto a very private, lobby. Big black security doors, he slides his key card in and it opens automatically, both sides. *How cool.* Inside, was a very large, double height, penthouse, with white walls, large modern colorful, paintings hung on the walls in places. The place was open plan, with a huge, stainless steel double oven and fridge, amongst the black two Pac kitchen. It was an enormous kitchen, just for him..

"Drink?" He goes to a bar on the far side of the apartment.

"Yes, claret, if you have it?" I walked slowly past the deep red, massive sofas, that were big enough to change the shape of, part facing the massive 2 storey beautiful vista, and part facing the wall. He handed me my glass, as I sat looking at the stupendous view. I looked around; it was his red and black, coming through just like the boathouse.

"When you're ready, I'll show you around." He sighed.

"OK I said." Sipping, and leaving my glass on the modern low black, coffee table in front me. *I have to get this over with,* there's *nothing here, to make him so edgy.*

"I'm ready, show me now." He put his glass of bourbon down next to mine.

"I have an obsession, I'm not normal, like you with sex. I don't want to lose you, but it's what I do. It's kept locked away, he grabs his key card, it's a part of me, and I want you to be a part of it too." He unlocks a room door, and beckons me in. As the door opens, I see it's a large bedroom, black wooden, I think, king-size 4 poster bed in the centre, with chains, on each corner post, leading to hand cuffs, to hold someone in place. The room is dark red, there are chains dangling from the ceiling, to the bed. Red silk sheets. The walls have what initially looked like pictures, but looking at them, I see they are whips, and all different types of leather hooked onto the wall. There's a large chest at the end,, which I can't see what's in it. There canes on the wall in racks, there's chains hanging on the wall, in varies lengths. I look at him, as he sits against the door, looking at me. The window has been complexly plastered over, so no light, or peeking to come in,

"What happened last night, when we had straight sex, wasn't normal for me. Rare for me."

"Why do you like all this stuff, all the whips, it must hurt?"

"My birth mother, beat me, and did other things to me, until I was 12, when the Carrington's adopted me, and took me to America, from England, to escape her. I still remember it, it plays out in my sex life, because that's all I knew, like I told you, yesterday. I'm in charge, so I don't get beaten ever. A partner does have to be willing, to do this, which is why I'm showing you, I want to show you what I like to do in sex. I want you to think about it. I won't ask you to stay, have a few days to thinks about it all. If you decide to be with me, then I'll tell you some other things, I'd like to do with you." I have one last look around, at the room of pain. *Shit, this is bad!*

Chapter 7

So tired, I haven't slept all night. Try and get some shut eye Nat. I've got so many questions Marcus, running round in my head. Must, write them down. How can he be so nice, then want to do things to hurt people, me, I don't get it. Why would someone agree to do that? They must have been happy at the time. My mind crowds with pictures of other sex partners, and Marcus bent over, their body, lashing them with the crops while they bend down. Ugh, *how could they want, to do that I don't get it. I do want to be with him, he's the one for me, I know that every time he's with me. But I haven't done anything like that at all; I'm scared he'll hurt me. Do I trust him? I've only just met him, if I asked myself that before, I looked at the room of pain, I'd have said yes. But now, I just don't know what he's capable of in there. I'd better get ready for work.* Opening my eye's I'm still half asleep. I pull myself into the bathroom, and lock myself in. *Wow, not a pretty sight in the mirror, mascara all over my face,* I didn't take it off last night when I got back. My thoughts were on something else. I pull everything off and have a swift shower, no naughty thoughts coming into my head, about Marcus, today, making feel all orgasmic. Actually all thoughts of Marcus all hard edged, at the moment. I hope that will change, if he's the one, I hope it will. As I get dressed in my dress for work, I feel a longing to see Marcus, to sort out some questions that have been going through my head. He told me he'll pick me up on Friday, for dinner, so I can get him to answer my questions. So I'll wait until then, I think, and try to stay alert driving, to work; I stop off at my favorite coffee shop, Gloria Jeans, and I order my large skinny latte. \with caramel sauce in it. *Gorgeous, just sweet and caramel enough for me*, it's perking me up as I get halfway through stuffing my takeaway cup into my cup holder, I get going for work again. Parking outside the office is normally easy, but I'm later, and have to go around the corner a bit.

As I go through to my office, with dark sunglasses on, and a coffee cup in hand, Trish notices me.

"What you up to, looking very shady there. Don't normally have coffee in the morning, what's up?"

"Nothing, just tired, needed something to wake me up." I dropped everything onto my desk, I was carrying. I hung my blue jacket over the back of my chair.

"Too much sex Nat?" I should have warned you about that, in a new relationship, you'll get some disease and die probably." She joked. *I wish it was too much sex, not enough sex, is what I have right now though. Sorted by Friday, if I decide yes, of course.* Donna sat down at her desk, luckily, not hearing the crude comments of my best friend.

"Morning to both of you, good night out Nat?"

She looked over at me.

"Yes thanks, Donna. Super in fact." *Well it's true I did have a good night out, up to a certain point, then I'm not sure, I suppose I was shocked, I wasn't expecting kinky, domination, stuff coming out of Marcus. I'd heard of people who were, dominating in relationships, and I'd heard of their partners being called submissive, sometimes. I didn't really know what it meant. Is this dominant, and submissive? Is that what Marcus is, and wants' me to be?. I'll find out, a question, I grab a notebook, from my desk drawer,*

1. Is this a dominant and submissive relationship, you want?

2. Will I get hurt?

3. How do I tell you to stop? -Can I stop you or is it up to you to use my body as you wish?

That's enough for now. I turn on my computer, ready to start my day now. My boos, Mr. Smith, is away for the next few days, so I have more to do, seeing his clients, I have 3 to see this morning, I see them, easily, but it takes up my morning totally. *I'm glad I don't normally see clients; I'd never get anything done.* Trish comes over to my desk.

"Want to go for lunch today, at 'The Deli again." Looking at my iphone, it was half an hour to go, until lunch.

"Yes, OK we'll catch up then." Lunch, comes quickly, and I'm glad. It's been too busy for my liking, I like to have easy days, which is why I've been working here for 4 years now. I could get paid more, somewhere else, if I wanted to go.

I pulled my new black bag on my shoulder. I'm at Trish's desk before she comes to me.

""Ready? Miss Townsend?"

"You beat me that never happen, just a sec." She put her rucksack on her back, and walked with me to the sidewalk.

"I could eat a horse." Trish sighed.

"Not sure you can get it at this deli. We can go to the mall if you'd prefer horse meat."

"Ew, here will do. Glad to see you're back to your normal self."

"Large, cappuccino and a chicken salad, please, to eat in." I gave him all my change.

"See you back at the table, as I took my order, to an inside table. Sitting down, I sipped my coffee, and thought about Marcus. I was feeling better about it all, I think. *He told me some awful things, which happened to him as a child. That can't have been easy for him to have told me. It happened when he was 12. That's not good, he can remember it all. Why weren't the authorities informed? If it happened here they would have put her in jail.* I get out my notebook:

4. Why did your Mum get away, with hitting you, and what happened to her? That's

2 questions. Putting the book in my bag, Trish puts her tray with, her drink, lasagna and chips on the small café table.

"What's with the notebook?" *Dam*

"Just getting some things, I have to sort out in my head, onto paper."

"Oh, OK everything still alright?"

"Fine thanks, I'd tell you, if I couldn't sort it all out myself." We ate out lunch, for a minute in silence.

"It's busy today for me, what about you Trish?"

"Normal day, for me. So are you seeing Mr. wonderful, tonight?" She sipped her coffee.

"No, Not until Friday, he has to run a multi-million dollar company sometime." *I thought I'd covered that well.*

"Taking you to dinner?" *Still probing*

"Dinner at the Plaza actually." *Covered.*

We talked about work, until it was time to go back to the office.

I was so busy again in the afternoon, 2 more clients to see that popped in without an appointment. Still it made it go quicker. I found myself wishing it was Friday already, so I could see my Marcus again, because that's how I think of him, mine. But do I want him now? That's the question, isn't it?

"Can I get coffee for you, it's my turn?" Donna was at my side

"Yes thanks Donna, I appreciate that. Just then I heard my iphone, ringing. *Oh it's Marcus…No Rosie Bugger* I answered it.

"Haws thing's Nat?"

"Great thanks Rosie. And bump ok still?

"Yes we are all three fine, How was your date last night?"
Must stop telling everyone.

"Great thanks Rosie, we went to an Indian restaurant, with a fabulous sea view, it was superb food to." Trish looks over.

"That's awesome, I'm glad it's all working out ok for you. You are seeing him tonight?"*Oh, no not again.*

"No, not until Friday, he has to work."

"Ok have a good day, catch up soon."

"Bye." I put my phone in my bag I catch up with the things I have to. *Dreams overtake my thoughts, Marcus is partly, undressed on the bed, tied up with chains and handcuffs. He is blindfolded, with a tiger skin blind fold. He begs me to release him. I refuse; climbing, on top of him, he has his nipples out which I lick tenderly, and then bite them hard, and it makes him squirm and moan. He has tiger skin Calvin Kline underwear on too, I touch him around his groin, he moans, in erotic pleasure.*

"Want a coffee Nat?" Trish was beside me, holding a tray of empty cups. *Fuck.*

"Yes thanks Trish." I try and catch up with my dream, but the phone rings, and I deal with the client's problem, and put the phone down. Trish hands me my drink, I put it on my coaster.

Perhaps being with Marcus, in a kinky way, is ok, that dream showed me something I don't normally think about, it was erotic, and made me feel horny, while I was thinking about it. There's something in that, it means I liked that, but I was in control not him. I sip my coffee, too hot. I grab my notebook,

5. Can I be in charge or will you always be?

The afternoon draws to a close, at work; I catch up on as much as I can, then leave the rest for tomorrow. Pushing my chair under my desk, I grab my jacket and bag, checking my iphone is in there. *No messages from Marcus at all today, he did say he had a meeting to deal with, probably kept him busy all day.*

On the way home, I stop off at Gloria Jean's for coffee and a think.

"Hi, can I get a large, caramel frappe, please." I hand her my cards.

"With cream?"

"Yes Please." I wait for my drink at the end of the counter. *As I think of Marcus, my body feels wet and wanting, he's in the boatshed, tied to the sofa, with handcuffs. I have total control over him, I put my lips on his, tongues, entwining, lusting..*

"A large, caramel frappe with cream? The young, uniformed, barista calls. *Oh my god.*

"That's me." I take my drink to a table, sipping my cold drink, with a straw. Dreaming again of Marcus, *He's hanging from chains, in his room of pain, handcuffed, and all mine to use. I lick his slightly dark brown, haired chest, going over his nipples, it fills me with excitement. His moans, as I touch his cock, that's huge, and erect ready for me, in my hand, I rub it, giving me such pleasure. I bring him to my body, pushing his erection, fully into me; it feels so good, as he comes quickly. Oh my, oh my, oh my, I'm wet again. Wow he really does have a really good effect on my body.* I finish off my drink. And go home. Andy's not in when I get home. So I have an early night, after watching some TV.

Waking to a new day, I got some sleep thank goodness. I go to the bathroom, Andy's in the kitchen making toast.

"Would you like some Nat?" He points at the toaster.

"Yes please, Andy, Pandy, with coffee if you're making it too?" *My mood was certainly one I liked today.*

"Ok, 2 bits?" He got the bread out of the freezer. ""Just 1 piece thanks." I close the bathroom door, and shower and dress quickly. As I do my makeup, I realize that I'll see

Marcus again tomorrow, and it made me excited. *I must be getting used to the idea, of kinky sex, in the room of pain.*

"Breakfast's ready." Andy shouted from the lounge room.

"I'm coming." I did all my final make up, and came out in to the lounge room. I sat on the sofa, where Andy had put my breakfast on the coffee table.

"Thanks for making that, you're a star." I nibbled on my slightly burned, toast.

"I'm off tonight, if you want to go out, unless you're already going out with Marcus?"

"Not until tomorrow, so yes love to Andy thanks." As I finished my toast I sipped my coffee, and watched the early morning news, on TV. *It will be nice to catch up tonight with Andy, we haven't for ages.*

I missed Gloria Jeans, this morning not feeling the need for it right now. I parked outside the office, and ran into Trish, just getting off her motorbike. She locked her helmet into the top box, and looked at me.

"Hi, just going to "'The Deli' for a coffee, do you want to walk down with me? I might get some breakfast too."

"Didn't you eat this morning?"

"No, just wanted to get out, from my mothers, glare."

"Ok," We walked down to "The Deli'. I looked at my iphone, it was only 8.45am.

"Hi, latte and bacon, lettuce, tomato, in a white six inch sub, please. Do you want anything Nat, while I'm here?"

"Thanks, but no." As we waited for her order, at the counter.

"What's your mum done now?"

She's just being mum, wanting to know everything, I do. I'm an adult, but I can't wait to be able to move out of home." She picked up her order, and we walked out on to the sidewalk.

"Look, I'm going out for a drink with Andy, tonight, you want to come? He won't mind at all."

"Just check with him first." I called Andy's number.

"Hi, Trish is a bit down, would you mind if I asked her to come along tonight?"

"Course not; I haven't seen her for ages either, so yes please." Thanking him, I put the phone down. I was feeling excited about tonight, now.

The morning was busier than yesterday for me. I tried to stay calm amongst, the chaos. I had to see, 3 clients in Mr. Smith's office, which I preferred, due to the locked door. After I had seen my second lot of clients, Trish bought me a coffee and piece of birthday cake. I'd been so busy, I forgot, it was the receptionists 33rd birthday. I went down the short stairs to the reception.

"Sorry, I forgot, I've been so busy. Happy Birthday Megan!

"That's ok I know you're busy, Nat you're still going to "The Stagg Bar" across the road after work, aren't you?" *Fuck I forgot I was going there, Trish must have forgotten too.*

"Of course, do you mind if I invite, my flat mate, Andy, we're going out later, and I may as well get him to meet me there.

"Of course not, he's very welcome." I got back to my office, and whispered to Trish.

"We forgot, about "The Stagg Bar tonight after work. I'll get Andy to meet us, there, and we can go on, after that. That ok with you?"

"Course, that's fine." I rang Andy back.

"Hey"

"Hi, I forgot a birthday drink, after work at "The Stagg Bar, across the road from here. The birthday girl, is happy for you to come straight after work if you like, we can go on after that."

"Sounds perfect, I'll get a cab down, so we can leave your car there if you decide to drink." *Tonight was getting better and better, all the time.* I went back to Mr. Smith's office, with my last clients for the morning, I went through everything I was supposed to with them, from the file notes, and the conversation I had on Tuesday with the boss. As I saw them out, I sat in the boss's chair for a while, swiveling it to the window. He had a good view of the street from here. My thoughts turned to Marcus who I hadn't heard from, yet today. *Perhaps just a little text to him. No just leave him, he's probable busy.* It was lunch now; I went to get my bag, hanging on my chair. I turned to Trish.

"You are going out for lunch?"

"Yes, like to go to the mall, if you don't mind driving us."

"That sounds like a wonderful idea; I want to get some bits." We walked out to my car, leaving the top on; I drove to the nearest Mall, which only took a few minutes.

"I'm looking forward to tonight, for a good booze up, haven't done that for a long time.

"Me too, should be fun." We parked on the ground floor car park, and walked into the Air-conditioned mall, called "

Silverlake Mall." Walking through the shops, we looked at the different window displays on show.

"I haven't got anything with me, to go out tonight; I'd rather find something here, rather than have Andy going through my drawers." I laughed.

"Nor me, that's what I want too." We went into the nearest department store, *pity they don't have a Carrington's store here, too small a place I suppose.* I found some black sexy jeans, drainpipe style, in a perfect size. Trish found blue jeans, drainpipe too. We each found the perfect casual tops to wear, trying them on just to make sure. I can wear my court shoes, I'm wearing now. Trish was happy with her shoes too. We looked for somewhere for lunch, heaps of places. We settled on Sushi Bar, and taking it outside table, to eat in the beautiful sunny warm air, and perfect blue sky.

"So you went to an Indian, with Marcus on Tuesday night?"

"Yes, it's out on the seafront, I hadn't been there before, it was very good food, and company." I nibbled my tuna avocado sushi roll.

"That's good; bet you're missing him, not seeing him until Friday, aren't you?" *I was missing him; still I'll see him soon.*

""Yes, I am."

The afternoon wasn't as bad as the morning; again I managed to get more of my own work done, before close of play. Now it was 5pm and I was ready to party. Trish and I got changed, in the ladies, Donna was coming as she was, as was Megan the birthday girl. Mr. Rumble went home already, he never liked to party after hours, and left that to his younger partner John Smith, who was away today. We walked over the road to "The Stagg Bar," On the outside it was modern, and had wooden tables for people to sit at. It was just getting a little darker now out here. On the inside, it was getting full of people just finishing work, and filling quickly. I looked for Andy; he was at the bar, with a drink. I waved at him and he got up. I sat with the girls, and Trish, on a couple of modern red leather look three seat sofas, the backs short and square, edges to them. Andy appeared, and he sat between me and Trish, whist Donna and Megan, sat on the sofa opposite us. We introduced her, and Donna, who Andy couldn't remember meeting before. Megan only joined in the last year, so that may be true.

"Whose birthday is it? Megan put her hand up, the drinks are on me. If you could come and give me a hand with them Megan" Andy *never buys a round -ever.* Trish and I look at each other he goes to the bar with Megan, as we all give him our drinks orders. We watched Andy do his stuff at the bar with Megan.

"I hope she's not after a relationship, so soon after her divorce? Andy's more into one night stands. He never has anyone staying over." I look at them deep in conversation, at the bar, the usual routine, I've seen many times before. They come back with Andy holding the tray of drinks, Megan behind him. "There we are, the tray is put on the table, and he moves to the other sofa next to her.

"Happy Birthday." They chink glasses. We all congratulate her.

"I'm just staying for one drink, then I'll be off Nat, I have to cook for Glenn and the kids."

"That's ok; we may drink well into the night anyway." I sipped my red wine.

"This place is quite good place after work, isn't it?" Trish says to me and Donna, as the other two clearly not listening.

"We could go out, after work more couldn't we Nat, just got into a habit of going home afterwards." Trish sips her beer. *It was actually getting a little embarrassing now, watching Megan and Andy, perhaps I should say something to him, I know I'll see if Trish thinks I should.* I say I'm going to the ladies, Trish come too. I tugged her arm. In the ladies, Trish and I were alone, to talk.

"What is it?

"Do you think I should have a word with Andy, or Megan? Andy only wants sex with his women, no sleepovers remember?"

"They are both in their 30's they know what they want. If they both want just sex tonight, then thanks what they'll both have. They are both adults just leave them, I don't see it's any of our business to butt in." Trish was a straight talker, which I liked.

"Right I'll let them be, and if she comes back for sex tonight, I'll just have to ignore it." *Ew the thought of it, made me queasy, mostly because if I'm honest, Andy's activities never really affected me, but Megan is a work colleague in a very small firm.* We exited the ladies, headed for the sofa, Andy and Megan, had started to hold hands now

"I'm going now, Thanks for the drink Andy, see you tomorrow girls. Have fun tonight all of you." Donna picked up her wine glass, and finished it off.

"Goodbye Donna, thanks for coming out," said Megan.

We had planned for tomorrow. We all had another drink, and then decided to move on somewhere else. We decided on "Moo Moos Café." which was a cab ride away, as I wanted to leave my car, and drink tonight. *It was my suggestion for Moo Moo Café, obviously, I thought he might be there, to take me home himself. But I knew he was in L.A. until tomorrow, I still clung to hope anyway.*

Moo Moo's, is still crowded, it's only 6.30pm, and still full of office staff. As soon as I walk in, in brings back memories of me and Marcus, I don't want them to disappear, I want them to stay. I want him to stay with me. He's not in there as I look around.

'What would you like to drink Nat?'

"It's my turn Trish" I get my tiger skin purse out of my bag, to pay. Andy and Megan have got a table in the corner, near where Marcus and I sat, tears start welling up in me, as I realize I miss him so much, *perhaps shouldn't have come here.*

"You ok, are you crying? What is it?" Trish is anxious.

"Nothing, just missing Marcus, I'll see him tomorrow."

"That's what I thought it was. If you want to talk about anything, you know I don't blab."

"It's ok thanks, I might text him in a minute." I wanted to now. I ordered the drinks; Andy and Megan already told me what they wanted before grabbing a table. I got my iphone out. *Rather do this here than over there. I sent the text.*

"Missing you, out for drink with friends at Moo Moo Café x" In a few seconds, I got a text back.

"Missing you too, this is hard for me to keep away from you, for so long, just letting you have time to think x" *OMG that's so good to hear from him, why didn't I text before.* My iphone beeped again

"Have fun with your friends, I'm looking forward to seeing you tomorrow, hope you are?" I typed back, with a massive smile on my face.

"Course I'm looking forward to it. X" I sent it.

Trish and I took the drinks tray, to the others, who were now kissing. *I was truly over the whole Andy and Megan thing; I really am being missed by my boyfriend, so I don't give stuff about anyone else. We stayed until 9.30pm, then went on to a club, nearby, which I hadn't been to in years, dancing the night away around my and Trish's handbag. Got a cab, dropped Trish off, and then back to mine, where I fell asleep on the sofa, next to my iphone with my boyfriends messages over and over in my head.*

Chapter 8

Marcus, is doing everything I ask him to, as I lie on the bed, handcuffs around his wrists and ankles. "I have a surprise for you darling." I was opening the tiny package, I'd beautifully wrapped for him in gold, with a silver bow, as he couldn't. I took out a gold ring, and pushed it onto his marriage finger, "No, no I 'm not getting married, please Nat, don't force me, please. I then had sex with him on the bed to seal the deal. "Now it's done" I looked at him, lying there, in an erotic haze, shit what I have done!

"Fuck my head hurts, what was that all about?" Opening my heavy, tired eyes *fuck I'm on the sofa, and my body hurts.* I lift the quilt off me, and look at the clock on the microwave, it's 8.15am.

"Shit, I got to get up now." I walked slowly into the shower, which I did as, quickly as I could. I remembered last night, as I did. *Had a bloody good night out with everyone, even went to "Chino's" I haven't been there since my teens. Wow what a blast it was, dancing around Trish and our handbags. I want to go there again now.* I got the towel around me, as my clothes were in the bedroom. I put my makeup on in super quick time, and opened the door to go to my bedroom. As I walked past the kitchen, I saw Megan, making a cup of tea, she saw me.

"Hey Nat, how are you this morning?" She stirred 2 mugs and picked them up to take with her. *Shit, Andy's had (literally) Megan here overnight, wow did he mean to? Or was it, was just that they fell asleep afterwards? Shit.*

"Hello Megan, hope you had a good night?" *Fuck, why say that, I don't want to know about her sex life.*

"Yes I had a good night, in all ways, you rocked last night, didn't realize you were such a party animal?" I walked into my bedroom, to get dressed. I grabbed the closest thing I could find, black trousers, and long white blouse, looked a bit dressy, but it didn't matter. I brushed my still wet hair and put it up in a ponytail, as I didn't have time to dry it right now. *I wonder how Trish is feeling this morning, she got back before us?* I opened the door to get some breakfast quickly. Andy was in his PJ's and Megan was dressed in the same clothes, as yesterday. *Fuck this is embarrassing. I'll get breakfast on the way, or when I get there at "The Deli. I just wanted to leave them to it. Fuck the car, it's at work, this is why I never do this."*

"Megan, how are you getting to work?"

"Normally go by bus, but as its 8.40am now, it will take too long."

"I'll call a cab, which will be the quickest." I grabbed the phone handset, and the directory, found the number; they were going to with us within 10 minutes." I grabbed a coffee mug, and put some coffee in from the jar, then added luke warm now water, from the kettle, which would be quicker to drink. Whilst there I put a piece of bread in the toaster, and got the peanut butter out, and a knife. *Hope my car's ok.*

"Do you want some? I looked at thin as a rake Megan." Who shook her, blonde head.

The toast popped out, I spread it as quick as I could. Megan was all over Andy, getting his phone number off him, before she left. Andy was trying to get away, at first realizing that it was ok to give it to her. The door buzzer went.

"Cab for Hungerford." The gruff man's voice echoed.

"Thanks, be straight down."

Andy had a last kiss from Megan. I held the door open for her, with one hand, toast in other as we walked towards the lift. Pressing the button, the lift came quickly, and we stepped in, it already had four people in it. Megan and I were in virtual silence, until the lift door pinged, and out into the lobby we went. I ate my toast.

"Have you got something against, me and Andy dating, Nat?"
I ran towards the cab, and got in. Megan climbed in with me
in the back.

"Rumble and Smith Lawyers, in the High Street, Do you know
them?"

"Yes, the cab driver started driving."

"No of course not, Megan, what makes you say that?"

"You're not talking to me Nat." *I should have warned her,
he's not into relationships Perhaps he's changed his mind with
Megan; I don't know what to say to her.*

"Look Andy has his relationships, and I don't really have
anything to do with them, has he arranged to see you again?"
Probing, to find my answers.

"No he's going to call me, tonight and arrange to go out."
*There's a get out right there, for Andy, if he wants it. It's
nothing to do with me.*

The cab was stuck in traffic, the cab driver cursing, at the still
cars. I finished off the last bite of toast, and licked my long
fingers. *I realized I haven't even had a chance to think about
Marcus, I'd been so full on. I was seeing him today, did I have
my notebook with my questions, as he's picking me up from
work. I was suddenly so excited knowing that at just after 5pm
today, I'd be with Marcus, it made me smile.*

"Do you think Andy won't phone me? Is that what you think Nat.?" The cab luckily pulled up outside, Rumble and Smith, I looked at the clock in the car it was 9.05am. I paid the man $20, telling him to keep the change; he was instantly full of appreciation. I got out the cab after Megan had, she tried to give me money, but I said it was on me. In the street, just where I left it, was my beautiful car. We went into the office.

Megan, arranged herself in reception, and turned on the phone system, as I went past. she smiled at me.

"Thanks for the cab, Nat, I really appreciate it."

"My pleasure, Megan." I walked up the stairs, into my office. Donna was on the phone, Trish had her head on her desk, I put my bag on my chair, and sat down.

"You awake, Trish?" Silence.

"I'm getting a coffee, anyone want one?" I looked at Donna, and she nodded.

"I'll come with you." Trish's head appeared, and stood to follow me to the kitchen.

"How are you feeling today?" I was obviously more awake than she was.

"Not good, had too much to drink, will never do that again, ever"

"Heard and said that before Trish, and it got broken, just like your new year's resolutions, only last for a few days normally." I put the kettle on and putting our mugs on the tray.

"We had a good time last night didn't we? With Andy and Megan, were in their own little bubble. What happened to them at your place? Did she stay?" She whispered.

"She stayed the night, a first for Andy I think. I was so embarrassed this morning, got up from sleeping on the sofa, and Megan was making them tea, in his t-shirt. "

"Ew, that's horrible, did Andy get rid of her, in his usual way?"

"Well I think so; he took her number and said he's going to call tonight, which I don't know is a brush off r what?"

"She seems to think, he's going to call." The kettle boils. "How did you get here this morning, I got here and thought you were already, here, then I remembered last night."

"We came in a cab, together, it was embarrassing, Trish. I'll take my car next time."

"That's so funny. " Trish laughs.

"It's up to Andy now, nothing to do with me."

"You think? Hope so for your sake." We bring the tray of drinks into our room.

"Good job Mr. Smith's away, with you two looking as out of it, as you are."

"You're probably right there Donna." I put her mug on her desk. Trish got back to some work, and I turned my computer on. Whilst it booted up, I thought of Marcus, I'll send him a message.

"Hi, had excellent night out, with friends, now bearing the brunt of it, this morning. Looking forward to dinner, later x" and sent it. A few seconds later, ping.

"Glad you had good time, hope I can out do that tonight?"

"I hope so too, see you soon. x" I'm all wet again.

"Looking forward to it, like you wouldn't believe, I have a meeting, see you later. "The morning had two unexpected visits, from clients wanting reassurance, on some things before they came into see John Smith, next week. It only took a short moment, but I dealt with it in reception, aware of being watched by Megan at the same time. I managed to get quite a bit of my work done, right up to lunchtime.

"Where you want to go for lunch today?" Trish was picking up her stuff, and getting ready to go.

"Why don't we go to the place we went last night, "The Stagg Bar.?"

"What an awesome idea, hair of the dog, right?"

"Not really, off alcohol, thought you said?"

"Oh yes I see what you mean, let's just go and have fun." grabbing my bag, we set off across the road to the bar. In reception, Megan was waiting for us, with her bag over her shoulder.

"Where are we going?" *Shit* I looked at Trish and smiled.

The bar was different in the light of day, as we made our way to a red sofa first. Megan sat opposite, and Trish went to get the menus, as there were none on the table.

"You have to order and pay up there. What drink you want Nat?" We normally paid for ourselves, and I wanted to keep that going.

"I'll order mine thanks, Megan, you coming to get your drink?"

"Oh ok" at the bar she ordered a Pepsi max and went to order a salad at the cash register.

"Trish ordered beer, lasagna and chips again? "I ordered a claret wine, and a whole meal, sandwich, *I am going for dinner with Marcus, tonight.* A smile takes over my face, as I walk back to the sofas, with a low mahogany table in between.

"So do you think Andy will call me tonight, Nat?" *I knew this was going to happen, its*

Nothing to do with me, leave me alone.

"I really can't help you with that one, Megan. Andy and you are both adults, making your own choices, phone him, if he doesn't." *Has same conversation with Trish I n the Ladies here last night, I remember.*

"So you think he won't?"

"Look Andy's a big boy, *ew, wrong choice of words* He can call you right now If he wanted to. He's not that into relationships, Megan, You want me to be honest with you?"

"Yes, I do just give it to me."

"Well Andy likes sex, but not into relationships at all, so far. He has never in the years I've known him, have a proper relationship with anyone. He has never even let anyone, sleep over. "

"So I am special then, because I stayed over?" *She's exasperating*

"This is new for me and for Andy; you really will have to speak to him yourself. He may have just let you stay, because it was convenient at the time."

"Convenient?"

"Speak to him, Megan, no more talk of Andy during lunch. Ok?"

"Ok." Luckily our lunch arrived at that point; I sipped my wine, hoping that Andy did call her and put her out of her misery. We ate our lunch in blissful silence. Looking around, this place looked bigger today, It's white walls with large mirrors dotted around, the floors were white tiles, reflecting the warm sunny day outside. As I finished my food, I sipped my wine, and looked at Trish, who was trying not to laugh.

"Do you see you boyfriend tonight?" Megan had finished her food, and sipped her drink

"Yes he's picking me up from work at 5.00.pm."

"So I'll be able to see him then." Trish did so want to see him, to get the mystery man out of her head.

"Yes, if you're still around? I'll introduce you."

"I'll make sure I'm around." Trish smiled.

"I'll see him when he comes into reception then."

"Yes Megan, you will see him too." *I didn't realize that having Marcus as my secret was appealing to me. Having to share his identity, with the office, it had to come; I just wasn't ready for it.* We finished lunch, and started to walk over the road to the office, when I really fancied a "The Deli" coffee, so we managed to farewell Megan, in the nicest possible way.

"My god, I didn't realize how annoying Megan is at times" Trish looked at me.

"I know, I think after her divorce, she told me once, that she just wanted to have a baby, but her ex didn't. Knowing that, Andy is not the one for her?"

"Oh, now I feel for her, you're right about Andy though." Trish walks into "The Deli" with me. "Could you see Andy with a baby, I couldn't?" I smile at the thought.

"Not the way he is right now, but he's the perfect age, if he does like her. Remember she did sleep over." We order and pay for our coffees. As we stand waiting, a huge grin comes over me again, as I imagine Marcus actually coming into the office, to pick me up.

"You're thinking of Marcus?" I nod.

"I hope you guys stay together, as I'm not sure I can survive if you ever broke up."

"I'm not breaking up with him ever."

"Would you marry him?"

"He's not into marriage at all, so no." I was quite happy with that, I had no urge to have kids, like Megan, so our relationship, will flourish because of our, wanting to be with each other. We had about 10 minutes to sit and have our coffee, before the afternoon onslaught. We sat outside on the, café chairs, on the sidewalk.

"I hope you'll find someone, like Chris, and marry them if that's what you want."

"I do date Nat, but I've not found anyone I like enough, to have a relationship with. Seems to be a few dates and that's all I want from them."

"Take last month, Jerry, was nice, just lasted a couple of dates. What was wrong with him?"

"Just not for me, we were so different in so many ways, whereas I thought we had a lot in common at the start." We finish and throw our cups into the bin. Walking on to the sidewalk, it occurred to me that Trish was still in love with Chris, and was rejecting everyone else, but kept it to myself.

Back in our office, I felt a new vigor, for the place. Marcus I would see in now just 3 hours time, I was beyond pumped up.

I got all my work done, saw 2 clients of Mr. Smiths in record time. Trish really was looking forward to seeing him too. My iphone rang, and I picked it up, out of my bag. *Marcus, Rosie*

"Just wishing you all the best tonight, you are going to dinner right?"

"Thanks Rosie, yes I'm planning on having a good time. Feels like I haven't seen him for ages, but it's only a few days"

"Are Sebastian and the baby all good?"

"Yes everything is going as it's supposed to with the baby, and Sebastian, wants me to give up work now, I want to wait until, I feel uncomfortable to work, I do type, at a desk, as well as reception, so we'll have to get someone in at that point."

"Ok, well if I hear of anyone, I'll let you know."

"Thanks Nat. talk soon. Have fun"

"I will, see you." I put my iphone down; I was getting a little stressed over the Marcus date now, had I written down all the questions I wanted to ask him? I got my notebook out and held it to my chest, so no one could see, and took it to the kitchen, and made a coffee for just for me, and took it back to Mr. Smith's room, to go through again. *Do I have any more questions, for him? I seem to have mellowed a lot since I saw him last, having erotic dreams, makes this seem like a good thing, in a way. I have no more questions, so as long as I'm happy with the chat I have with him about these, He's going to tell me something else; he'd like me to do. Shit, I have no idea on what that could be.* Taking my notebook back to my office, I put it in my bag. Look at my iphone, less than an hour to go. I take my bag and redo my makeup and perfume. *Shit, I completely forgot to go to the Dr's for the pill.*

I ring the number and make an appointment for next week. Apologized, been so busy. It's finally 5.00pm and everyone starts packing away, I've already done that. My iphone goes, *Marcus*

"Hi, I'm coming in you ready?" *oh yes.*

"Yes, come in now." A few seconds later the front door opens, just as I'm coming down the stairs. *OMG he's even more gorgeous than I remember.* Trish is behind me, mouth open, and Megan, peers out from behind her desk. He takes me in his arms, and a full passionate thrilling tongue twisting kiss, that lasts for minutes, not wanting to release him. Eventually I do, and introduce him to Trish and Megan, work colleagues. He's wearing a black suit, with, my favorite, white linen open necked shirt.

"Ready?" I nod, let's go now." He whirls me out of the office, and into the Bentley Limo outside. I can see the two of them speechless, at his good looking hotness and devotion to me, and obvious wealth.

Chapter 9

As we get into the Limo, Barker has a smile on his face, as he sees us together. When inside, our lips, meet again, electric thrills go through my body, as he holds me tightly, and our tongues entwine again, this time even longer. *OMG I've missed you, never go away from me again do you hear Marcus.* He comes out and kissed my lips softly and gently, leading to my neck. *He's making me hot, and wet.* As we sit up, our arms still entwined, he gives me a huge bouquet of pink and yellow flowers, with a handwritten, note.

"I've missed you, Nat"

Marcus

"Thank you, so much." I kiss him tenderly on the lips. Then his throat, gently, and he moans in erotic pleasure, the car starts to slow down, and then stop. We're outside"The Plaza" which is what I hoped for.

"You glad you're here, Nat.?"

"Yes, you know I love the views up there. It's nearly sunset, which I wanted you to see."

Carlton nods as we go through. He grabs my hand, tingles run through me, and we walk to the private lift. To any outsider, we're two people in love, staring at each other, because, we've missed each other so much. The lift opens and we go in. He moves in front of me, and kisses me more passionately than he's kissed me before. My tongue ached afterwards. When we reached the restaurant, he still had his around my shoulders, as we walked into the empty "Seaview Restaurant". The manager Max shows us to the best seats, in the place. He takes the seat out for me to sit down, he smells delicious, manly body wash, and expensive perfume. He sits down, the drink waiter comes.

"Nat what would you like to drink?"

"Red wine, a sweet one today please." I look at the waiter.

"And I'll have a Bundaberg rum, and coke." The waiter goes.

"So have you had a good day at work?" He touches my hands gently. *Chills!*

"Very busy the boss has been away for the last few days, so it's busier than usual."

"What about you, good day?"

"It is now." He kissed my hand; a he bought it to his face.

"I'd like to see your office, see what you do, one day."

"Does that mean you're staying, with me?"

"That would be telling, wouldn't it?" The waiter bought our drinks, and the menus. I tasted the wine, and he filled my glass. The sunset was the best I'd ever seen. We had perfect views all around, just stunning. We sipped our drinks still holding hands. Our legs were now entwined around each other too, giving me such a warm feeling of love inside.

"What do you want to eat?" I looked through the menu again then, look at Marcus.

"I want you, for dinner." I whispered

"Later, if you're coming back to my place, you have me then." He smiled lovingly at me.

"Ok I'll have the fettuccini, please." I said to the waiter, as he came to see us.

"I'll have, spinach and ricotta ravioli, please." The waiter took our menus.

"Can I get my questions, out of the way, before we eat?"

"Yes, fire away" He moved back some he was upright again, still holding my hand .I grabbed my notebook from inside my handbag. *What to choose first?*

"Is this a dominant and submissive relationship, you want?" He looked at me.

"Not really, I mean, I don't want you to act all submissive, if that's what you mean. I nod. It's more about the erotic side of it. It turns me on to be dominant over you, in a very big way, to see you tied up like the bed is sexy, to me. It turns me on that's all. Does that cover it?" I nod. *I'm glad, I want a say in my sex life too.*

"Will I get hurt, with the whips, and chains and stuff? If I did tell you to stop, would you immediately, or would you get to use my body, as you want to, for as long as you want to?"

"Fuck, that doesn't' sound too good does it. I need your permission to do anything with you, if you're tied up, so you tell me and I'll stop."

"Can I be in charge sometimes? Or will you always be?"

"I've never been asked that before. I like to be in charge, so if you do too, we can work it all out, I'm sure."

"Why did your mum get away, with hitting you, and what happened to her? "

"Wow, you really want to know? I nod; she was on drugs, and for all my 12 years, of being with her, she allowed me to be raped, and many other things, so she could get her fix. She got away from the system; she only started sending me to school at 12, and the authorities jailed her for life, and that's where she is right now. I hate her, all thoughts of her I tried to forget, the Carrington's adopted me, we all came out here, I was privately tutored to catch up. And here I am, fucked up sexually, because I'm not normal as I said before. But I care about you very much Nat, I don't know the reasons, I just know that I feel better, when I'm with you, I hope you feel the same?"

"I think you know that I care very much about you Marcus, that's why I want to sort this all out, so we can be together more." I kiss his hand, as he moves closer to me. Our food is here,

"Another drink Nat?"

"Yes another wine please, it's gorgeous."

"Just like you." He whispered. I smiled as he took my hand across the table trying to eat pasta with only one hand, his was easier to prod with his fork, I had to daintily twirl. In a race, if there was one he won. I sipped my wine that the waiter bought. We sat staring at each other, like people in love, but I knew it was too soon for that. As I finally finished, he said

"Do you want a sweet?"

"You know me, of course I'd love one, I looked at the sweet menu, and he'd been given.

"Too many choices again, I'll have the lemon meringue pie, with cream please."

"That sounds good, two of those please, and the waiter took the menu. We touched legs again, sending pulses through me. Our hands were locked tight, as he gripped my hand in a loving way. I sipped my drink, and he his. Just then our puddings arrived in super quick time. They looked delicious, and they tasted it too. It melted in my mouth, with a slight lemon tang, beautiful. This place is awesome; well we are their only guests.

"This is sublime. Compliments, to the chef. What time have you got this place until tonight?" I ate mine as slowly as I could, manage for such a delicacy.

"All night if you want, but I'd rather go to my apartment, wouldn't'you? He grinned wickedly at me. *He's so hot.* I put down my fork, finishing in super quick time.

"Do you have any more questions? He grabbed my hand gently, and kissed it lovingly. You said there was something else you'd like me to do, what's that?" I grabbed my handbag.

"I find it erotic to watch a woman, playing with your body, using toys, and licking you. *Oh shit.*

As we ascended in the private lift, he took me in his arms and kissed me passionately, we were entwined; he tasted of meringue pie, mmm. The lift pinged and he took my hand, leading me to his door, he unlocked with his key card, using his free hand. Inside I saw the beautiful penthouse, because it was light and beautiful the tall double storey frameless glass. In fact I'm sure my fear of heights has now gone, since being with him. He had marble flooring in the lounge room, with thick, black wool rug, under the huge sofa. Which I sat me on, whilst he went to the kitchen. *How hot he looks tonight. His hair messed up, by me and specks of sun streaks, makes him, look even sexier – he must have a lot of willing sex partners, ew. I do feel so secure with him, so grounded.*

"More wine? My favorite bottle of wine, He *remembered,* He opened the bottle, and got two glasses from the bar, put them on the coffee table in front of us.

"Thanks Marcus." He poured into the glasses. *Wow this is a dream come true, I can't believe it, I'm finally here in my Marcus's apartment, having the most blissful time. He wants to be with me, and I could stay here forever.* I sip my wine, put it on the table, putting my arms around his head, I put my lips to his, gently kissing him, then moving to his neck, little kisses as he moans in delight.

"I want to have sex with you here on the sofa, normal sex, right now." His voice had an urgency to it.

"Couldn't agree with you more." I sounded as sexy as I could.

"Do you have condoms? I'll be back on the pill next week."

"Of course." He took several out of his pocket, and put them on the coffee table. I lay there on the sofa, as he pealed my trousers, then my sexy lingerie off. *Shit, I haven't time to shave, or wash.*

"I can go and shave, now if you prefer?"

"I'm happy with you any way I can get you, just want have sex with you now Nat. No problems, you're fine as you are." His finger went inside my wet wanting body, in and out, in and out slowly, getting me hot and steamy. I pulled his trousers off, then his Calvin Klein's off, his cock was hard, and he moved on top of me, filling me with his, back and forth slowly, then quicker, and quicker. Moans of delight came out of my body; I was getting unusual orgasmic feelings, welling up inside me. He had his hands out to; keep his body weight off me. Orgasm, took over my entire body, pulsing over and over. He came at the same time, thrusting hard, into my body as he did. Moans of ecstasy came from Marcus's mouth, as he pumped, his come into my body. Luckily the sofa was wide enough for the 2 of us to lie, side by side. For a few minutes, we just lay there in each other's arms, until our breaths, slowed. He removed the condom, tying a knot in it, and putting it in a bin nearby. We sat up and cuddled on the sofa, for a while. About an hour had passed, and then we dress.

"I want you to stay the weekend with me, will you?"

"I' can't think of anything, that I want more." *I really am falling for you Marcus; I can't believe that I've found my soul mate. Apart from the erotic bit's in the room with a woman. I don't understand that, so much, only doing it, I'll know whether I like it or not. I would do anything for him, that's the problem, that's why I'm still here.* I grabbed my iphone, and texted Andy, so he knew I was at Marcus's all weekend, he replied with his usual, 'Well done' comments. I put my iphone away.

Marcus stands, walking to the kitchen with the used condom, and put it in the incinerator.

"This is all new to me Nat, having sleepovers, I'll show you around, if you'd like to?"

"Yes, love to see where you live." I was like an excited chipmunk. We walked, hand in hand, electricity pulsed through me. We went out of the main room, down a hall past the locked bedroom.

"You've seen the room in there, he opened the next door.

"This is another bedroom, as is the next door." Looking inside it was furnished in modern, men's colors,. "It's nice. "He walked past the next door, as it's the same. Then we went on to a dining room, with the most stunning views, again.

""What a great place to eat!" He smiled. We came back out into the main lounge area again, where his security room was.

"Who uses that, then?"

"If I want Barker in here for security, he stays in here, with anyone else; there are 2 beds in here for them. As well as an office, with everything they need." Next into a door, it's a very plush, 12 seat, movie theatre, with black leather recliners, and electric blinds, completely obliterating the view and light, by the touch of a button. Next door is his office, with his huge modern desk, facing the view. The filing cabinets line the wall at the rear.

"That's it on this level, just the master suite left." I look at little confused, thought we'd seen all the bedrooms. He walks me across the lunge room, and presses a remote. A set of glass steps, appear to a hidden mezzanine level, I thought was just a wall, but as I watch the wall is changing to clear glass.

"I normally keep this down, during the day, but just want to show you how cool it is."

"Wow, I've never even seen a wall do that before, it's so clever." I can see his black king bed frame as I stand there, I move up the clear glass steps, which feel like there's nothing holding them there. In the master suite, there's the bathroom off to the left, overlooking the view, all privacy glass. Then walk in storage, wardrobes. Then the humungous round, black leather, sided, and built in headrest.

"It's one of the best waterbeds around, cool eh?" I sit, and then lie on it, it is so comfortable, all over, not that I'd sat on many waterbeds, in my time.

"Are we going to sleep here this weekend?"

"Yes, unless you'd like one of the other bedrooms, but I'd prefer sleeping here."

"Can I have a shower now, so I feel a little cleaner? I don't have any other clothes to wear either this weekend?"

"We'll sort that out tomorrow, go into our L.A. store, if you like, you can get whatever you want there. Tonight, I have t-shirts you can use. I'll get your clothes cleaned by the service here that does all that, and back to you tomorrow. Ok?"

"Wow that's wonderful, thanks."

"Oh, nearly forgot, I'm having lunch with my parents on Sunday, that ok with you?"

"That's great, they're in San Diego, and so are we flying?" *Meeting the parents too, how awesome. It may be a little soon, but I don't mind, not with him.* I have a quick shower, using the razor; I bought with me, to trim myself. *That feels better, now.* Then I get dressed into one of his t-shirts, which covers my girly bits, just. It's a simple black T-shirt, obviously quality made. *I look good in it.* I tied my wet hair up, whilst I do my teeth, with a brand new toothbrush, I found in his cupboard. *I'm sure he won't mind.* I looked at my iphone whilst I had it there in the bathroom, no messages, was 11.10pm now, I wasn't feeling that tired. I undid my hair, and put the soft, white hand towel around it, as I came out he was sitting on the bed.

"Do you want to go into the playroom, and play on the bed with me, you look so dam sexy?" He stood, putting his hands around my waist.

"Yes, I'm not feeling tired yet."

I walked to the playroom which he unlocked. Inside, was what I'd seen before, but this time it had a new sense of fun to me. *Knowing Marcus found it erotic to have me tied up here whilst he did what he did to me, made it exciting for me, I could see that now from my new perspective as his lover.* Marcus laid me down gently on the bed, and took his borrowed t shirt off completely; he gaped at my body, in all its white nakedness and didn't say a word. The bed had a quite firm mattress on it, covered in blue silk sheets, which were quite, fun as I moved in the bed on them. He put my hands then my feet into the handcuffs; it felt binding, holding me there in place, they were hard on my wrists. Then he put a blindfold on my eyes, It was exciting, not being able to see him, just the feel of his skin on me as he did it, and only his deep erotic breathing to hear, taking me to a place of sense that I'd yet to experience, in all its glory.

"Trust me? " Was all he said I lay there in anticipation. He got something off the wall, I could hear. Next minute he was very softly beating my tummy, then my clit, with leather, or some other soft cloth, with lashes on it. It was done so expertly, and gently, making it very erotic for me, wanting more. Then he, put it down and started licking my clit, which was wet for him already, he was so expert at it, for that I was grateful. licking me gently in the folds of my skin, circling round and round first slowly, then harder, as his tongue, went deeper into my clitoris. Bringing me to such a phenomenal orgasm, because I couldn't see, this was so focused, such momentum of pulses, throbbing delightfully through my body. He was on top of me now, guiding his sheathed erect cock inside me. Filling me with the full-length of his erection. I moaned as he moved back and forth on my body,, filling me with more pulses, as he came inside me, clenching my buttocks as he did. I wanted to hold him, but couldn't. I just laid there wanting him more, pulling my cuffs towards him, so they hurt me; I just wanted to hold him. He lay on top of me, careful not to hurt me for a while, then as he stood up, he took my blindfold off, and then the handcuffs he came out of me taking off the condom tying it and throwing it in a bin.

"Well, did you like it?" His hair was all over the place.

"Yes, I had an amazing orgasm, the best I've ever had, don't know why, whether it's the fact that I'm handcuffed or the blindfold, works for me." I grinned at him in my second post orgasmic flush tonight.

"Here" He gave me his hand, as he pulled me up, still unable to stand straight. He pulled me into his arms and kissed me gently on the lips.

"Thanks for saying yes tonight; I wasn't sure that you would, especially after I told you my other fetishes." I left the room with him, beside me.

"I'll have another quick shower."

"Sure" I hugged him.

I headed for the shower in the ensuite again, picking up his t-shirt to wear afterwards that had got thrown on the floor. He went to the bar with his t-shirt, and jeans and underwear, back on. Getting him bourbon, in a short glass, sitting on the sofa to drink it, whilst I had my shower in privacy. *I'm glad he let me do that, as we have only just met really. 2, stunning orgasms, in the last, few hours of being with him, this is unheard of for me. To find someone who can make me feel so horny for him in such a short time.* I wash and shave my body again, leaving my just washed hair in a ponytail, to keep dry. Afterwards, I come out in his white toweling, bathrobe that I found hanging on the door inside. He has finished his drink, and goes into the shower, after I come out, whilst he's gone I towel dry my slightly wet hair and get into his t-shirt, in his bed. I looked at the alarm clock, beside the bed, it was 12.03am. When he's finished, he comes out with just his pajama shorts on, nothing on his delightfully clean, muscled body. He smells, of body wash, as he comes into bed with me.

"I could have sex with you again, right now; you look so hot in my bed. I'll give us both a break though, so you have plenty of energy for tomorrow," He has a wicked grin on his face.

"Let's save that for Saturday please, I'm worn out." I snuggle up to him. Then I will, he sets his iphone into the charger, and sets the alarm.

"What time do you wake up?" Surprised he was setting the alarm on a Saturday, when I like to sleep in.

"Usually 6.30am, but I can leave it if you want to lie in. I'm used to getting up and, doing stuff at that time, what would you prefer?"

"I prefer to sleep in, with you next to me."

"Ok done", As he changes the alarm to off.

"Have you never had anyone sleep in your bed like this at all?"

"No, you're my first, I hope I don't snore or keep you awake?"

"I'm sure you don't, but if you do, I'll tap you.."

"Thank you for letting me get you in my playroom, tonight it was so erotic and hot for me. "I do trust you already, Marcus, you make me challenge the idea of normal sex, and think outside the box."

"It's me who should be thanking you for that."

He put his arm around my shoulders.

"I'm being challenged too. Not having been in a relationship, I must admit, was a little scary, at first, because I had nothing to compare it too. You'll have to tell me, if I'm not doing something that I'm supposed to do, ok?"

"Of course, if that's what you want."

"I do."

"Then I will." He kissed me passionately with his tongue tasting of fresh mint.

"I just want to lock up, I'll be back soon." He disappears into the lounge room, making sure all locked, then comes back to bed *and ki*sses me on the lips. *He likes the right side of the bed, and I like the left, as we cuddle up together, I hear him breathing softly, he falls asleep quickly, as I listen to him breathing, I fall to sleep to*

Chapter 10

Marcus, where are you my love. He's hiding from me, must be," Please show yourself Marcus, I can't bear it any longer." Searching the thick woods, surrounded by thick bush, please find me. "He can't be lost, I've just found him." I move and sit on the log in front of me crying, he comes to me. "Why are you crying? It was just a game." He falls to his knees next to me. "I'm here now, nothing to be scared of." "I wasn't scared, I just thought you left me here alone." "Why would I do that?" "I don't know, I don't know really." I cried again, he held me in his lean muscular arms.

"Nat, are you dreaming? You're saying all sorts of odd things." He shook me so gently as I wake up.

"Oh sorry, I was dreaming, about you I think."

"You didn't make any sense from here, all fine, I dream nightmares sometimes. So If I wake you up? can you wake me too?" He leaned his naked, slightly tanned top half towards me, and kissed me gently on the lips.

"Good morning beautiful."

"Good morning, Marcus." I smiled as he, went underneath the covers, and took off the black sheet with his teeth, coming out from the end of his bed, removing his black satin quilt cover as he went. He moved up my wet body, and took his t-shirt off slowly. Laying there in my nakedness felt ok with him. Even though we seemed like new lovers, it felt like I had known him for years.

"What do you have for me today, Natalie?" He moved up to my clit area, and licked it gently, seemingly expertly, back and forth, and I couldn't move, I was scared to move, it felt so good. He could sense, it felt good for me, after a while, I climaxed, keeping me in one spot whilst he devoured me more. My orgasm built, he put two fingers inside me, pushing them gently, in and out, over and over. I was lost to him my orgasmic climax, pulses right through my body.

"You are so good Marcus, you now that?" As my body, rested, and came back to earth, I lay there in a glowing haze.

"Thanks, you are a great body to work on, tight and ready always ready for me." I moved to take his pajama, shorts off. I could see him in all his beautiful nakedness. I moved my hand up and down over the top of his erection, he moaned loudly. I put my mouth on top of very long thick cock, sucking and moving my hand up and down at the same time.

"Yes, yes, more like that." Marcus moaned in ecstasy, as he came in my mouth, I spat it out. He was all tired after that, and curled up next to me, back to back, we fell asleep. I woke about half an hour later, and had a shower in his en suite. Washing my bits again and shaving this *is truly like a dream, being here with him, he is a sex god, truly. Does he actually know how good looking he is to women? Well if the looks at office that he got from Trish and Megan are anything to go by, if he saw them. He was looking at me. Why me? I really wonder though, that's why this is dreamlike for me, he could have any girl he wanted, and he chose me, why? Not sure he knows really, he's never been in a relationship, that I find so hard to believe, he's in his early 30's, he must have had someone in a relationship, he just must have had, and perhaps didn't realize it at the time. The bathroom was huge, I hadn't really noticed it before. He had all white, very modern. It had modern flick switches on all the taps, in silver, the huge spa bath, I hadn't used yet. and a modern dual flush* toilet. *There was his and hers matching vanity units, with matching taps again. The walls were black tiles on the floor and halfway up the wall, then white tiles, up the rest of the wall. He had all white towels on the towel heater, so they were warm to use. On the floor he had a black bath mat and toilet mat. It all looked very masculine and very Marcus, I'm beginning to realize. The window was small, and had an electric vent, so the steam could escape easily, without opening the window.* I could hear Marcus stirring, as I turned the water off.

"Nat, I'm just coming in." He called.

"Just coming out, you can come in if you want." He opened the door, and I kissed him gently on the lips, as I passed by him, with the towel wrapped around my body."I bought your cleaned clothes, on from the overnight laundry." I stared at my clothes from yesterday, which did seem a bit weird to wear the same clothes, despite the fact they are laundered and ironed, and looked just like brand new, on a clothes horse in the bedroom. I put them on.

"I'll get you some more clothes, when we go, into the store in Los Angeles today. You can have anything you want. Then I know you have some clothes to wear here." I heard him turn the shower on, and sing which I hadn't heard before, he was quite good, but I didn't recognize the tune. I got my makeup in the bedroom, vanity mirror. I just bought mascara, and blush and powder, which I keep in my bag for work, luckily. Marcus comes out of the bathroom, looking super hot, wearing just a towel on his lower half, his wet hair is all over the place, is so sexy. *I could fuck him right here and now, but I'd have to through the shower routine again. I prefer to watch him, as he get dressed,* I growl at him, *as he takes the towel off, and puts black Calvin Kline underwear on, they are so sexy.*

"Leave me alone, you're hot too, I'm doing my best not to have sex again with you, you're insatiable you are Nat."

"I haven't had anything so gorgeous to look at for a while."

"Haven't you had a partner for ages then?"

"No not for about two years." *Not ready share that yet.*

"Why, any reason in particular."

"Something happened to me Marcus, but I'm not ready to share it with anyone yet, so please can we get off the subject." I got ready, to walk down the steps as Marcus, was now dressed, n his black trousers and white shirt open at the collar, to match my clothes. We went barefoot, down the stairs, to the kitchen.

"You know, whatever it is, you can tell me, I am good at understanding problems, and sorting them out. " He looked me in the eye.

"I'll tell you one day just not yet, it's too soon."

"Ok, what would you like for breakfast? Choices are 1, go to the restaurant here, and might have to put shoes on for that. 2, I cook, and I am quite good I think, I try to keep up my skills as much as I can, because Claire cooks most of my breakfasts, at home. 3 go out somewhere else, of your choosing." He sits on the modern black high-backed barstool, facing me.

"Well as both other choices, involve shoes; I'd rather have something cooked by you please. What can you cook?"

"Anything, as long it involves a microwave, or the stove top. Not as good on oven stuff." He smiled.

"Then what about eggs and bacon, can you do that?"

"Yes, I believe I have all the ingredients for that. Want anything like mushrooms or tomatoes in with it?" He got out the eggs and bacon and a fry pan, and some oil to spray. As he cooked, I put the coffee machine on at the wall.

"No just that thanks, he added mushrooms for himself, washing them first.

"Do you use this much?"

"Not really, I'm mainly live at my home, where I have them dotted about, but don't come here as much as you might think. I'm only here in Long Beach, because you're here." He started cracking the eggs, and putting them with the bacon, in the pan. The machine, I turned on, I loved freshly ground beans, for my coffee. He pointed toward the fridge, for the beans, he had an open, but sealed with a zip lock.

"I'll give these a go." I pulled them open and put them into the grinder part of the machine, it was noisy for a few seconds, but smelt great. The machine was a a fully automated Delonghi, I hadn't seen before, but easy enough to get the menu up, when Marcus showed me. I made 2 delicious cups of coffee, a black for him, and a cappuccino for me. He had proper coffee cups, which I preferred because you can really taste the coffee, rather than a mug which just makes it too weak. I put his coffee cup on the black marble breakfast bar.

"Thanks, do you want to have the view from the dining room, with your breakfast madam?"

"Oh, yes please." I put the cups on a black tray he gave me and walked to the dining room behind him. As he opened the black micro fiber, mini blinds automatically, I got the wow factor of the room. The view over Long Beach and the sea were magnificent. We put our breakfast down on the, modern black wooden table, seats for 8. I was starving by now. I sipped my coffee, magnificent. Then I tasted m two eggs and bacon.

"This is gorgeous, the eggs are very tasty, are they organic?"

"Yes, they are a better taste, I ask Claire to get them normally, and I got some for here too as I knew you might be coming the bacons organic tot."

"The best breakfast, you've cooked me so far." I eat it all quickly, and sip my coffee in between. I put the plates together, and put them at the end of the table.

"Can't believe you don't use this place much, the view all round is worth coming for."

"Perhaps I will more now, I have you, that's if you're planning on staying?" He gazed at me.

"I am, nothing is going to keep me away from you." I kissed him on the cheek as we sat looking out of the window. It was a beautiful, sunny Long Beach day, and only around nine am at the moment, plenty of time to fill in our day. He took my hand and walked me to the lounge room again, sitting on the sofa; he pulled out a black acoustic guitar from behind the bar, which was lying in a hard case. He played it beautifully; it was a tune I knew, Hotel California by the Eagles. He was good at it, no singing just the ring of the acoustic guitar in the penthouse, truly was a good place to play it with the sounds echoing through the place. When he stopped he sat near me.

"Do you play guitar, or anything?"

"No unfortunately, tried to learn years ago, but couldn't keep doing it, it hurt my fingers, so I gave up." Sitting next to me, he started playing again; I didn't recognize it this time.

"What is that called?" He put the guitar down

"It's one of my own compositions, not called anything. Are you ready to go to "Carrington's" store now, and get you some clothes?" I got up off the sofa.

"Yes, you don't have to buy though; I have a credit card on me." His face was a scowl.

"Ok Yes thanks, love to go shopping, you come with me while I go through, won't you?"

"Yes If you want me to, I will." He stood putting his arm around my waist, as we moved to the bedroom to get shoe's and my hand bag. A few minutes later, we were at the lift door.

The lift didn't open where I thought it was going to, instead we were in the basement, parking level.

"We're going by car to the airport this time, ok?" He opens the securely locked garage, with his key card, and a passkey he typed in the keypad. The doors opened slowly, and there was his bright red Ferrari Italia, one of the most beautiful cars, I'd ever seen.

"We're going in your Ferrari, yes please, it's gorgeous." My enthusiasm was a little over the top perhaps. Sitting in and watching my boyfriend Marcus, who had a massive grin on his face, drive beautifully. Normally it only takes 10 minutes or so to get to the airport, I was wishing it was a longer drive. We came out of the underground garage, as the automatic gate was up, then he slid his key card for it to go back down afterwards. He was like a kid with a new toy; I looked at him as he drove, to the airport. Our short drive was exciting, like driving in a race, except, he was careful, obviously loving his car. When we got there in a few minutes later, he parked in an undercover security garage, which was obviously his to use. We left the car, and he took hand as we, walked to the airport together.

"You really love that car, don't you?"

"Yes, it's my newest boy's toy; I suppose that's why I love it. It's the best car I've had, so far."

We walked into the airport towards the security gate, that I'd been to before.

"It works for me too." I beamed.

"I can see that for myself." He pulled himself in front of me, and kissed me on the lips gently, and quietly, so no one could see. Then we went through the security gate, at the side, so we didn't have to wait in the queue that had formed.

"Wow you can get through anywhere, how did you get through the gate at the side?"

"It's just a case of them knowing you're a pilot, and then they help you rather than slow you down. That's what I did as soon as I got my helicopter, last year, and bingo, works every time now." We carried on walking through the short terminal, out the other side onto the tarmac of the airport. It was a beautiful warm sunny cloud free day here in gorgeous Long Beach, we were set for a good ride, I could feel it. We got into the helicopter, which was parked not too far away. Getting in, I made myself comfortable, and put on the headphones, so I could hear Marcus, talking. He did his pre-flight checks, inside and outside. *He is a very cautious person, I'd decided, and that's a good thing I also decided. He looked so dam sexy with his hair all windswept, and pushed under his headphones.* He sat down, and looked at me.

"Ready?"

"Always." I nodded. The blades started to move, slowly then faster. He got his ok from the control tower, to proceed, after a few minutes, and the helicopter went higher, as the planes and cars, and streets, got smaller. I watched my bird's eye view, in the few, little puffy white clouds; it was getting warmer, now. I could see people, walking and enjoying their Saturdays, just as much as we were, some in their gardens.

"You like?" He looked briefly at me.

"Love it, remember, I love it." I'd forgotten to turn my iphone off, which he asked me to do, when he was checking stuff outside. I had a message from Trish, but I'll see it later. I looked over at Marcus, he looked every bit the adventurous pilot, who his black trousers and white shirt. He looked very handsome too. As we flew over the tiny houses, and then freeways and sometimes green areas, we made our way toward the big city of Los Angeles. It only took 20 minutes max, before we were heading towards a modern tower, about 4 storey's high, with "Carrington's" in gold letters on the outside wall. We headed for a big H on the roof; he hovered, and then slowly descended to the helipad.

As the blades stopped, and he did a post flight check. Then turned his phone on and made a call to someone. He grabbed my hand, and helped me out, shutting the door after me. We headed inside through a door, and went down, past a door.

"This is my penthouse suite here, I'll show you later." He took my hand, as the stairs became a wider passage. At the end of the white painted hall, a woman, in a grey suit, greeted us. She was in her thirties, and looked like she was in charge. She shook his hand.

" Hi Marcus, She looked at him and you must be Natalie? She shook my hand.

"I'm Martha, Marcus's assistant." *She was younger and sexier than I thought she'd be about the same height as me, she had eye's that twinkled every time she focused on my Marcus.* I sat there assessing her, for a while, and then decided it was pointless, he was with me after all.

"I want you to show Natalie around and get everything she wants, on my account. " He looked at me.

"That's ok Nat? Come back to the office, when you've finished, alright? I want you to get everything from sexy underwear, to pajamas. From casual whatever you want no limit ok?" He whispered in my ear. *He is supposed to be coming with me, I know, but this way I can find out about her and get some things he hasn't seen.*

"Yes ok Marcus, see you soon." I kiss him passionately in front of her. We walk off into this huge store; *I feel like a kid in a candy store, he's good at making me feel like that.*

"Where would you like to start?"

"Underwear, please." she nods as we walk to the escalator, and head down.

"Have you worked for Marcus long?"

"Yes a couple of years that's all."

"You know we all thought he was gay, he's so good looking, and never a woman at his side, until now." She got off the escalator and went towards the lingerie department, it was huge, I literally had never seen anything, with so much lingerie to choose from. I'd decided to make sure I had all the brands I would love to buy, but didn't. I had a small basket to put them in, so I filled it, with Calvin Klein, Elle, Triumph, and all the pretty but sexy things I could find. I actually had twenty sets, so I was happy, plenty of choice.

"Where to next?" Martha looked at my basket and put my goodies on the counter, so we could use it again, and held it for me.

"Pajamas, then casual clothes, and then going out stuff, and shoes." I think I've got it covered; she was actually quite fun to have around, holding anything I couldn't carry. When we'd finished, we went to the checkout, where we'd left this mountain of gorgeous clothes, and Martha put it through his account, it came to $3,467.87. *Shit, well he did say, whatever it cost.*

"Do you know how wealthy his family is, they make well over a million dollars? every day in their stores worldwide. It looks like it's you that has to get used to it. He loves you Natalie, it's written all over his face, when he's with you. Get used to being treated by him. He deserves to find someone like you to love."

"Oh Martha, He can't love me, it's too soon?"

"Love is blind, and so are you, you're besotted with him too." She sorts it through his account and gets one of the staff to bring everything to the office.. We walk, in silence up the stairs, as I realize that I have loved him from the start, just didn't know it. As we reach the office, Marcus catches my eye, and smiles.

"Hope you spent all my money."

"Well a few thousand of it anyway." I kissed him passionately.

"Let's show you the penthouse I have here, and put your clothes in there for a while, whilst we go out to lunch, that ok?"

He took my arm and led me to the penthouse, the man with the clothes, hanging behind us.

"Oh lovely, Marcus, I can change in the penthouse, into something new, that I bought?" We all went into the penthouse, after the man left the clothes hanging on a clothes horse and left, Marcus thanking him. The penthouse was a large modern décor again like his one in the Plaza, but this had more black furniture. A big soft thick cream carpet was all over, the open plan lounge and kitchen area. Marcus grabbed my waist, not able to control his appetite any longer. Carrying me all the way, he took my clothes off and put me on the bed in the master bedroom,

"I want you now." He panted. Taking his clothes off too, so we were both, naked. There were no handcuffs or other things that I could see, I felt a little relieved. Getting on top of my body, careful with his bodyweight, he licked my clitoris, which was already wet, round and round, not wanting me to come yet. He put his sheathed erect cock into me, filling me with his aroma of body soap and expensive cologne. He put his mouth on mine out tongues twisted in ecstasy as he came inside me, and I pulsed from within, as I came around him, continuing to orgasm blissfully, on to another ad another. *OMG thanks you Marcus, for breaking my spell. The only person, who can make me come whilst having sex,, thank you Marcus.* I kissed him passionately, He tasted of coffee.

"Thank you that was a nice surprise, always wanted of course."

"Pleasure is mine, I've wanted you since we got out of my helicopter, and hung around waiting for you to come back." He came out of me, threw the condom in the bin, he curled against me, he nuzzled into the side of me.

"I like relationships, don't you?"

"Well I like this relationship, the best of all." We had a little stay in bed, and then got showered separately, to avoid more wanting. I went through my clothes, founds some sexy leggings and a beautiful top to go over it, with new court shoes I got. As he came out the shower, I showed him my clothes, including my lingerie.

"That's gorgeous, looking forward to removing it from you. I'm glad you got lots of clothes, wasn't sure you would, I'm proud of you. I have lots of money, just say if you see something you like, and your fairy godfather will buy it, ok Nat?"

"Oh ok, but if I want to buy something for myself, with my credit card, I'll buy it, ok Marcus?" He laughed.

"Ok" He kissed me gently on the lips, then got dressed, in the same clothes he had on before.

"Do you have a suitcase, or two, so we put all this into your helicopter easily?"

"I do of course." He got a large, expandable suitcase out of the wardrobe, it was black and just big enough for all my new clothes, which I put them neatly in before we left. Marcus got his staff to put it into the rear of his helicopter. Once I'd finished off my make up in his en suite, I tied my hair into a ponytail, as it was still slightly wet, and I couldn't find a hairdryer, as he probably didn't use one. He came back into the bathroom, and took my hand when I was ready.

"I do have a hairdryer, in one of the other bedrooms, which is more kitted out for my Mother, I can get one if you like?"

"I'm fine, but thanks for that Marcus, least I know you have one."

"Are you ready?"

"Yes let's go," He didn't tell me where we were going, so I didn't ask.

As we came off the ground floor on the lift, going outside I held his hand outside, I saw Barker opening the Bentley Limo side door for us, smiling openly, at us. I grinned at him as we got in, closing the door, he got in to drive slowly away. The privacy window was up. Marcus held my hand again as we sat there looking at the river as we went past, it took about fifteen minutes until we were at our destination.

"We're here." Barker announced on the speaker. He stopped the car and opened our door.

"Thanks Barker." We were at a restaurant, right on the river's edge, the restaurant, was actually over the river in part. It looked very expensive, looking by the cars outside. As we walked hand in hand to the door, we were greeted by a man, who opened the door for us, welcoming us in.

"This is "The Rickenbacker" supposed to be the most exclusive restaurant, but I haven't had the perfect person to bring here, so now I have and that's why we are here. Tell me what you think later." He guides me through, the throng of people at the bar, to the food area, the man at the desk

"You have booked Sir?"

"Yes, Marcus Carrington plus one." He smiled at me.

"Oh welcome Mr. Carrington, he recognized his name, come this way please, you can have our best table here on the water's edge" We overlooked the river that was slowly meandering past.

"This is beautiful Marcus, thanks for bringing me." He sat opposite me so we both could see the wonderful view, together..

"What would you want to drink Madam? The wine waiter asked.

"Bundaberg rum and coke please. Hasn't had that for a while thanks."

"Sir?"

"Just a cascade in a bottle please."

"Yes sir." Our drinks were bought in super quick time, whilst we perused the menu. I ordered a prawn salad, when the food waiter came, and Marcus ordered a Steak Diane, with pepper sauce, medium rare. The waiter took our menus.

"You are full of surprises aren't you? All of them good, so far. Today is fun, thanks Marcus." I kiss him gently on the lips, as he leans towards me. Behind I can hear people talking about us.

"Marcus do you get people talking about you, behind your back, there's constant chatter here today."

"Ignore it as much as you can Nat, they haven't seen me out with a beautiful woman, as a date, they'll get used to it. If they don't it's no concern of mine. If you feel uncomfortable about it, tell me and we'll go, I mean it." He gazed at me with concern.

"I'm just not at all used to it obviously, but I will get used to it I hope." Sipping my drink. I go of to the ladies, before the food is bought. It's a bright modern large, place with halogen down lights. Inside I enter the toilet, whilst in there some ladies come in, and start talking.

"Who has Marcus Carrington having lunch with?" One of the ladies asks.

"Don't know, but no one to worry about, Margaret, she's not stunning to look at, or much up top, so he's still available. You have more money than she does that's for sure." I came out into the vanity areas, to use the sinks. They ladies looked at me with distain. I moved towards the door, just wanting them to have a last thought of me.

"Marcus Carrington and I are engaged to be married, so get your sweet ass off my fiancé." I stormed out. I explained to Marcus what happened, and luckily he laughed. Our food came, it was such fun, I felt heaps better. I didn't feel like a dessert today, but I had a coffee, as did Marcus.

We laughed as we came out towards the Limo.

"I'm glad you have a fun sense of humor, like me." By the time Barker drove us back to the store, and then on to the helicopter, it was 5.00pm already. I've arranged something else for tonight, totally different from today, if you're up for it?" Now I was excited, thought's racing through my brain like fireflies.

"Another surprise, not like today, what could it be Marcus Carrington, bring it on."

Chapter 11

The helicopter began to ascend, slowly, it was getting darker. A beautiful sunset yet again a la Marcus. Going above the cars looked like ants again, racing around in a manic way. The houses we flew past got darker and smaller as we flew higher. Green forests turned to darker blobs in the then night sky. We were only in the air for about 15 minutes, when I recognized, somewhere I'd already been with him. We landed at his walled acreage home, Smith approached to secure the helicopter.

"Thought we could stay here tonight, Claire's expecting us for a home cooked meal. "

"Really, she's going to cook for us, how awesome!" *How does he arrange all this? Without me knowing, must have been at the office, when I wasn't with him.* He talks to Smith before leaving. We walk towards his home, and into the main hall, it's as huge as I remember it. Claire comes out to greet us, taking Marcus's arm, then mine. *She really is like having your own mum around.*

"Come on, I've made your dinner for 6.00pm, so if you get your drinks, I'll be ready by then, in the dining room." She scuttles off to the kitchen, clearly happy to see us. Marcus takes me to the bar in the lounge, finally able to have a proper drink; he gets himself a double bourbon straight,

"What would you like, do you like liqueurs, Bailey's Irish Cream, got that or gins and tonic, vodka?

"I'd like a Baileys, please, haven't had that since last Christmas." He pours it in to a shot glass. Then gives it to me, then shows me where the dining room is, we sit sipping out drinks, and Claire who has already set the table, with solid silver cutlery and green, modern art design placemats. She comes in with our starters, and sets it on the table. "Now, Marcus says you like all the food I've cooked tonight, so I hope he's right Natalie." She sets down proper prawn cocktails served on a bed of lettuce, in a wine glass.

"Thanks Claire, I love prawns." I taste it, it is the best tasting prawn cocktail, I've ever tasted. I gaze over at Marcus who's devoured his already.

"Wow, that's so good." I finish mine. Claire comes in to take the dishes.

"Claire that was the best ever, thanks." She nods, and goes for the main course.

"Hope you like roast beef, with all the trimmings?" My mouth watered and my nose was filled to the aroma, as she bought our food in. as she places our massive white plates, in front of us, and then went for the food.

"I really do, we have them at my mum and Al's, when we go there at the weekends. She put a bit of everything on the table, roast beef, roast potatoes and pumpkin, peas and carrots, enough to feed an army, along with gravy, and sauces in dishes.

"Just eat what you can, Natalie we have dessert after." She went out.

"Wow, that's a lot of food for two Marcus, Does she normally feed you like this?"

"No, think she wants you to like her food, Nat. And you will." He puts some beef in his mouth. I tasted mine, the woman is a genius, and she's a food guru, food heaven.

"It's beautiful, absolutely gorgeous." I sip my drink. Eating as much as I can, feeling totally stuffed and full. Putting my cutlery on my plate.

"That was the best tasting roast dinner, better than my Mum's but don't tell her. I can't eat any more, I do want to try and fit in my sweet, she's gone to such trouble. "I know she's a good cook, isn't she? Sometimes I stay in rather than go out, because the foods better tasting at home." He finishes, takes a sip of his bourbon, and holds my hand across the table. Claire comes in, so soon after, she must have heard us talk. She takes the dishes on a trolley, smiling.

"That was gorgeous Claire thank you." I smiled at her.

"Thanks Natalie,, glad you enjoyed it. Hope you like dessert, I'm told you do." She glared at Marcus, as she left the room. A few minutes later, she appeared again, with, lemon meringue pie.

"That's my favorite sweet, thanks Claire." I looked at Marcus, who adored it too. *It has the perfect consistency, and tasted sublime, melting in my mouth.* We slowly devoured each mouthful, sipping in between. *It was blissful.* Putting my spoon and fork down, I felt more stuffed than ever.

"Want another drink, Nat?

"Not right now, not sure I'd get it in, perhaps later a coke or something light."

"Sure thing." He put his cutlery down, and finished off his drink.

Claire came for the dishes, again.

"That was blissful Claire, beautiful, thank you again."
"Thank you, glad you enjoyed it."

Marcus got up, and took my hand, and took me out into the hall again, then up the huge wide steps of the stairs. Holding on to the white painted banister, as I went. The stairs were carpeted, in a tough carpet.

"Where are we going, Marcus? *Haven't been up here yet?"* We get to the top.

"Wanted to show you round, so you know where everything is." He walks down a wide open area with a very comfortable chair in it, and a coffee table next to it. Turning to the right there was bedroom 2, which was quite large, and overlooked the garden. Next, on the right, another bedroom overlooked the garden again. Next again on the right, bedroom 3 overlooking the garden, although couldn't see anything as it was dark. Then on the right, down a wide corridor, was a gym, fully kitted out, with new things. Then, coming back, the next door led to a movie theatre, with everything for 10 people to sit and enjoy themselves comfortably, even a bar, which he grabbed 2 cans of Pepsi max, handing one to me.

"Here if you want it now."

Yes please. You have a huge gorgeous home, I love it. Gina has put the same theme upstairs too?

"Yes, as I said I may change it soon, as you know I prefer modern. And this is the master suite, where you'll be staying."

"Wow it's gorgeous, Marcus, you are so lucky to have all this around you."

"I don't think luck comes into it, just years of hard work." He smiled.

"Oh I didn't mean it like that; you are blessed, then to have all this beauty around you."

"Yes, it's nice to wake up to, I must admit, but tomorrow I'm going to wake up to something even more beautiful." He caressed my cheeks, kissing me gently and softly on the lips. He sat on his huge king size bed, pulling me into his arms and holding me tight. He looked so tired, his hair all over the place, he looked so sexy. We lay down on top of his bed it had a manlier quilt cover on it, than the décor around the room, with its black and silver horizontal lines. As I lay there wrapped around his back, I heard him fall asleep, I didn't move as I didn't want him to wake. He was obviously worn out, and he slept so soundly. Looking around the room, I saw my suitcase full of clothes, had been bought up, *that's what he was talking to smith about.* I took Marcus's shoes off, put them on the floor, then his trousers, as slowly as I could, *oh my it's so erotic, and he's making me hot, as he slept.* I left his underwear on, but I had a lovely feel of his cock, as he lay there, he didn't get any bigger, so he must be asleep. I then got myself, some new sexy bed clothes out of the suitcase, slipping into the double sized modern shower, I have the most exhilarating cleanse as the power shower, it threw, water at me like a massage, *wow these are good.* I dried myself on a freshly laundered towel, white, and so soft. I put on my new pajamas, they looked hot, I must say. *Pity he's fallen asleep really, never mind, I feel so good now.* I got out of the huge en suite, he was still asleep, my iphone said it was only 7.30pm, I replied to the text Trish sent, I'd forgotten about. She'd asked if everything was going well, and I told her I was staying the weekend with him. I didn't feel that tired, so I lay cuddling next to Marcus, and gradually fell asleep listening to him breathing.

Marcus can't hear me, I'm hurting, he's hurting me, I can't stand the pain any longer. He comes over in his face mask, made of tiger skin, whacking my back with his canes, he's getting harder and harder, please stop, I'm bleeding, the pain, he won't stop, laughs at my agony. Please stop say louder, stop, stop "Stop Marcus!""Nat are you ok, *it's him he's here.* Nat please wake up, you're having a nightmare."

"Oh ok, a nightmare, wow it was so real." Opening my eyes, I'm next to my sex god, in his underwear, and his shirt from last night still. In his bed in his huge home, this *I like.*

"What happened last night? You took my trousers off?" He grinned.

"Well you fell asleep, so yes I enjoyed the view."

"You also changed, into these sexy pajamas, if I'd seen these I wouldn't have fallen asleep."

"You were totally knackered, so I had a shower, and put these on. They are great aren't they, thank you so much for all my gifts, you are so generous."

"Well I was expecting, to take them off you last night, but as it's now 8.30am now, I guess I've have to have you twice this morning. He threw his shirt on the floor, and moved on top of me, gently, teasing and moving the strap of my black silk, baby doll outfit, off my shoulder slowly, then the other. Then his nimble hands, undid the three black buttons, down the middle, peeling it slowly off my pert, supple breasts, one side at a time. He licked my cupped nipples, teasing them, with his tongue, making me want him more. Then he removed my bottom half, using his teeth, I smiled as I watch him, get harder, and harder. Then I removed his Calvin Kline's, showing his fucking hard cock, I leaned over, and smelt him, mmm putting my tongue against, him hard naked skin, I licked him up and around, the head, making him moan in ecstasy. I covered it with a condom. He was back to my wanton body, hot for him. Licking my clit, round and round, gently, then putting two fingers inside me, in and out, in and out, I moaned with aroused pleasure, and then he moved on top of me, He moved himself, inside me, moaning as he filled me with such a wonderful bliss. He moved slowly back and forth, again then again, then one last push, my body was pulsing with delight, as I felt myself coming, he came inside me and to my delight, I pulsed after him with such multiple, orgasmic pleasure, laying there to make it last as it could. He collapsed to the side of me, coming out of me. We lay there, in the afterglow for a few minutes. Feeling so hot and flush, I nearly drifted off, as I snuggled up next to him. Then he rolled to sit on the bed, put the condom in the bin, tied up.

"I'm just having a shower, see you in a minute." He turned the taps on, whilst he was in there I got out something to wear to his parents for lunch. I chose my new skinny black jeans, Calvin Klein ones, with a black camisole top. As Marcus came out the bathroom looking super hot, with his wet hair, all over the place, I smoothed it down, kissing him passionately before he got away, lingering tongues, tasting his toothpaste.

"If I could have you now, I would. But I will get you this morning, so watch out Miss Nat." I smiled at him.

"Looking forward to it, Mr. Marcus, Do you think this is ok to wear to your parents for lunch?" I showed him the clothes, including my new black court shoes, I'd chosen.

"Perfect, mum always overdresses anyway, she says it's her London upbringing, and she get 's dad to do the same so that's perfect, I'm wearing blue jeans today, because it will probably piss her off a bit, not that I mean to, but she has to relax, it's a family lunch, not going out to meet royalty." He bought out new underwear, I watched him put them on, slowly, just for me, so sexy. Then his jeans and a plain black t-shirt, he had casual black shoes, to go with them. I went into the shower, giving myself a shave, as I was going to get pounced on at some point this morning. When I came out he was combing his still wet hair, I messed it up with my fingers, he combed it again. I got dressed, dried my hair with a hairdryer, he found for me. He'd also moved something's out of a drawer, so I had some space; I put my sexy lingerie and baby doll pajamas in there. When I'd done my make up, I was ready.

"You ready, for a Claire Grogan, breakfast now?" *I was still full from last night.*

"Not really, but bring it on." We walked holding hands, down the stairs, and into the hall. Marcus bought me towards the kitchen this time. Claire was busy on the hot cook top.

"Oh I didn't see you 2 there, are you ready for breakfast now?

"Yes please Claire, Nat what would you like, she can cook anything for you, or cereal, whatever you want."
"You know what I really fancy right now, is some mini pancakes, with maple syrup do you have the ingredients?"

"Of course, and you Marcus, what would you like?" Claire grinned at me.

"Actually that sounds lovely, can I have some too, please with some blueberries on the side, you want any fruit Nat?"

"Yes strawberries please, if you have them?"

"We have everything, here. Get yourselves coffee from the machine, or I can make you something if you prefer." She started cooking the pancakes in a fry pan. We went to the coffee machine, another Delonghi, automatic machine.

Marcus helped me get my cappuccino, and he made himself a black coffee.

"We'll eat it outside, Claire on the patio, ok." Marcus put our cups onto a small black, café tray, and headed through the lounge room, through the doors outside to where, we went before, when we went to boathouse. It's a beautiful clear blue sky day, I hadn't been able appreciate the outside because it was dark last time. The patio area is actually covered with a solid, roof area. The chairs are good quality, bamboo they are covered with soft cushions on the rear, and seat. The table is glass with silver legs. We sit down, looking at the view of the lake, and the boathouse over the mowed lawn. It was truly stunning, as we sat there gazing at the beauty.

"Do you sit out here much?"

"Not as much as I could, I mean that's why I created the lake so you can sit here and look at it, but it has gone to waste a bit, hope you being around might change that?"

"I hope so too." I heard the clattering of the trolley as Claire bought out our breakfast. She came through the door way and put our plates onto the glass table.

"I've put your cutlery in napkins so you can help yourself from the trolley, same with some extra sauces, just in case you want them." Marcus smiled, at me.

"Thanks Claire."

"Pleasure, would you like some more coffee both of you?" She spied our empty cups.

"Yes please, cappuccino, please." I gave her my cup

"I remembered that already for you." Marcus's cup was taken to be refilled, as he nodded.

"What time are we going to lunch?"

"Probably, take 2 hours to drive in the Bentley, or I was thinking of going by helicopter, should only take roughly 45 minutes, if you want to go by helicopter that is?" He smiled at me.

"Of course I do. What time can we leave?" I tasted my pancake, which was delicious, light, melt in the mouth too.

"Probably about 12pm lunch is around 1pm normally. You're looking forward to meeting my Mum and Dad aren't you? Why?"

"Because they are the ones who are your family They adopted you, they took you out of something bad, into something good. Because they're your parents, that's why." I'd got a little animated, about it all. *He should be proud of them for helping him.* He finishes his pancakes, and takes the coffee Claire just brings in, *hope she didn't hear my ranting.* Looking at my iphone its 11am already.

"We only have 1 hour, for you to molest me Mr. Marcus, you'll have to catch me, and find me." Marcus was a little surprised by my sudden exit, but decided to play the game.

"Bring it on, Miss Natalie." I saw him look, around the lounge, area where I had disappeared off to in the first place, nothing. Then I saw him go into the kitchen, to find a surprised Claire, looking at him. Then, as I listened behind a door in the main hall, where I could hear from all around, he tried his office door, it was locked still. When I heard him go upstairs, he was gone for a while, so I ran outside towards the lake. As I ran across the garden I heard him, as he came outside.

"The boathouse, is the only place I've shown you, so I'm coming Natalie." He said, He crossed the lawn, down the steps, it was unlocked, and inside he couldn't see me, as he went around the corner, I was laying, on the sofa naked, at wet for him silently, he stripped naked too. He was rock hard, ready for me he got a condom, and I licked him first, slowly then sucked him, making him moan in delight, then put on the sheath, moving towards me, his need to fuck me was clearly urgent. He moved on top of my erotically charged, nakedness filling me with such pleasure for both of us, moaning again with desire, he closed his eyes and rocked me back and forth over and over, harder now, ready to come his body threw itself into pulses of pleasure on top of me, making me pulse at the look of his erotic sexy body convulsing on me, on and one the orgasmic pleasure pulsed through me.

The helicopter rotors, started to make that now familiar whir, I had remembered to bring my suitcase from the bedroom, as we're staying at the Plaza tonight. Marcus had the most delicious post fucked grin on his face with the matching hair and flush on his face as he sexily piloted us off the ground, silently. I gaze adoringly at him, *I know we've only just met but he, is so precious to me already, can't tell him that, he'd probably run to the hills. Remembering back to the boatshed fuck we just had, and how, I'd coerced Smith to let me in so I could hide from Marcus, the thrill, I had in him finding me, and the phenomenal orgasms, I've had more in just this weekend, than the whole of my sex life. He can make me come when he's inside me; no-one's done that to me ever. No wonder I want to be with him, all the time now.*

"We'll be landing in a few minutes," He tells me, as he confirms with San Diego International airport, flight control. We are still flying quite high, as he gets his path, confirmed, I hear through my speakers. He points, over to the sea front.

"That's where we're heading,.." I nod. I can see him line up, so I leave him to it. We start to descend, onto a huge white H. *This place is huge and very private too.* Bordering a National Park at the rear, the house is huge and white brick, standing in acreage of at least 10 acres, mostly to the back, there's a smaller garden at the sea front side. They had their own helicopter too, which was on another spot I could see was bigger than Marcus's; they must more than the 2 seats this one has. As Marcus slowed the blades, we waited until they'd stopped; he did his check, before we got out. The helipad was at the side of the driveway, not too far from the house. When we got out a man was sitting in a golf buggy to take us to the house. I could see his mum get out and watch us coming, followed by his dad shortly after. Marcus grabbed my hand.

"Well Nat, this ma and pa's home, hope you like it." He grinned at me. We got to the huge steps leading to the front of the house; Marcus helped me off, not that he needed to, something for ma and pa, I reckoned. We walked up the step, to where his mum, held out her hands to embrace him.

"Oh Marcus I'm so pleased you came, darling." She had a clear British accent, which Marcus didn't.

"Mum this is Natalie Hungerford, my girlfriend." His mum came over to me.

"Great to meet you Natalie, I'm Mary, his mum, but you must know that." She went to shake my hand, so I did. Then a tall man in his late fifties, with grey short hair, and a moustache, came out, to shake my hand too.

"Hi Natalie, I'm John, Marcus's dad." He was wearing a full suit in black, as predicted by Marcus. His mum was, dressed up too, like she was going out to dinner. She had a black dress and black court shoes on. Her hair was dyed blonde, and tied in a bun. We all then went inside, into a very luxurious, interior, it was a typically British home, as I looked at the mock, Georgian *or were they,* chairs and tables. There were beautiful old paintings on the wall, although not knowing what they were; they were good to look at. We moved to the area at the back of the home a more formal area, which had the most phenomenal sea view. John told me the history of the house, and how much it cost to get the right protection from the sea. We all chatted and they gave me a drink, I asked for Bailey's as I had a thirst for it. Marcus sat beside me on the very comfortable sofa, holding my hand.

"Are you ok? He whispered.

"Yes, thanks."

As we were, going to lunch, behind hid mum and dad, he kissed so passionately, taking me off guard a little. His mum turned around just as we started pulling apart. She smiled at him, but didn't say a word. I was sat opposite Marcus, at the table, with his mum at one end, and his dad at the other. Marcus was touching my legs with his all the way through, I grinned at him, as he took his shoe of and tried to get in between my legs with his foot. We had a lovely lunch with a few choices, their chef had, I had the pasta bake, and Marcus had beef wellington. After we had coffee, Marcus doesn't even like to have 1 drink when he's flying. We took our coffee outside, to the table with the most spectacular view.

"Let Natalie alone for a while Marcus, then I can get to know her."

"Ok Nat? Come on dad," he took his father for a walk around the other side of the house, staring back at me to make sure I was ok. Which I was, of course.

"You know he's in love with you, don't you Natalie?"

"That's what others seem to think, I'm not so sure though, it's too soon."

"You are too, Natalie it's so obvious, take your time, I couldn't bear it if he lost you now. He's not bought any girlfriends, home ever and he's 32 years old." She sighed.

"Has he told you what happened to him, by his birth mother, he doesn't normally tell anyone."

"Yes, he told me she treated him like shit, and that she made him do things so she could get drugs. Up to 12 when he found by you, and bought to the States to escape her. He hates her."

"I hate her too, she had him raped by men, for drugs, she left him all his life, threatening him, if he told anyone, what he'd get. She didn't want him, she was drugged up and got pregnant, with her supplier, but she didn't tell him because he would have killed her and him. She sobbed, who could not want this beautiful man?"

"I don't understand it either, that's why I wanted to meet you this weekend, to talk to you as you know him the most. He says he has nightmares, but I haven't seen any yet. He asked me to wake him, if I'm there, because he hates them I think."

"When we left England, We found the best shrink for him of course, he was 12 years old, didn't talk much, but after about 6 month's he began to believe that she was in jail, and couldn't hurt him. He started talking more to the males Dr Thomas, and his dad, but still not so trusting of me, it took a few years, of love before, he'd cuddle me. He was so starved of love for 12years, she hated him.

"Wow, I didn't realize, how awful for you, Mary?"

"He was and is a beautiful child; I just want him to be safe. Natalie, he was beaten, and sexually abused for all those years, he never really talked to anyone openly about it. His father and the Dr both said he changed the subject. I did begin to think he might be gay, as he never bought any women home. But he didn't show any signs of that either. His sex life is his business, Natalie believe me, but I just want to know he's now happy and moving on with his life. He does seem to be turning a very good corner with you, I hope it lasts for both your sake."

"So do I" I was shocked still.

"Just be gentle with him Natalie, promise me, he's so precious to me." She sobbed again. *What am awesome woman, to have for an adopted mum.*

"I have no reason, to do otherwise, Mary. In the short time we've known each other, we are totally addicted to each other, haven't wanted to spend any time apart. It's so powerful; I want it to last, just as much as he does. I will take as slowly as I can though, for both our sakes." She hugs me tightly, round my shoulders. Just then, Marcus and John, come around the corner, he runs and put his arms around me., kissing me on the neck.

"What is it Nat? Tell me?' He's totally confused.

"It's all good, just having a little cry together, as we women do." I tried to pacify him.

We have a final coffee together, making sure I have Mary's phone number, if I need it, and she has mine.

Chapter 12

As I wave goodbye to Mary and John Carrington, I feel a pang of slight sadness, we'd become quite close, Mary and I, in the end. *Whilst we were having lunch, John told me of the history of the stores empire they've built as a family. Apparently the first "Carrington's" was in London, they'd built it up for 10 years, it was going very well. Then they adopted Marcus, and came out to the USA. They built a chain of luxury department stores, based on the popular English one, which they still have to this day. It worked, each one is in a capitol city, and they have over 200 stores in America and worldwide now, all privately owned by them, they don't franchise them because they want the control, in the products. John was as proud of Marcus as he was now mainly in charge, we'd all call a meeting if we want to buy or build a new store, just to make sure we all agree. We like to stand back a bit now though, in our 50's, both of them now, just work as part time as they can. Mary has found lots to occupy her time, as she's into a charity, they set up for abused kids, helping them get out. He said he can't keep himself away from the business; he loves it, talks with, Marcus most days. He said that they had plans to build, another store in Paris that looks like it's going to go through soon now. They have a huge staff, of trusted people. And managers in each store who report everything to them, every week so they know all the figures. The managers all deal with staff problems; because that's their job, so   hopefully only get the good stuff reported to them. He was so animated, talking about this wonderful, American Icon. I felt proud to know them and especially as they were Marcus's parents.* Marcus flew higher above, his parent's home; I looked at him with adoration

"What is it Nat, what are you looking at?

"Oh just some hot erotic guy I met in a bar, and can't get off my mind." I smiled.

"Oh, what were you crying about with mum today, are you going to tell me?"

"Maybe when we get back, I want you to concentrate now."

"That wasn't too bad, having lunch with ma and pa was it?"

"It was good Marcus, Your mum and dad are very proud of you, as they should be. I totally had a good time. I think your mum and I will be good friends, she's such a lovely person." *And she was, she had a London accent, standing strong. She was not all pretentious, she was down to earth and approachable for such wealth they must be billionaires between them now, I don't know if that's right, but not far off probably.* Marcus flew on, over the sea for the start of the flight, so I got a good view of their home. As we headed back to Long Beach Airport, *staying at the Plaza tonight, good sex, sex and more sex please Marcus* I looked over at him in his gorgeous padded headphones, looking every inch the pilot. *Mary had told me at the lunch table, that they so wanted kids, but none came, they then looked at adoption, and that's how they got Marcus, he was new on the adoption agency's list, and they got to meet him first. It was love at first sight for Mary, they adopted him, and then they thought it would be nice to come over here, so they could start a new life with him. I can't believe they've been through so much together, especially Marcus, I wonder if it's worth trying to get him to remember stuff with his birth mother. I know I don't want to talk about my attack, not even to him, so why would he want to talk about it. Now I could see that unless he talked to me, I wouldn't ask.*

"You quiet, are you asleep?"

"Not with this view to look at." I gazed at him and he laughed.

"We'll be about another 40 minutes; you can sleep if you want to."

"I'm fine thanks, do you have a drink, in here, Pepsi or water, and I'm quite thirsty now?"

"Yes, got two cans of Pepsi, in the cubby." He pointed to the secured area in front of me. I got out a can.

"You want one?"

"No, I can drink some of yours though, if you don't mind, just a sip." He took the open can and tipped it up, trying to drink and fly.

"You could get bottles, instead, with a straw." I suggested, as he wiped his chin free of the Pepsi drips.

"Great idea Batman, you really are quite clever aren't you?"

"I try to be." I took a sip. As we passed over the freeways, it wasn't as mesmerizing during the day. I looked at the mountains in the background, the many homes that we passed over. I did fall asleep.

Marcus was naked in the playroom, handcuffing my bound body, to the bed. He had an evil look in his eye. I want to go now, I screamed. He just laughed. Please Marcus please release me let me go. I cried, terrified sobs were ignored, by him. He got his cane, the thickest one out and beat me over and over, blood gushes out of my wrists, my legs, my tummy, he kept on going, please stop now. I've only just begun, so get used to it. You will love it like I love beating you. I don't love it I hate it. Please stop. I cried sobs and sobs came down my red cheeks. He laughed at me, you are weak, I am strong, and you will like this. He kept hitting me.

"Ah, don't touch me". I screamed.

"What is it Nat, I'm here now, everything's ok" he touched my cheek. *Marcus oh shit it was a dream again, fuck that was real.*

I opened my eyes; Marcus had got me out of the helicopter, in his arms and was trying to keep me asleep, whilst he took me to the car. He had got me out past the security in the airport that *would have made them all laugh no doubt. . He was just getting the garage opened, with the remote, when I woke up.*

"Thanks, I could have walked though, I must be heavy."

"You're lighter than you think." He set me down on the road. The garage door opened, and we went in. he unlocked his car and we got in. *How come I keep having those horrible dreams I want it to stop, he's not like that at all. It's all very distressing at the time.* Driving back to the Plaza, I gaze across at him.

"You like driving your Ferrari don't you? I love your happy little boy look right now."

"Yes it's great to drive; do you want to drive it now, to see what I mean?" *Not sure I'd keep it in one piece, never driven a supercar before.*

"No thanks, one day maybe, when I have had a lesson from you maybe. I might crash it, and then you wouldn't be happy."

"It's just a car Nat. It's insured, or I just buy another one. Over the years I learnt not to get attached to things, as they are just things, and it feels much better than obsessing over things, I really let go when I drive up the freeways now, not worried about it, or me, and I have a much better drive. I can teach you one day though if you like, it's very responsive, you get used to that." He drove towards the Plaza entrance, then pressed the remote, and drove us in, closing it behind him. We parked in his garage, and then walked to the lift.

"How many garages do you have here, I've only seen that 1."

"All belong to me, so I could use any of the 100 plus spaces, or turn them into garages. But I just use this 1 and about 2 others for me." My mouth was open. As we got into the private lift, he kissed me passionately; thrills ran through me, as he touched my wanting body. Holding me, around the shoulders, until we reached the penthouse lobby, as we went into the penthouse he turned off security.

It was only 4pm but it felt later, it was getting a little darker outside, and the place seemed to darken at the same time.

"Wonder if it'll thunder, that must be stunning to watch from here?" Marcus came towards me, and put his arms round my shoulders as I stood overlooking the beautiful view. He kissed the back of my neck, gently.

"You will have to get used to how rich I am, Nat. It's a fact, I know we've only just started dating, just let me know if you want something ok? I mean it. I care about you very much, I can buy anything I want to, I have taken a longer time to get used to it, it's a fact though, I'm a multi billionaire Nat, and so are mum and dad individually, I wanted to tell you myself, but you didn't seem to know just how wealthy we all are. So now you know, and I'm glad told you." He kissed the back of my neck again. *Wow, that was a bit of a long speech, why'd he come out with that now?*

"Oh ok didn't know you had so much money. It's so different for me Marcus; I'm really trying to come to terms with that. I earn $50,000.00 a year Marcus, I work full time for that, but it's a little different for me to suddenly go from that, to having a rich boyfriend who wants' to buy me things. I'll get used to it, just ease me in gently, don't buy me a Ferrari tomorrow, wait until my birthday or something; I have to get used to it, or it doesn't feel right, I'm sorry."

"Nothing to sorry about Nat, I just want to spoil you, let me." He grinned.

"I know, and it all sounds lovely, just take your time."

"Ok," He kissed me on the back of my neck, just as a rumble of thunder, came from outside.

"Going to stormy in here tonight?" He had a wicked grin on his face.

"Do you have Monday off, like I do, it's a Holiday, I don't but, I will arrange it right now," He grabbed his iphone, and phoned through to someone, told them he wasn't coming in, but only on emergencies, can he be called on his mobile. And so within a couple of minutes, he had Monday off too. *How awesome was that to watch.*

"It must be great being your own boss? Wish I was sometimes, at least I could choose, when to work."

"Have you never wanted to do anything yourself." I hugged him.

"Yes, when I left school, I thought I'd love to be a self employed business owner, but I think it's what all people dream of doing. But I didn't have the resources to do that. Then you have to start making money, and I had to get a job, which paid immediately, I became a paralegal. I guess thinking about it, I put in the same hours as a business, except someone else, made the money from me."

"Sounds right, if you could start up as a paralegal on your own if you want to, would that be good?"

"No, I've been doing this for years, I'm over it now. If I wanted to start up something now, it would be a business of my own I think." *Wow where's this coming from, didn't even know I felt like that.*

"You sound pretty certain about that, I thought you liked your job before?"

"You know, I think it's you and your mum and dad, building something, I wished I could have done, years ago."

"But your only 29 Nat, you have plenty of time, if that's really what you want to do, Want a drink?" He went to the bar, and got out the bourbon, and filled his small glass.

"Yes please, sweet red wine, I like please." I wandered toward him as he gave me the glass.

"You know I can make your dreams come true?"

"You already are Marcus, just leave that thought there of any business ideas. I want to get to know you, If we are meant to be business partners at some point, then we'll both know at the right time. 2 weeks into a relationship, where we've only seen each other for a few days, in that fortnight, is a bit too soon, even for you, surely?"

"Not for me Nat, I'm ready now, just so you know. " I smiled at him Clinked glasses with him.

"You know I really want to get to know you more, you said you wanted to watch a woman do things to me, while you watched, right?" His ears pricked up."

"Yes I do." *This I wanted to know, because it wasn't making any sense to me.*

"Is this because, you were made to watch it as a child, and that's how you know that you like it?" *The questions been asked now.* He looks at me and doesn't move, as he recalls something, not too good.

"Yes." is all he said.

"Ok, so you want to do this tomorrow?" *I wanted to get it out of the way, it was something that I'd never come across before. Not being lesbian or bi.*

"Are you sure you want to, and that you're ready?" *No not really.*

"Yes I'm ready, Marcus." And he went to use his phone in the office, whilst he was gone; I started to feel differently about it, I felt all sexy, and just wanted him back, to make love too. He then came back a few minutes later.

"All done now Nat, it'll be 10am, tomorrow here in the playroom." I grabbed him by the t-shirt, and dragged him towards the master suite, going up the glass steps in bounds. He pulled his t-shirt off slowly, revealing, his taut muscular slightly hairy chest. I kissed him, on his nipples and he moaned in pleasure bending to kiss his chest all over, not wanting to miss one bit. I took my top sexy underwear and jeans off; he bent to kiss my breasts, releasing them from my sexy black bra. Flicking his tongue on my nipples, made me moan. I took his jeans off, then his underwear; he'd been erect, since he came back from the office. I pushed his naked body onto his bed, as he did, I held his cock licking the top, then sucking, licking the top again than sucking, not wanting him to come yet, I put the condom on him slowly, squeezing his balls gently as I did, he moaned in delight. I put my wet, pussy on top of his cock sitting on top of him as I was in control, slowly, I moved my body, back then forwards, *OMG I'm gonna come,* I let out a ecstatic moan, as we come together, in the most orgasmic moment that we've shared so far, as I continued to move slowly into him again, I pulsed as another orgasm took over my body. Exhausted, I lay down next to him, as I did I felt him come out, I cuddled up next to him, he fell asleep, as did I for half an hour or so, just cuddling.

When I awoke, I was quite hungry, he was still asleep. I looked at the gorgeous lean hunk of a man who was mine, his hair, was all over the place, I touched his face it was slightly bristly from a day's growth, it was actually quite suited him, make him look even hotter, if that could possibly be, I touched his red lips they were so soft, and gentle. He turned to take my arm.

"Enjoying the view?" His voice was beautiful, he opened his eyes.

"Are you horny for my body or something that was awesome, thank you?"

"My pleasure and thank you." After showering we decided to go out for dinner. I wanted him to pick somewhere He hadn't bought yet, or planned to, this made him laugh. He wanted to drink. He

made a phone call from his mobile, as we got in the lift. We'd dressed up well. As we got to the lobby of the Plaza, I saw Barker outside with the Bentley, he opened the door with a smile on his face. And we got comfortable.

"Doesn't Barker get days off? He's always there for you."

"Yes of course, lots actually, and he's paid to be on call, like right now."

"Oh ok, does he have family?"

"No he's single right now as far as I know. Ex wife, with a much older child who lives in England."

"How do you know that?" I whispered but I knew he couldn't hear.

"Everyone I employ has security checks on, always." As the car moved down the road, the thunder started to roar, it was getting almost dark now We drove out towards the beach, then Barton went through a "Barney's Fish and Chips" drive through. I looked at him, as he asked me what I wanted from the menu that was just outside the door. I couldn't stop the giggles then, as I keeled over in hysterical laughter. The privacy flap went down, Barker, was in giggles too, I could hear him trying to stop.

"What would you like?' He asked us.

"I'll have the special, for $10. Please," chuckled Marcus. I was now rolling in hysterics around the Limo, *focus Nat please, this is fun.*

"I'll have the special too." I held it together.

"Get whatever you want Barker. Marcus handed him a $50.00 note.

"We'' have 3, $10 specials please." He spoke gruffly into the automated speaker. The Limo moved on to the next window to pay, and get our food. We waited for a couple of minutes. Then Barker handed our food back to us, keeping his, and then drove to the beach and parked the Limo so we had sea view, it started to thunder, and then lightening. We opened our fish and chips still not able to stop giggling.

"Well I don't own this place, we have a lovely sea view, and great food, this place was recommended to me by Barker, apparently it's excellent. And I can have a drink, he opens up the bar fridge, and the slide out cupboard, which has cutlery, glasses tissues, and just about anything a person might want. He had plates if we wanted them, *but I was happy to take this all in.* He poured me a glass of my favorite red bottle, and then got himself a bourbon. Cheers, to us." He said digging into his food, with a massive satisfied grin on his face. *The grin on my face said it all, I was happy, after the talks and places we'd been today, this has just topped it off, as we sit here on the beach car park, in a new Bentley Limo watching the thunder and lightning together, with our $10 specials, from Barney's on our laps. What great fun he is to be with.* We had another drink because we weren't driving the rain eased off, leaving the thunder and lightning to disappear about 20 minutes later. Barker went for a walk, to give us privacy I think. We finished off our food and drinks, I cuddled up to him, I was so happy, just being there with him.

"Well this has topped, everything off so nicely, thanks Marcus, you know how to make me laugh, thanks for this, it's such fun doing this." I kissed him passionately, He tasted of bourbon, and fish. We sat there just cuddling, and looking the now full moon that was standing bright, in a now clear night sky, it was perfect.

"Thank you for being with me."

"It's my pleasure." As we watched Barker coming back the car, grin still on his face, we decided to go back to the Plaza, Marcus had a talk with Barker outside, then we packed our stuff away.

On the way back, Barker drove the Limo though "Wendy's" so we could an ice cream.

"I should have guessed, shouldn't I, I'll have one scoop of, choc mint ice cream with flakes mixed in please.

"I'll try one of those too, one for yourself Barker."

"Not for me, but thanks. Can I have 2, one scoop of, choc mint ice cream with, flakes mixed in please, he asked the lady at the kiosk. We waited for a minute, then she came back with our orders in cone holders. Barker handed them through, the privacy screen, trying not to laugh, as he gave the change back Marcus. We parked up in a nearby park, so we could eat them

"This is one of the most fun nights I've ever had I think, Thank you." I licked my gorgeous ice cream.

"This has been fun, only because of the company." He did really know what to say, to me. Finishing our ice creams, we hugged and kissed passionately, I really wanted his body, but now was not the place, for either of us. Even though the Limo was sound proofed and non see in glass, it just didn't feel right to attack him right there and then.

When we got back, we had hardly enough time to turn the lights on, before we both hit the master suite. Marcus rolled beside me, giving me the most delicious erotic look that always took my breath away. He licked my fanny which was so wet and ready for him, round and round, I wanted to orgasm, but I so wanted him inside me, now, I put a condom on him slowly, he put his hard cock in me, a wonderful feeling of fullness, came through my body as he did. He moved back and forth, quickly, and hard so fucking hard and as the most orgasmic, tingles pulsed through my hungry sex starved body; we came together, as the waves pulsed through me.

Chapter 13

"No, don't get off me please, no more, I can't take any more, get off me."

"Marcus, wake up please, you're having a nightmare." I caress his cheek, as he tosses and turns, in his bed.

"No, no more, it hurts, stop."

"Marcus, you're having a dream, please wake up, you're scaring me." I tried to get him to wake up.

"Oh, Nat, I had a nightmare I think.

"I know, it's ok, it's just a dream, and it can't hurt you." I kiss his forehead.

"I'm so glad you're here." He cuddles me, like a baby would.

"I'm not going anywhere." *I thought of what I'd agreed to yesterday, sex with a woman, now the reality of it has hit me, I'm not sure I can do this, she's coming at 10am, it was*

8.55am already on his alarm clock, beside the bed. Shit. Not sure I can do this now, He said yes, when I asked him if he knew he liked this from watching it as a child, that's just yuk, so is his mother, gay, bisexual or did she so it just for drugs, which is the most probable, of all these, in my mind. Perhaps she had friends that were gay that came to the house. Some friends if she let him sit and watch. No wonder he's so messed up sexually. Mary said he was beaten, over and over, no wonder he likes to have control now. I wonder how long, he took, after being adopted; it was until he started experimenting and getting his own way in sex. He'd been sexually abused for basically 12 years, oh I can't bear the thought of that, I start to well tears in my eyes. Wiping them away, I hug him tighter, perhaps one day, he'll be able to tell me all that happened to him, in a way I didn't want to know, but knew, from personal experience that, it was better to release it, talk to someone, then let it go, and move on. I cuddled him for the next 20 minutes, tightly. When I looked at the clock again it was, 9.29am.

"Shit, I'd better get a shower Marcus, your friend is coming at 10am." I moved him until he was fully awake. He grinned at me

"Oh yes, looking forward to it, are you?" *Oh shit.*

"Yes, want to know what it's all about I suppose, so this is more like a test, to see whether, I want to do this ok, just want to make sure you know that."

"Ok fair enough." He rolled out of bed and into the en suite with me. I undressed, and got in the shower. Marcus moved under the 2nd head, in the double shower, and smiled at me.

"I'm here for a wash, Marcus. Nothing else, we don't have time." I got on with my shower.

"Ok, maybe later?"

"Of course." He was certainly very sexy, in and out of the shower, drying his hair with a towel, he looked so hot, I was about to change my mind. *Focus, woman, here for a shave, for a woman. Oh, that made it worse. I'm shaving to have sex with Marcus later, like I just promised.* I dried my hair, with hairdryer, to speed things up. Once dried, I dressed in jeans, and a t-shirt, to cover as much of my body, to the woman when she got here. It said 9.50am, now on the clock. I decided to eat breakfast, with him afterwards. Marcus got a coffee, from the machine for both of us, to chill me out I think, he must have been able to sense my stress over the whole woman thing.

He unlocked the playroom, and was in there for a while, leaving the door open. I came into the lounge room, sat on the sofa and drank my coffee, quickly.

"Ding" went his phone; Marcus came out of the playroom, glancing at me, then talked to her and let her in. He went out to the foyer, leaving the door open and he swiped his key card, allowing her access to the penthouse. *So that's how he does it, no staff downstairs, know she's coming, she just looks like she's here for anything, like a coffee, or to meet a friend. He must have used her before then. Shit how he has-been watching doing this before me? How many woman has he had do this over the years? Because that's how long, he's had this penthouse, years. Or perhaps it was somewhere else before, shit how many times has he done this? Fuck now I'm one of many, shit I can't do this, I can't. Why did I say yes? Because I adore him, and want to make him happy I suppose, that's it, isn't it, in a nutshell yes. So I'll try not to think about the others and just do this, for him, for Marcus, my boyfriend, because I'm a true heterosexual, not in any way gay.*

At that moment, a short, thin, woman with long blonde curls hanging from her head comes in, wearing jeans; fuck me boots and a camisole top. Marcus brings her to me.

"Nat, this is Kelly, Kelly Nat." He smiles.

"Hello." She says, in an American accent.

"Hi." I back away a bit.

"I'll just go have a shower first, ok Marcus?

"Yes in the shower, near the dining room", He shows her again, but clearly been here before. *But I must have known that, he phoned her and asked her to come, shit I just don't want to do this anymore, I don't even wish it was over, just*

that I'd never said yes, in the first place. Shit, fuck, shit.
Marcus comes in the room, I back away from him.

"It'll be ok Nat." He assures me.

"I have all these crap thoughts going through my head
Marcus."

"I can tell her to go right now. Just tell me." I stare at him; *I
know he would do that for me, but I promised, and I was happy
with it all yesterday, or so I thought.*

"No I said I would and I will, just ask her to do it quickly and
get it over with, would you?" He gave a little laugh.

"Of course." Marcus walks me to the playroom, which now
has red silk sheets on the bed. He sits down with me on it. A
few minutes later Kelly comes in, through the door, she has on
a tight black leather outfit; it's a baby doll, with black lace,
with ribbons on the top and very short shorts, with holes,
around the front and back, for easy access, her top has holes
where her nipples come through and fuck me boots up to her
thighs. Marcus talks to Kelly and then just stands inside the
door, watching. Kelly, doesn't say a word, she undresses me
so I'm completely naked, standing before both of them feeling
silly. Then she points to the bed and I get on, and one by one
she handcuffs me to the bed, then she puts a blind fold on me.
Now that's better, now I can't see her, so much better. She
puts some cold oil, or liquid on my top half smearing it in, and
them licking it off, I pretend it's Marcus, she then licks my
nipples, rubbing it around my clit area, I feel her licking my

clit, gently *oh that's nice, not like Marcus, but nice, like she knows where to lick because she's a woman. I pretend it is Marcus, imagining he's her, and not just watching.* She puts a finger inside me, *ow, fingernails, oh not so good,* then she stops, and gets something, then a buzzing noise, *a vibrator? She puts it on my clit, and then it vibrates on the cock vibrator inside me and my clit, oh my god, I'm going into orgasm, she hold it there for a while, my whole body, pulses as I orgasm, once, twice oh bring it on, more please. As my body stops, climaxing, I hear Marcus wanking himself to come, he moans, as he watches my orgasm. Fuck, didn't even think he'd do that, it must have been how he released himself as a kid. Kelly came off my body, and undid the handcuffs, then I took my blindfold off, I stared at him. Not sure of what I was feeling for him right now, pity ranked up there pretty high. I didn't want to be feeling that for him, that s for sure. Kelly left, and went with Marcus to the lift. And to pay her no doubt.*

"I'm going to have a shower." I said but wasn't sure if he heard me .I washed, more like scrubbed off all the oils, and everything else that I possibly could that Kelly had done to my body. *Oh shit I'm not sure how I feel about him, not sure if I had to do that on a regular basis.* I scrubbed my body with the flannel, so it was red raw, in parts. The soap I used twice, to make sure every part of her was taken away. When I was finished I'd been in there for over an hour, it said 12.06pm on the clock. I was now really hungry. And where was Marcus, hiding away somewhere? I got into some new fresh, new black, jeans and a white camisole top, and went down the steps into the lounge room. He was nowhere to be seen. I looked in the playroom, no but, the place had been tidied up. I went to go into his office, which he normally has locked, it was open. He was sitting in his desk chair facing the picturesque window, with his iphone in his hand.

"Get them to come in tomorrow, I'll sort it all out then, they are good suppliers, but if we can't agree on price, then I'll go elsewhere. Just get them to come in around 11am on Tuesday,. You can sort that Martha see you tomorrow." His manner was businesslike and dominant. He put his phone in his pocket, and turned round, when he heard me come in.

"Hello Nat, tell me how you're feeling, I was going to come and see you, but caught up on the phone sorry."

"I'm not sure how I feel right now Marcus,

"Talk to me Nat please?"

"I want something to eat I'm starving, now."

"Here or out somewhere?" *If we go out I can avoid the subject more, or I could just go home? Would prefer to be with him, for some strange reason right now.*

"Out please, in the Ferrari, to somewhere nice in the countryside, you choose, because I can't think for some reason right now."

"Ok are you ready now?"

"Yes, I put my bag over my shoulder checking my iphone for massages, as I go, nothing. We walk to the lift, Marcus grabs my hand, and the usual thrill is missing. We're silent as we enter the lift, he still keeps my hand in his, as the lift descends he kisses my hand. We get to the car park and as we walk through the doors to the garage a few steps away he opens the garage door. We get into the Ferrari, in awkward silence, on my part, not sure about him. As the doors close on the garage, the mighty roar of the engine echoes beautifully, as we come out into the street he drives, without a word leaving me to think.

As we reach the suburbs, he goes into a more country area, towards the National Park. We climb up a hill going towards the mountains; he keeps driving for about 40 minutes, then stops the car at the side of the road.

"Great eating place." *well at least it had a view.*

"I want to talk to you; first, it's just round the corner." The engine is quiet.

"Talk to me Nat, I really want to know how you feel about this morning. Tell me please" *I was still so angry the words couldn't come out.*

"I just don't get why you want to watch me do that"

"I just do, you said you would do it, yesterday, I thought that, was just nerves of something new, this morning?"

"I'm not sure how I feel about the whole thing Marcus, it felt odd to me."

"In what way"

"I'm heterosexual, not gay. I have no urge for a woman to do that to me."

"I get that?"

"But do you?"

"It's just a different experience sexually, that's how I see it"

"Well I don't see it that way."

"Why did you say you wanted to then?

"Because you said you liked it so much, I wanted to see for myself at the time."

"See you did want to, it's just erotic sex for me, something that makes me feel good watching, I thought you wanted to have that feeling I felt too."

"It doesn't give me the same feeling as a woman."

"I'm starving can we please just get some food."

"Done"

He drove liberally round the next corner, to "Ramblers Country Restaurant", and parked outside, with the other few cars. As we walked he grabbed my hand, bringing it to his lips, he kissed it gently.

"Hello sir, can I help you?"

"May I have a table for 2 please?"

"Certainly." He shows us to a window seat, and gives us the menus. *Oh good, somewhere he doesn't own and they don't recognize him,*

"What would you like to drink sir?" The waiter takes his order.

"Just a black coffee for me please." He looked at me.

"Pepsi Max, please." He nodded, and we looked at the menu's .Marcus got the waiters attention again

"Sir" Marcus looked at me, so I could order first.

"I'll have Lasagna and salad please."

"Roast beet salad with mayonnaise." The waiter took the menus. The drinks appeared. We sat in a few minutes of silence, whilst fiddling with our drinks. He took my hand and played with my fingers, but wasn't in a playful mood.

"Ok, I said yes, to try it out, but it wasn't as pleasurable for me as it was for you. Let's just not talk about it, right now. Ok?" *I remember hearing him wank off to the sight of it all, it makes me feel sick. He's been through this crap childhood, and he's playing it all out in his adulthood. But he can't see that, do I tell him? Fuck knows, I just don't know what to say to him about it all, so I'll ignore it, and deal with it another time, when I'm not with him, that way, I can get my head round it, I can't when we're together.*

"Yes I think that would be good right now." Our food arrives. And I tuck in, not as good as "The Seaview" but it's not got any stars here. It's filling though which is what, I've wanted all morning. Looking across at Marcus, I feel so sorry for him. All I wanted was to bundle him up in blankets, and start his life all over giving all the love he deserved. I grabbed his hand, and we ate one handed for a while. When we'd finished, I stood up, moving us to the sofas, in the bar area, taking my drink, that still had a bit left, putting it on the table in front of us.

"Want a drink, Marcus?" I got out my bag,

"Yes Pepsi Max, please." He looked at me, but didn't stop me as I went to the bar, to get our drinks. I returned and sat as close as I could to him, he put his arm around my shoulders.

"Thanks for the drink and wanting to move here." He kissed my lips gently, then down to the back of my neck, slowly and gently.

"I want you, in my life so much Nat; I couldn't bear it any other way. I'm just not sure you feel the same way after this morning, am I right?" His voice was nervous.

"Marcus, it's a relationship, we have up's and down's in them, I know it's your first, its ok we'll get though this ok promise." I kissed him gently on his lips; we sat there cuddling for a few minutes. *I do feel more amorous, towards him. But not ready to have sex, which felt so odd to me, this is my sex god, Marcus,. I gave you my promise we can sort this out, I hope I can, come good on that.*

"I'm so glad, we found each other, at Moo Moo Café, I'm so glad I fought off my doubts and called Rosie and Sebastian's place. None of this do I regret, at all. The only thing I do regret, is not getting to see you for a more than a week, after our first date, so that we could have got to know each other better over that time, and not the few days that we've actually had together." *ah, that's so lovely.*

"That's lovely, but we got to spend this long weekend together, and it's been eye opening, in lots of ways. We had fun, with takeaways in the Limo, we have got lots done in these three days, Marcus, because if you want to go somewhere, you get in your helicopter and fly there." I kissed him with my tongue gently, sexily; he was now looking so much hotter to me, than he had all day. I stayed kissing until it hurt my mouth muscles. Then I went back for more. I moaned, that he hadn't been able to touch my wanting body now all day, I was now so wet, but where to drag him, the cars too small, and not here. There were not many people left, as the food was now closed.

I grabbed his hand unexpectedly and pulled him to the back of the place, outside, where it had lovely ground bushes and trees for perfect cover. He ran with me as I climbed down to an area outside the perimeter fence of the restaurant. We slowed, then caught our breath, in a clearing, far away from anyone.

"Come here, I want you right now!"

"You think I don't," His jeans, are huge with his hard cock. Releasing his zipper, he frees himself, leaving his jeans on. He undoes my jeans, and sexy lacy black G string, pulling them down to my feet. He puts a condom on, and holds me pinned up against a big tree trunk, it feels so erotic out in the open. He kisses my mouth, long and hard, then I put his erect cock, into me *oh how I have wanted this, right now, with him, my screwed up, little boy.*

"Oh Marcus yes, yes I want you now" I moan in delight, as he thrusts, his body against me, using the tree as a buffer, from the huge force, which he's using. He comes inside me; *just listening to him sendsm e off in blissful, orgasmic pulsing through every fiber of my body* We stand there pinned to the tree as he kisses me, his tongue tastes so good, Not wanting to let him go, I hold around his shoulders, keeping him close so tightly, and he me. Eventually he moves out of me, and removes the condom, and does his zipper up, I pull my underwear and jeans back up. *How sexy was that? I love, having sex outside.*

"We should do this more often out in the open." He says, as if he's just read my mind.

"Definitely, it's exciting, not knowing it anyone it watching."

"Yes, But I prefer it if they didn't see us."

"I see your point, of pictures in the press you mean?"

"Yes that wouldn't be good, would it?"

We walked back up to the car, and had a lovely fast drive, back to Long Beach, twisting, and turning, around the curves, having fun together. We drove along the beach front, ending up in a café right on the beach, where we decided to stop for a drink.

"This is a great view again, thanks for a great time this afternoon."

"I' had fun too, we had good time in the woods, a nice surprise, thanks. "We're at a 2 seat café table on the balcony, of the café. The view of the ocean was mesmerizing. The sound of softly rolling waves brushing lightly into the shore. The gentle sea breeze, flicking my loose hair away from my face making Marcus move, his hand through his tousled hair, making him lot so hot. Sipping my coffee it tasted fabulous. We sat there holding hands and gazing out at the beautiful sunset.

Chapter 14

The woman with sexy clothes, got on top of me, I cry out, for her to get off, now, before I get angry. She stays on, I'm hooked up to the bed with handcuffs and foot cuffs. I have a blindfold on. I can't move at all, they're so tight. Please let me go, Marcus lets out a moan of satisfaction, and ecstasy, but I can't see him, I know exactly what he does, while she's here with me, it disgusts me. Marcus kisses me.

"Morning Nat, and what a beautiful day it is, to wake up with you beside me."

"Oh, morning Marcus, I open one eye, you're looking hot this morning, in your nakedness, thanks for that lovely surprise last night, much appreciated." Glancing at the clock, it's 5.00am.

"Why are we up so early?"

"I've got to get to L.A. before 7.00 to sort something from yesterday. You can sleep in, I'll get Barker, to take you to work; your car's there isn't it?"

"Yes, thanks, what time are you leaving here?" He smoothes my messy hair.

"By 6.00am if possible."

"Oh so we don't have time to get dirty again then?"

"I'll make it up to you, promise." He kissed my lips.

"It was only a couple of hours ago, though so you'll have to last until tonight." *I really wanted some time to myself today, just me, so I could think things I needed to think through. I've been ignoring it, but I do want to get it sorted, before it comes up again.* He got out of bed to go to the bathroom, as he did I grabbed his arm.

"I'd really like to have some time to myself tonight, catch up with friends, you know?"

"No, I don't"

"I want to talk with my friends, who I haven't seen because I've been with you so much." *That's a bit of a lie, because we don't go out all the time, and Trish and I catch up every work day and weekends sometimes.* He put his hand through his hair a little agitated, and went to have a shower.

When I heard the water stop, he came out into the bedroom, toweling his naked body, And hair he kissed me gently on the lips.

"If that's what you want tonight, ok, I'll see you Wednesday then?"

"Yes that's great, thanks for understanding Marcus." I grabbed onto his wet hair and pulled him towards me, pushing my tongue into a long deep passionate one, after a few minutes, he pulled apart. He went to get his suit on, black, jacket and trousers, with a fresh white shirt. He had a red thin tie, this time. He did look the rich business man, and he looked so hot, as he towel dried his hair, then combed it through wet. I put my fingers through his hair playfully; he smiled at our refection in the bedroom mirror.

"It's 5.40am, got to go and get a coffee, and toast, do you want some?" e got up to go down the steps.

"Just coffee, I'll come with you." *The thought of eating right now made me feel sick, but coffee I can do anytime.* I got out of his bed in my new black baby doll, pajamas and went to the kitchen with him. He put the coffee machine on, and got the bread out of the freezer, and put two slices, in the large stainless steel toaster. "I can make our coffees", as I heard the machine beep ready. I put a cup in the machine, pressed black, then did mine, flat white, I added sugar, but preferred sweeteners, *must remember to buy more so I have some more on me .*I took the drinks onto the huge, breakfast bar that jutted out in the kitchen, and pulled out my barstool. He sat opposite me. He had peanut butter on his toast. He held my hand across the counter, thrills buzzed through me. I watched him, eat, and then sip his hot coffee; I didn't want him to go right then.

"What time do you normally finish?"

"Between 4.00pm and 6.00pm, usually, depends on what I have on, and when I want to go, although I've never had anyone, I want to leave early for, up until now. If I wanted to I could work from home, and I do sometimes, the manager's report to me, daily, weekly, and monthly. I go through everything I need to, and call them if I want to sort something. It's pretty much automated now, which is good, but can get a bit boring. I like it when we get something new, and I go out and check it out, like our Paris store, will be setting up and running, I'll go out there, and sort that, I know exactly all the pieces, to fit. Once they do we open, the store." He's excited as he tells me.

"That's so cool, that's running your international business, and you love the buzz don't you?"

"Yes I so love the adrenaline rush, from it, knowing I'm in control, is awesome, choosing where to open or buy next, is my decision, and I love all that." He finishes his toast and takes a last sip of coffee.

"It's 6.10am I've got to go. He put his dishes in the sink; I do have a cleaner that comes in whenever I ask her to, so leave the dishes for her please."

"Ok, Have a nice day at the office, Marcus, email or text me if you want" I was feeling a little lost now he was actually going. He kissed me passionately, then grabbed, his iphone and wallet off the breakfast bar, putting them into his trouser pocket, as he walked the door, blowing me a kiss.

"Barker still be outside to take you to work when you're ready ok,"

"Thanks, ok see you." The door closed, it was really quiet without him. I went back to bed and lay down, checking my iphone was going to ring at 7.30am which is the normal time I get up. I lay there hoping to dose off, but couldn't, I was too awake now. I wandered, into the lounge room, *the place was huge for just Marcus, but that's what you get if you want a penthouse, I suppose. I wonder if the playroom is open.* As I try the door it doesn't open. *Knew it would be locked, that's ok, sure it would re kindle memories of yesterday, which I didn't want right now.* I wandered around the penthouse, looking for something that would show what Marcus liked as a person. In his office, which was open, his huge desk, was facing the view, with his office swivel chair, that was so comfortable to sit in, I opened the blinds, with the remote on the desk, wow, *what a view, if I were him I'd work from here, although I'm not sure he'd get as much work done.* I didn't want to open his drawers they were private, but I did anyway. *Just wanted to see something of the real Marcus.* There was a few normal office oddments, in the top drawer, on the right set of drawers in the desk, then in the larger drawer below, he had some files, hanging, I rifled through them, the first had a file, with phone numbers and lots of names, and I saw "Kelly Slater*" Perhaps that's Kelly? I suddenly felt like I was invading his privacy.* As I looked through the file, she had a security check, and lived in L.A. and a photo, *yes definitely* her. *I shouldn't be doing this.* There were other files on the other people he'd had sex with pre me, all with full details , security checks and photos. *I wish I hadn't looked now, but it's there in my head, the pictures of the women, he had sex with, I know because of who he is, he had to be careful, but this put it all into real life for me, I couldn't get The pictures out of my head now, there were about twenty photos and files, altogether.* I closed the drawer, and went to get a coffee, and some toast now, I made one piece, with just butter on it and sat on the breakfast bar, trying to think of something else. *What was I expecting; he told me he had sex, just sex, right from the time I met him, so it should be ok, finding the proof of that. All the girls were pretty, thin, sexy to him, I suppose. He's with me now, so I'd really like him to destroy the file but that means I have to say I've seen it, shit what to do?* I make another coffee, as they are just normal cup size, I'm used to mug, but I prefer his machine it really tasted of café coffee, which I'm addicted to. I sip my hot drink, as I hear my alarm go off on my Iphone, *shit, its 7.30am I forgot to turn it off.* I went to his bedroom, to turn off my alarm. Then I decided to have my shower and get ready,

as I came out of the shower In my towel,, as I dressed in the bedroom, *I noticed that he had no personal pictures of his family. I'm sure I remembering him having some on the tables in his home, but none here. Perhaps he just wanted this free of any personal things for the people he had sex with, that makes sense, I have a feeling that this place is his, and that his parent's never come here, or they'd see the playroom. Which he keeps under lock and key anyway. He's quite a private person, I've noticed.* I put my make up his vanity mirror; in the unit is a drawer, which I open. Lots of condoms, in different Styles, it amuses me, as I remember last night, *the sex was stunning, with an orgasm like I'd never experienced before.*, he can give me an orgasm *during penetration, which I love, the best, bit at the moment, he takes my breath away, literally.* As I'm ready I move downstairs, to my cold coffee. Plenty of time for another, as I don't have to leave until 8.45am really, unless I want to check my car before. It's only 8.20am now. I get myself another coffee, with a fresh cup, as I don't have to even clean up after myself here. *How cool is that, this penthouse is great, apart from the room of pain, it's got everything anyone could want.. I sip my coffee on the very comfortable sofa, opening the blinds, with the remote, to give the place, such a gorgeous all round view, the hills, of the national parks, on one side to the Pacific ocean on the other, and way above other towers, that's what I love about this place, it's the depth of the view, as there are very few other buildings this high.*

At 8.40am I get ready to go, I've closed the blinds, and he never showed me the security system, so I can't do that. I go out of the front door, as it closes behind me, I realize that if I wanted to get back in, I couldn't. It was ok when I went down in the lift, I thought, someone here would be able to call him, and use a master key, no doubt.

Good job I had everything with me then, I smiled. As the lift opened onto the, foyer,

"Morning Madam." Carlton was surprised to see me.

"Morning Carlton." I looked for the black Bentley Limo, and luckily for me there it was, right outside.

"Morning." Barker said with a smile on his face as he opened the door for me. As I got in the privacy screen went down, as he sat back in the car.

"Rumble and Smith Lawyers in the High Street, is that right?"

"Yes that's right, do you know where that is?"

"Yes, I have sat nav, here. I found it when Mr. Carrington, spoke with me about it this morning." I hadn't been able to have a conversation this long with him, so I kept it going for as long as I could.

"How long have you worked for him?"

"Almost 10 years now?" He slowly drove off.

"So is he a good boss?"

"Yes he is, always surprising."

"Oh, and you have a daughter living in England, Mr. Carrington, tells me. How old is she?"

"Liz, will be twenty five this year, she is now engaged to a man in England, and so I go over there when I can, Mr. Carrington helps me with getting there, in the family jet, he is a good man to work for." *Family Jet, shit can Marcus fly that too? Wow how exciting, to have your own plane.*

We arrive outside the office, I can see my old Saab parked outside, still looking good, as I knew it would be safe. Barker stops the Limo, and I get out myself so he can stay on the busy main road.

"Thanks Barker, I really appreciate the lift and the chat."
"My pleasure, see you on Wednesday, after work." *Wow he'd been given instructions*

already from Marcus.

"Yes see you then." I waved as he went off, but he was concentrating on the traffic. As he pulled off, I felt slightly alone again.

As I went into the office front door, Megan greeted me cheerfully.

"Hope you had a good weekend, Andy tells me you've been with Marcus all holiday weekend?" *Shit I forgot all about*

Andy and Megan, perhaps they did last more than a one night stand.

"Yes, I had fun, Megan, thanks for asking." I walk up the mezzanine to my office, and go to put my bag on my desk. Trish grabs me and walks me to the kitchen.

"Love your new clothes; did Marcus buy them for you?"

"Yes"

"Well, tell all, that is some gorgeous looking hunk, you had glued to your lips."

"He is nice isn't he."

"If I'd met someone who looked like that, money or not, I'd be looking for him like you were, I totally get it now. So tell all, what happened on Friday night?" "We went to the Seaview Restaurant, the revolving one in the Plaza that he owns. I had a great time all night."

"And Saturday?" *She looked really interested so I'll tell all the good bit, because let's face it there are too many to explain.*

"We went to his store in L.A where's he's based by helicopter, then out to lunch in the Limo, then back in the helicopter, to his home in L.A. where his cook made a fantastic meal for us and stayed there overnight."

"And Sunday?"

"He flew us to San Diego then, to have lunch with his parents. Then stayed at his penthouse in the plaza" *As I retold the story, it sounded like I was reading it out of a fairy story book. I realized just how, phenomenally rich he was, and that I'd just added a private Jet, to the list of toys, he enjoyed.*

"Wow, and Monday?

"We have a lovely lazy morning *that sounds better,* and then we went in his Ferrari, to a restaurant, in the hills, then to a coffee shop on the beach near here. Then back to the Plaza overnight." *I missed out on some fun things, but right now they feel so private, because we went through them together.*

"Wow, you did so much, I'm really happy for that, you know I am, you are really lucky to have him in your life, I did a Google search for his family they own hundreds of stores all over the world, they are billionaires, did you know that?"

"Yes he told me, and I had the whole family history from their first store in London, all those years ago, to over 200, now all owned by the 3 of them. It's amazing isn't it. I'm really proud of them, actually." *And I was, they all deserve it.*

"Tell me Trish; are Megan and Andy, going out together? As I came in she insinuated that they were?

"All I know is what you know. You probably find out tonight, if you 're going there?"

"Yes home tonight, see Marcus tomorrow. I'll find out and let you know."

"Thanks."

"So is he good at sex? "

"Too personal, but yes, I've never had so much good sex, ever, we're a perfect match in that department."

"Oh good at last, I'm truly happy for you."

"So am I." I grinned at her. Picking up out mugs of instant coffee, I really love Marcus's coffee machine, but it will have to do, but just didn't have the edge any more. We came into our office and I answered the questions from Donna in an evading way. My iphone, buzzed, it was Marcus, wishing me a good day at work, I sent one back to him, with a big kiss at the end, wishing him the same.. My morning was slow; because I had to catch up with the work from yesterday that I wasn't able to do. I was glad the boss was back though, we caught up on everything and he said everything seemed to be in order; he was pleased with my work.

"Ready for lunch at "The Deli" and a catch up?" Trish is pushing her chair in.

"Sure, let's go." I put my bag on my shoulders and went out of the office with Trish. We walked out to the footpath and slowly towards "The Deli"

"How do you feel going out with one of the, most eligible bachelors, in the world?"

"I hadn't thought about it like that before. He's just Marcus, with his faults, just like you and I." "I fancied him, before I knew how rich he was, he's a good person, and I'm getting to know him better and better each time we meet. This weekend was manic though, If he wants' to do something, he just does. I like that about him" We go into the shop, it has a small queue, whilst we wait, I notice, the newspapers, The L.A Times, has a picture of Marcus on it, running up the hill with me, *shit, that's the restaurant all the way out we went to, how on earth did they get there, I didn't even see them.* I buy the newspaper and look at the article; *thank goodness they didn't mention the sex scene, before we ran up there, just a lot of innuendo*

"What's that it's Marcus and you Nat, wow you're in the papers, shit Nat.?"

"I don't know who was there from the papers, but just missed what really happened in the woods, which wouldn't have been a good picture, for him." I call him on his mobile.

"Did you see the picture in the paper, of us at the restaurant yesterday?"

"Yes, normally I can spot press for a mile, its good job they didn't get the picture they really wanted. Are you alright, we'll have to watch our step, Nat, I'm sorry you're in the paper, but again it's part of life for me, and my parents, so we are used to it. Just watch out if you're going out anywhere, they know who you are now, so keep the talk about us to a minimum if you go out ok?"

"Yes Trish and I are out for lunch, I'll take note though, thanks Marcus, see you soon."

"Missing you, but I have a lovely photo of you now to look at, see you soon"

"I'll cut mine out for my desk photo of you too. See you soon, Marcus." When we got our lunch, I wanted to back to the office, but checked the out the park, which was free of people, so we went there. Sitting on the park bench, we sipped our coffees, and opened our sandwiches.

"Wow, so you had sex, in the forest, then ran back up the hill, and that's when they got you?"

"Yes, I'm going to have to get used to it, as Marcus just said, they have my picture, so more people will be looking for me I don't mind but I haven't done anything except go out with him, and it's page one news, there are more exciting and newsworthy things to go on the front page as far as I can see.

"It's a good picture of us though"

"They don't have your name yet though, it's all pretty vague as far as I can see."

"Yes but it's what they do, the press they find out things, they're good at it."

"I can't believe you're a celebrity Nat."

"I'm not" and that point my iphone rings *my mum's picture comes up* shit its mum, I look at Trish with a help me, look of desperation as I answer the phone.

"mum, How are you?"

"Great thanks Nat, Is that you're picture on the L.A Times today, with Marcus Carrington? It is you isn't it?

"Yes, mum, it's me."

"How long have you known him, why didn't you tell me?"

"We've only just started seeing each other mum, I didn't want to tell anyone until, we were a bit further along in our relationship, just to make sure we were going to last more than month, that's all."

"So are you sure Nat, I'm so happy if you are, not for who he is, but for you moving on after your attack."

"When we've gone out for a month, I'll tell you mum ok, it's too soon for both of us to know any more at this early stage." *Couldn't tell her he's fallen for me, I don't know that for sure, he'll tell me if he has.*

"Ok Nat, take care, see you soon, invite him for lunch" the phone ends

"Shit, she invited him for lunch; this is just too weird today." Trish laughs.

"She's just being your mum"

"That's true; it's just weird because, I don't know who else saw that, I feel a little invasion of my privacy, but Marcus has to deal with it, so I will too."

The afternoon was going much quicker, I had a little time to myself to really think about the things, I wanted to about Marcus. *The whole woman thing on Sunday morning, I've been able to ignore, now I have to sort this out, every time I think about, it makes me sick. The very fact that he's standing there, wanking himself off, whilst she does those, supposedly sexy things to me, which I assure you are not sexy to me. It's depraving, that's the word, and depravity at its lowest is what it is to me. But I can't tell him he's playing out his childhood; I can't even talk to his mum about this, it wouldn't be right to Marcus. I will have to have it out with him on Wednesday, tell him how I feel, then if he doesn't want me, and then I'll leave.* I sipped my coffee that Trish had brought me, in from the kitchen; she could see I was having some thinking time, just assumed it was to do with the photo. I left work on the dot of 5.00pm

As I got into my car someone flashed the camera at my face,

"Hi, it's Natalie, Hungerford, isn't it? Good day at work Natalie," The female blonde reporter asked quickly as she got between me and my car. I didn't say a word.

"You're dating Marcus Carrington, aren't you?" I ignored her, got in my car, and drove off as quickly as I could. *Shit now they know me.* I drove back to my apartment, and put the car in the undercover garages, and walked, to the lift. Closing the lift door, I was alone, thank goodness. I didn't trust anyone I didn't know now. I let myself in to our apartment, seemed a long ago that I was here with Marcus. Going in, I remembered just how big his penthouse is compared to mine. I took my shoes off and threw them by the door.

"Andy?" silences.

I went to my bedroom and put my things bag on my bed, I lay down trying to chill, from all the excitement and stress of the last few days in general. I really needed to have tonight here, I *hope Andy's around,* I wander to the fridge in the kitchen, and it's our message board, because sometimes we barely see each other, with our different work hours.

"Not working tonight, gone to see a movie, with Megan after work, back around 7.00pm" So *he is dating her.* Going to the bathroom, I run myself a bath, and put some of my favorite, relax in bubbles in. I get some of my most daggy pajamas I can find, so I can chill here tonight, *I was going to take Andy to the pub, to get him drunk, and get all the info, but after the photos today, I'd rather stay at home, hopefully Andy will come back after his movie and I'm finding the gossip out them. It was a plan, in the meantime I want work out what to say to Marcus tomorrow.* Getting in the bath, that was now the perfect temperature now, I put my head under, the water and sat there for a while, chilling, surfacing, I dried my hands and put my iphone on the loudspeaker near the bath, I choose, music to chill me out and put it on quite loud. First, was Enya, then Chris De Burgh, Whitney Houston, all on shuffle, I was so blissed out as I sang along.

"Well tonight is the night, that I'm feeling alright, and I'm gonna hold you tight" as I my version of Whitney, hear a knock on the door, I turn it down."

"Is someone drowning you Nat?" Andy's voice hollers

"You're back that's early. Did you see the movie?"

"Yes finished early, I wanted to come and check up on you, as I haven't seen you for days now."

"I'll be out in 10 minutes; put some coffee on would you please?"

"Sure" He put the kettle on. I dressed in my comfy pajamas, and cleaned the bath out. *Marcus gets his bath cleaned for him, I could do with his cleaner.*

Andy has blue jeans and his red t-shirt on and has kicked his trainers off at the door.

"It's good to see you." I slap his back playfully.

"Well what's happened, with Marcus, what you been up to?" I told him most of the events of relevance to him that had happened over the last few days leaving out quite a lot. I told him about the photos, just in case they tried to go through him.

"Wow, your life has changed massively, since you've met him, but are you happy Nat when you think about him right now?" *That's an odd question to come from him. I thought of us this morning, and the excitement of being with him, the fun few days we had especially our takeaway in the Limo night, with a sea view, to rival no other. I loved being with him.*

"Yes I am happy being with him, we all have ups and downs in relationships, but yes, he makes me happy."

"Now I want to know everything, about you and Megan"

"Well you know how we met, I did like her, it wasn't a one night stand, which you thought it was. Anyway we went out on Friday; she went to the bar I work at, which was easier. Then Saturday, the same as I was working again, then Sunday, we didn't see each other, then yesterday, I worked and she didn't so she came to my work again. We're just chilling getting to know each other. You know me I don't do relationships, and I told her that at the start so she knows that, we don't have sex though, because we're just friends, she knows that, I made sure she knows that Nat."

"Cool, she didn't say much, at work, just that she'd talked to you."

"Awesome." We chatted about other stuff from work, and anything else. After watching TV for a while, I felt really tired, from getting up so early, and went to bed.

Chapter 15

Driving to work, I didn't get as good a sleep as I'd hoped for last night. Trying to think of ways that I can tell Marcus that I don't want to do what happened on Monday morning ever again. *I'm over it, it isn't me at all, and in all honesty, I don't want it to be him, he's just dragging his past into the future, and it's not a good one, I agreed to do it, and then hated every minute of it.* I drove to Gloria Jeans, for a coffee to wake me up. as I ordered, waiting, I noticed the local newspaper, "The Long Beach Bulletin, had my photo they took last night, *shit* taking it to the table with my coffee, I sat reading it.

"Marcus Carrington's girlfriend, Natalie Hungerford is the headline, and then the text said."We caught up with Natalie outside her workplace Humble and Smith Lawyers, where she works full time as a paralegal, doing legal transactions. She's worked here for about 4 years, according to our source. She only met Marcus Carrington a couple of weeks ago, but is she the one to capture his heart? The Carrington families have made a 'no comment,' on their son Marcus. Who is a multi billionaire in his own right. Is Natalie, in it for his money, or love? Catch up with more news tomorrow, on the latest events" *Shit and double shit, who is their source? What a load of crap.* I drink my coffee, I call Marcus, I just want to hear his voice. The iphone rings.

"Hello it's me,"

"Hi I know, how are you, have you seen the Long Beach Bulletin, this morning, I presume that's why you're calling?"

"Yes, I'm in Gloria Jean's for a coffee stop, I'm beginning to hate the incident at work now. I saw it sitting there, the woman came, with a photographer, last night after work, and tried to ask me questions, I ignored her and drove away. I just wanted to hear your voice, before I go on to work."

"I'm glad you did I'm really missing you, I realized that the nightmares I have of my birth mother are there every night, but with you I've only had one, you're like my lucky omen I think. I miss you so much; just want to be with you every day. Would you move into the penthouse with me?" He stopped.

"Marcus its way too early for that, right now. But thank you for asking me. I miss you too, but that's just too soon at the moment, for me, sorry."

"But I'll pick you up tonight around 5.00pm, miss you .Nat, so much."

"I miss you too, see you at 5.00pm, I blew a kiss into the phone."

"See you later, got to go now." He ended the call. I finished off my coffee, for a few minutes more, then put my cup in the bin as I walked to the car. Flash, another photographer, and the same blonde, from yesterday.

"Natalie have you spoken to your boyfriend today?" silence.

"Are you meeting him today?" I was being watched by the bemused Gloria Jean's employees and customers through the windows, *shit, didn't ask for this. Marcus deals with it, so can I.* Unlocking my Saab, I got in and drove away, as fast as I could. I parked outside, the office, and walked to the door, I could see, the reporter's car, coming down the street. *Shit, what if they're here for a photo shoot, later when he picks me up?* I text Marcus,

"I'm being followed by reporters; they will photograph us together, when you arrive,

just warning you." I sent it.

"Bring it on I want everyone to know about us. Our lawyers will sue the pants off them, if they print anything, not right, so bring it on, x" he *put a x at the end, that's the first one.* His text comforted me, and I walked up the stairs into my office.

Trish, was on the phone as was Donna when I got in, I realized that I was five minutes late. I started up my computer, and put my bag on the floor under my desk. Trish came off the phone, and walked over to me.

"Are you ok?"

"Yes, fine thanks, just being ambushed by the press, last night and this morning, same paper." I got out the files I was working on last night.

"Do you want a coffee, I'm just going?"

"No I had a large one at Gloria Jeans, on the way here. I'm a bit out at the moment, but thanks." She put a hand on my shoulder.

"Are you sure you're alright, they seem to be making you stressed out to me. It's a big thing for them; they think you're a celebrity?"

"But I'm just me; celebrity is just something people make up, about people, mostly newspapers. I don't want to be a celebrity Trish. When I first met Marcus, I had no idea who he was, he was just so god dam attractive to me, and know I know him a little better, he is so much more than, a celebrity." *I was quite animated about, because I was in the middle of it.*

"I know, but it's a part of his life, and if you' want to be with him, then it's always going to be there."

"I know." I started my work; *I wonder who the source they mentioned in the article is.*

"Nat, you ok? I saw you in the paper this morning." Donnas was concerned in a motherly way.

"Yes, I'm fine now, just try and concentrate on some work, so I can take my mind off it."

"I'm sure he must worth all of the hassle, Nat."

"Yes he is Donna; he's the best thing that's happened to me." *I realized he was.* Getting on with my work, the morning went quicker than I'd hope for. Trish and I decided to stay in, for lunch and at five minutes before, lunchtime; Megan called me saying there was someone here to see me. *Shit it's the press again.* I walked slowly down the stairs, to see who it was.

"Barker, what are you doing here?" *I was totally surprised,* he had a parcel.

"Mr. Carrington sent this is for you." He put the parcel on the reception table, by now; the reception area had Trish, Donna too.

"Wow, thanks." I looked at the parcel.

"He said, it's a packed lunch, as you didn't want to go out." I open the huge package, in reception. It's got a top of the range Delongi automatic coffee machine,

"Wow" then I opened a wicker picnic basket, and sorts of luxurious delights, were in there.

"Thanks for bringing that, it's perfect, the coffee machine is awesome,, he's too generous. I'll phone Mr. Carrington and thank him. Do you have to go back to L.A now?"

"No he's flying down, I'll pick him up from the airport. He did say that if this wasn't ok, for me to drive you and your friend Trish, is it, somewhere for lunch. His treat, so which do you want?" The girls were ohing around me.

"He's got it perfect already, with this wonderful, lunch, I couldn't ask for any more, thanks again Barker, I'll see you at 5.00pm." He smiled at the attention I was getting.

"Great see you then." He went back to the car, which he'd parked in the private clients car park to the rear, avoiding the press, How *thoughtful*. We carried the box together, through to my office. Put the coffee machine in the kitchen, read the instructions, filling with water. Marcus had got my favorite coffee beans in the hamper, as well as some other flavors to use, about five different packs. I filled it with water, and waited for it to heat up. It was the exact same one from his apartment, so I knew it well now. The hamper also had a selection of freshly made sandwiches, sushi rolls and even a salad, with chicken mayo dressing, all in a bag to keep it cool.

It was from his store, I recognized the logo. We had a bottle of red wine, my favorite of course, with 4 glasses for us to drink from and a corkscrew. I had my favorite sweetener, in packets. Then I saw, some sweet things, wrapped up in the cutlery, tea towel, on top of 4 plates, was individual lemon meringue slices, and Pecan tarts. "Wow Nat, he totally knows what you like; Trish opens the wine, and pours glasses for me and her.

"He does," I ask to see if anyone else wants' to share in this huge, 4 person picnic. Full of fresh things. We are allowed to drink in the office thank goodness, but I just have one glass anyway. I phone Marcus.

"Hi, thank you so much, you're so generous, and I like that part of you right now.

Thanks Marcus, it's perfect, absolutely perfect, especially my coffee machine, thank you."

"My pleasure Nat, Barker said it was what you wanted, I'm so glad you had a happy lunch hour" I walked to the coffee machine, it was ready for me, I put a cup in which he'd provided.

"You do know what I like don't you?"

"I'm getting there aren't I?"

"Yes, you are. Thanks again, see you soon>"

"Pleasure Nat, see you at 5.00pm" we ended the call. I made myself and Trish a coffee and bought back to the office, as Donna had gone out to get one of her kids, who was sick from school. I put her cup on her desk.

"Here you are perfect tasting coffee."

"But it's only a small cup"

"Yes just taste the difference you can always make a mug, just put 2 scoops in, for this great coffee flavor."

"Wow, I swear you are a different person Nat"

"Still the same me, just an understanding, having used, this machine all weekend, that's all." I sipped my drink.

"Still this is some great present, right, perfect, you are very lucky to have him in your life, you are." I sat and drank the rest of my coffee.

"I know I am." Finishing my coffee I picked up a sushi roll, chicken avocado, it was divine of course.

"This is one of the hampers Carrington's sell, he's handpicked the insides, I saw it when I was in the L.A. store, on Saturday, it's great, I love it."

"You love him, Nat, it's so obvious, just admit it to me, we're on our own." I drank some of my wine, and a piece of lemon meringue pie, putting it on a plate, *this tasted divine, just like The Seaview Restaurant, one. I wonder if it is?*

"This is beautiful, you should try some Trish."

"I will if you tell me how you feel, I'm your best friend, I won't tell anyone."

"Well maybe I do, but I don't want him to know yet. I have a few things' to sort out with him that are personal to us, he did ask me to move in this morning."

"Did he, what'd you say?"

"That it was too early, of course, we barely knew each other." Trish took one of the lemon meringue pies, eating it on the hard plastic wrapping in came in, she tasted it.

"Wow that is nice, not too lemony, and just right." She finished it off. Sipping her wine and as she did. I cleared away the debris, into the bin, but washing up the plates, glasses and cutlery we'd used, putting it all back into the hamper, and keeping it under my desk.

After lunch I went into Mr. Smith's room.

"Hello Natalie, our own local celebrity, I see." He shows me today's Bulletin. *Shit.*

"Yes I do seem to be, don't I, it's totally unwelcome, I assure you."

"What can do for you?"

"Well Marcus, my boyfriend, *oh shit* well he just gave me an all in one coffee machine, which I've got working in the kitchen now, for everyone to use, I mean. I just wanted to check that it's ok to have it there?"

"Yes of course, I'm all for a decent coffee, they are thousands of dollars, which is of course, why we had a jar of instant, and a kettle. But yes, it's fine Natalie"

"There is something else, would you mind if I could to avoid the press, when I go to my car in the street, use the clients private car park instead. Sometimes I have been leaving my car overnight, *oh shit*, and I'd like to make sure it's safe, when I return."

"Yes, do you have a key; it'll be safer that way?"

"No, I don't"

"Ok I was going to say, go and get one cut now, but probably best if I ask Trish, right?"

"Thanks so much, I really appreciate it." He took the key and some money, and walked with me to Trish's desk.

"Trish, I would really like this key cut, as soon as possible please, then give the copy to Natalie, ok here's some money." I mouthed thanks, to her. Trish was a little shocked but went out to get the key. I started to get on with my work, and then my iphone went *Rosie*

"Hi Nat, you're on the front page of the Bulletin, did you know? *Did I know?*

"Yes I did thanks Rosie, and on the front page of the L.A. Times yesterday. Running up a hill, "I stopped myself.

"You sound pissed, not pleased, kind of gets to you after a while, they lay in wait for you, giving people no privacy Rosie. I've got get used to it, Marcus is coming to take me to dinner tonight, he's quite happy to have our picture in the paper. I wouldn't mind if I knew that one picture would be enough, but once they've got you, they want more."

"Wow they are making you angry, if you need a refuge come round to ours?"

"Thanks Rosie, I hope I can get over this, and have a lovely time tonight."

"So do I, call me if you want to rant won't you."

"I will thanks Rosie see you soon, I hope." I put the phone down as Trish came in and put the key on my desk.

"Sorry, about that, you seem a bit pissed with me. I really wanted to put my car somewhere the press aren't able to attack me before I get in."

"I get it, Nat it's ok, I thought I could keep my bike in there if I leave it overnight, like last Thursday too, if I can borrow the key?"

"Course, just let me know, I'll go and put my car round there now, it's only 4.00pm but they shouldn't be there until I finish. So I'll give it a go." Walking downstairs, Megan was on the phone, but glanced at me, as I went outside to my car. No one came over; I moved my car, around and into the ca park, down a short drive. I locked it and I locked the gate, mine was the only car in there, and I could unlock it if I needed to later, but as far as I was concerned, my car was out of sight.

At just before 5.00pm, my iphone rang, *Marcus.*

"I'm here; you ready, to have our photo taken?"

"Yes actually I am, bring it on." Moving down into reception, I said goodbye to everyone as they left, glancing at the surrounded, black Bentley Limo parked on the curbside. I walked outside, to Marcus who was at the top of the steps; he took me down to the car, holding my hand tightly. He stood outside the Limo passionately kissing me, a whole five minutes it seemed; the photographers were many now, with reporters asking many questions, I felt safe with him there embracing me. Sill holding me tightly in his arms, he cleared his throat, and the press silenced.

" Yes Natalie and I are in a relationship, you have what you want, now please let us enjoy each other's company." He was so in control of the situation, I was in awe of his self confidence. We got in the car and speeded off, to the Plaza to the locked underground car park, Barker put us near the lift and parked it out of sight, in a huge garage.

Going up in the lift, I held him so tightly.

"Thank you."

"Nothing to thank me for," As we got to The Seaview Restaurant, he put his arm round me; we walked through the empty restaurant, to our favorite spot. in the window, facing each other. We had a drink waiter immediately at his side.. He looked at me,

"Just a Pepsi Max, please, with ice."

"Bourbon with coke." He kissed my hand gently as he bought it to his face.

"Please move in to the penthouse with me?" *He didn't give up easily*

"I said it's too soon Marcus, you know it is don't you?"

"All I know is that I can forget all the crap, easily when you're around, that is a good thing Nat, if it's early in our relationship, then I'll have to wait until, you are ready. I'm ready right now, just so you know." Our drinks arrive.

"I'll let you know when I am, promise." I sipped my drink.

"That lunch was phenomenal, today, especially the coffee machine, thank you again."

"Anytime." We look at and choose our food, and give our order to the waiter.

"About what happened on Monday morning?" *I wanted this out of the way right now; it's been stressing me, since Monday.*

"Yes." He looked concerned.

"I was not happy with it Marcus."

"Yes, you had a different reaction to what I thought you were going to bearing in mind

I thought it was what you wanted."

"Marcus, I hated it. If you are going to leave me, because it's part of you, then leave, I just don't like it, it makes me feel cheap, and that's not who I am. I can't see why anyone would want to see their girlfriend like that, it's depraved to me. I'm sorry but it is, and I can't allow that to happen to me, again." My raving stopped.

"Oh, well I told you that my birth mother who I hate with a vengeance, made me watch it, as it were normal, so I just carried it on, as I didn't know any different, with the women I've had sex with. Do you really think it's depraved?"
"Yes, it is Marcus; it's not what normal relationships are about. I wouldn't want to see

you having sex with a man in front me, to make myself orgasm to. That's disgusting, it really is."

"Well if you put it like that Nat, I wouldn't do that either." He leaned to whisper across at me.

"She was disgusting; I had men put their cocks in my arse for, most of my 12 fucking years with her, just so she got her daily drugs, they raped me Nat, It's not something I have ever been able to talk about, even to the shrink, they got for me. Do you know how disgusting it feels, for me to have to admit this all happened to me as a child. I hate her so much; I try to ignore what happened to me, so far so good. But with you, you're so different, and now you know. She should have been, killed years ago by lethal injection, But they don't have that in

England, so she's in jail for life. Every day, I want her dead so I can have justice, in my life. Well now you know the truth. You don't have to stay." *Fuck our* dinners arrive. We start eating and thinking.

"Well I'm pleased were able to tell me what a slag, your birth mother was and is. It doesn't change the way feel about you, Marcus. I want to be with you, I really do. Perhaps more than ever now, because you were able to let me in, and trust me. I just wanted you to know that I wasn't going to do certain things, and I think we cleared that up."

"Yes, of course. You won't leave me?"

"No Marcus, I promise, just talk to me about it if you want, I'm ok talking about it with you, if you want to?"

"Thank you, for being with me." He ate his Roast Pork.

"Now that one really is one that I have to thanks you for. If you hadn't called and found me, we'd never have met up again, and wouldn't be sitting here now." We finish our dinners, my lasagna, was beautiful, as ever.

"Do you want a pudding here, or I can get them to deliver it, to the penthouse?" *I prefer the privacy of the penthouse, right now, just want you to fuck my brains out.*

"Penthouse, please."

"Glad you said that" he spoke to the waiter, and arranged for our chosen desserts to be sent to the penthouse, as soon as possible.

He took my hand in his as we walked to the lift. In the lift, he kissed me, passionately, and I was wet already, wanting his body as soon as I could. "What about the whips, you haven't used those on me yet?

"Only if you want to, I'll be very gentle Nat promise, so you get used to them." He smiled, at what he would be sharing with me for the first time. As we got out of the lift, into the apartment, he opened the playroom and turned on the lights and the security system off. His phone rang, as he was coming back to the playroom. He took it in the office, was gone for 5 minutes, then he came back, in an absolutely foul mood I think, it was difficult to tell. He wouldn't talk to me, about the call, or anything. He tied my hands and feet to the bed, front ways, so I was facing down on the bed. I didn't get a blindfold, but I couldn't see him because I was secure in position. He got a cane, and gently started to hit me. *This actually felt very erotic, hot and sexy; I was fully naked it felt nice.* Then he got a little harder, an*d I was able to bear the pain, in fact I wanted to see how much I could bear I suppose.* Then he got harder and much harder, it was in the same spot over and over again, I was totally spent.

"Stop Marcus!" But he didn't hear. *Fuck, stop now you bully.*
Eventually he stopped, and undid my hands, I was red raw,
literally I couldn't stand properly. I dressed and slowly and
walked, painfully out of the apartment.

Chapter 16

I left the penthouse, got into the lift, all the way down to the car park. I didn't want Barker to see me, or the press.

"Regent cab's "

"Yes how can I help you?"

"I'd like a cab as soon as possible, the Plaza Hotel please."

"Where are you going?"

"Rumble and Smith Lawyers in the High Street."

"Yes it'll be 15 minutes, is that ok?"

"Yes, can he come to the car park entrance; I'm on the slipway, rather than the main entrance please?"

"Yes of course." As I sat there, I thought what I'd do if Marcus came round the corner and saw me, but he didn't. I had to stand, because I hurt so much, I leaned against the car park wall. Eventually the taxi turned up, and I gently got in "Rumble and Smith Lawyers right?"He confirmed.

"Yes please." It only took a short while to get there, I paid the driver, and he went off. I unlocked the car park, put the ignition keys in, and felt relief that I had my own space, in the car, and drove it home, slowly and painfully. I parked it undercover, so no one, including Marcus could see it. My phone I turned off after I called the cab. I just didn't want to talk to him at all.

As I try to get comfortable, on my bed, I cannot sleep. I cannot believe what just happened to me. My arse is so sore; I had a warm bath when I got back, and Andy wasn't back from work, he'd have probably killed Marcus or something if he'd of seen me.. The bath was a little soothing, but it hurt to sit on my bum. After the bath, I sat on my side watching the TV trying to take my mind off the whole thing, which it did while I got into a movie, for an hour or so, then I went to bed, which is where I've been ever since, I heard Andy come in, but I've pretended to be asleep. I feel in total shock, *is that really how he is, with the canes, I can't believe it, or I wouldn't have thought it possible of him, before dinner tonight, but now, I don't know what to think. This happened to me, it's not one of my painful dreams, and although very close I think.* Rubbing my backside with cream helped, when I came out of the bath, I was actually bruised and bleeding on a part of me, I couldn't believe it of him.

As I drift in and out of dozing sleep, *my dreams, have come into reality, he must have been like this, and they were trying to tell me something, I guess*. Luckily Andy is off to work, or somewhere, early this morning, so I can still be undetected by him, as I lay still.

"Bye, Nat if you're here, I thought you' were going to be at Marcus's place. Anyway have a good day at work, see you when I get back." He was gone out the door, thank goodness. It's only 7.30am, I get up and, have another warm bath, and relax, I turn my iphone on to put the iTunes mix on again, through my speaker. 53 missed calls, several messages, *just don't want to listen right now*, so I put my iphone on flight mode. The music, just didn't make me feel the same way as yesterday, I chill out nearly falling asleep, in the bath. I send a good hour in there; my body is prune like at the end of it. I decided not to go to work today, *I couldn't sit comfortably, and basically too many unwanted questions about how my bum come to hurt. I'll take a sick day, I rarely have them anyway. I really didn't want Marcus turning up there either.* I came out of the bathroom wrapped in comfy pajamas,

In the kitchen, I put the kettle on, and put instant coffee into my kombi mug. I filled the kettle with water, *I've have to give back the coffee machine; obviously we are not compatible, any more. Which is a shame, but it's too expensive a gift now.* Making my coffee I put on a slice of toast, and cover it with peanut butter. I think of Marcus making his only a short time ago. I eat my toast and sip my coffee, walking to the sofa; it's quite comfortable, if I sit on my side. I put my breakfast on the coffee table. I put my iphone to ring the office, now it's 9.00am at last.

"Hello Rumble and Smith, can I help you please?" Says Megan in a cheery voice.

"Hi Megan, It's Natalie, could I to Mr. Smith please?"

"Oh hello there, how are you?" *I don't want to go there with her.*

"Ok, just put me through please."

"Hello Natalie, where are you?"

"I'm sorry, I'm not feeling that well, I can't come in today."

"I'm sorry to hear that, get yourself better and maybe see you tomorrow? "

"Hope so." Putting the call to end, I listened to the some of the, messages Marcus had left

"Nat please call me", they are all the same.

"Buzz." *The entry buzzer - shit I don't want to talk to him, I can't.*

"Yes." I answer

"Hello, is that Natalie?" Sounds like Barker.

"Yes, is that you Barker?"

"Yes, please don't hang up. Just listen, I don't know what happened last night, and what made you leave, it's absolutely none of my business. But Marcus Carrington is totally not good, over it. Natalie I'll be straight with you, I've known him10 years, I know how he is. He's been so in love with you, from the moment you met, he hasn't ever been in love, since I've known him. Now I'm not too known to give him relationship advice, because he's never had a relationship, and I'm divorced, so I know how important it is to be there for the one you love, rather than just letting a loved one go., But he's so upset over you leaving suddenly, not sure he'll ever have another if you've gone from him completely". *Wow Barker at the end of my phone, how odd.*

"Barker, I'm not sure he can fix this."

"Ok, but can he come up and talk with you, so you can see if it can?" *Shit, I don't know what to do.*

"Ok, send him up."

He was in denim jeans, and black t-shirt certainly hadn't shaved this morning. He smelt of last night's bourbon.

"Come in." He looked so sad

"Thanks, I'm sorry Nat" *it was a start.*

"Want coffee? It's instant,

"Yes please." I went to the kitchen, and put the fill warm kettle on again. I got him a mug, out, and put just coffee in it, and waited for the kettle to boil.

"You hurt me, so bad, physically and emotionally, I showed him some of my bum area, which was red raw, but less than yesterday. He touched my bum around the edge of so, gently. The kettle boiled, and I made his black, and put it on the coffee table in front of the sofa, motioning for him to sit down, whilst I sat the other end of it.

"I'm sorry, would you hear me out as I explain, what happened to you. Although I know there's no excuse for what I did..

When we were going into the playroom, normally I wouldn't have done that to you, I was going to start gently, then move on harder only if you wanted to, truthfully. Then as you saw I had a call from mum, telling me she wanted to see me so she could talk to me in person to me about something. I said, just tell me, and she told me, my whore of a birth mother, is due to come out of prison, because life in jail is only twenty years. The prison rang and asked if she can get in touch with me. As you know I hate her guts. There's no excuse for what I did to you, as I said before, I took all the anger for her out on you, I'm so sorry. When you left, I sank to my knees, I wanted to hold you, and talk to you. You just promised to stay with me, and then I was on my own again. I can't live without you Nat, I realized that so much, and I can't say how sorry I am, for not talking to you, just taking out on you, when it was not your fault." *Wow, that's crap for him.* He sipped his coffee.

"I'm sorry, about her, it sounds like crap timing all round."

"Yes it was."

"Have you had any breakfast?

"Not yet."

"Toast with peanut butter, is what I just had, and I'm getting another piece, if you want some?"

"Yes please Nat", we walked over to the toaster, he tried to put his arm round me.

"I'm not ready for that yet; I'm still pissed at you."

"Sorry ok." The toast popped out of my old toaster, and he spread his piece.

"Thanks for talking to Barker, it was his idea."

"He told me some stuff about you, I already knew, so I had so given you a chance to explain, ok."

"What did he tell you?" He sat back on the sofa, and eats his toast.

"He told me, you're in love with me?" *He has to know.*

"Am I?"

"Yes you are, he said in the 10 years he's worked for you, he'd never seen you in love."

"Well I don't know, if I've never seen it before, how do I know?"

"Your mum saw it as soon as you got there, on Sunday."

"She did." I eat my toast

"The reason I'm talking to you, is because, I have been in love with you, since we met, at Moo Moo Café. I didn't even know who, you were, just Marcus, my sex god."

"Sex god?"

"It was my nickname for you as I didn't have your surname. Do you know how much I wanted you to call me; I was in love with you, Marcus big time"

"Wow. I didn't know."

"It's understandable, if you've not been there before." I ate my toast.

"How do I know what being in love feels like, help me here please?"

"When you, feel good when, the person is near you."

"Well I feel that all the time."

"And when you want to move in with the person. Because you want to spend more time with them."

"I feel that as I told you, I want you to move in."

"Exactly, so now you have all these new emotions, you've been feeling around me right?"

"Yes, oh I get 'it now." He finished his coffee, and toast.

"Can I hold you yet? I miss you so much" he looked so sad.

"Yes, you can." He put his arms round me on the sofa, careful not to hurt me as I lay back on the sofa with him. He nuzzled up to my chin, kissing it.

"Is that ok to kiss your neck?"

"Yes, it's nice." *We still had a fair way to go as far as letting touch me fully again, but I was glad Barker had rang my buzzer, as I sat there, with, the most gorgeous man, alive as far as was still concerned, he looked even more hot with his stubble,* I touched it, and ran my finger through it.

"You like my stubble?"

"Yes, it makes you look hot."

"Oh, does it?"

"I haven't been in your apartment yet have I"

"No, you want to wander around?"

"Ok, come with me if you can," I got off my bum that was getting better all the time."

"We'll this is the lounge room, and kitchen as you can see," We walked towards the bathroom, I opened the door.

"Your bathroom is very nice." We walked towards, Andy's room,

"This is Andy's" opening the door was a man's bedroom, with lots of clothes on the floor. Then on to my room,

"This is mine", He went in so did I and I sat on the bed for the comfort of it.

"I always wanted to know what your room looked like, very tiger skin, by the look of it, it's nice." He sat on the bed next to me, putting his hand on top of mine, and just kept it there for a while, it felt nice. I lay down on my side, and he wrapped his body, around me, it felt so good to have that feeling from him, of him being close, but not too close. We lay there for a long time, he was careful not to hurt me as he, held tighter around me. I felt loved by him, again, it was so obvious that, he 'didn't mean to hurt me. After all, how do I know how could possibly know how he feels towards his birth mother. When my own mother, stood out, amongst the best as far I was concerned, bringing us up herself when dad died.

"We'll sort this all out, won't we?"

"Yes I believe we will" he kissed the back of my neck gently. We then fell asleep, in each other's arms, catching up for both of us.

As I woke up, I kissed Marcus, on the lips as I turned round; he woke up, still cuddling me, not wanting to let me go, now he had me, in his arms. He looked totally hot now; I was rested, especially with his stubble, and just, being him, who I found so incredibly sexy. I gave him a passionate kiss, his tongue gently entwining with mine, he tasted of peanut butter, delicious. I pulled his body tightly towards mine, and he realized what I wanted his erect cock, was under his jeans.

"Are you sure you want this?"

"Yes. I am feeling a lot better now all over"

"I don't have any condoms on me, do you?"

"No I don't." He thought about it,

"Are you on the pill yet, I missed the appointment, so I'm going again this week. It's up to you Marcus?

"Let's leave it, until you're feeling better, I still don't want to hurt you Nat, and it's so important to me." And clearly it was, so we just cuddled again, which he poked me with his hard erection, It said 12.05pm on the bedside clock.

"Can I go and get some lunch for us, to eat here?"

"That would be good, thanks; I don't feel like going out just yet. I'm supposed to be sick after all."

"Ok, if Barker hasn't fallen asleep, I'll go and get us something. What do you want most, right now?"

'I want sex slowly with you." I hold him tight around the shoulders.

"To eat I mean?"

"You I want."

"Food, Nat, anything your heart desires."

"Sweet and sour pork with fried rice and prawn crackers."

"Great, I don't want to leave you, you know that don't you?"

"Yes, I know I'll let you back in if that's what you're thinking."

"I know do you have any alcohol here we can drink with it?"

"Just a box of cheap red, get what you want."

"Ok see you soon." He was going for the door, I handed my keys to him, so he knew he could get back in.

"Thanks Nat" as he took them and put them in his pocket, with a grin on his face as he left the apartment.

He returned, within half an hour, which was amazing, but he did have chauffeur.

"Barkers happy now", he said, as he emptied the dishes of ten different Chinese out of the bag on the coffee table, in front of us, he got cutlery and plates, for us.

"Thanks for doing this, it's great, but I do think ten different dishes is maybe too much for us at lunch, but thank you."

"Pleasure, he got out a bottle of my favorite wine and a bottle of bourbon to leave here, so we can drink when I come here next time, if you like?" *He clearly wanted to come back and chill here with me too, as I wouldn't more in with him*, I supposed.

"Course, you can come anytime you know that now don't you?" Nodding, he put Chinese food for himself and me, and we dug in. He poured wine into a wine glass He got from the kitchen, and half filled another wine glass, with bourbon, smiling as we chinked glasses.

"To love, and to wherever it takes us" wow *that was lovely* we sat and pigged out on lots of food, feeling totally stuffed and partly drunk. He cleared all the dishes away for us, putting any spare in the fridge. He took me by the hand, and let me to my bedroom, lying down behind me, he showed me the condom's he'd just bought.

"Are you sure?" He checked, as I nodded.

"I will be as gentle as I can." He so, didn't want to do anything wrong. Moving his body, in front of mine so he could see me properly, he took off my pajama bottoms, he flung them on the floor at the end of my bed, and he undid the buttons of my not so sexy tiger skin top, so slowly, taking in the view, which he obviously found sexy. I pulled his t-shirt over his head, and onto the floor. He took his jeans off, and then his underwear, so I didn't have to move too far. He kissed me so very passionately. Then he got out something and put it on my body, he massaged, the oil into my erotic charged, body, licking it off with his tongue. I felt so sexy, hot and erotic all the wanting of the last day, was now here. He then licked my clit, he was so gentle, it was sending me off into frenzy. I felt him move over the top of me gently guiding his hard cock, into my wet fanny. I felt his wonderful fullness inside me, he gently moved back and forth, and after a while, sending my body into spasms of orgasmic pleasure, he came after I did, I love watching him as he came in me. He moved out of my body, dealt with the condom. We lay next to each other for a long time, closing my eye's I felt the true pleasure of having him close, my naked body against his. He saw the warts and all version of me today, as I'd been in my cosy pajamas, and hadn't put make up on. This place was a mess, but he's accepted me for me, it felt good knowing that, like we'd moved on leaps and bounds because of it. I smelt his delicious hair, as it cascaded over my face, as I reached my head round to kiss him passionately.

I woke before him, smel

ling his cum, on us. Looking at the clock it was, 5.00pm *wow, caught up on some sleep that time.* The bedroom door was closed, as I thought Andy might come home and see us when I went into my bedroom. I didn't hear him, though. Marcus stirred, holding him tightly against me.

"Would you stay here tonight?"

"Thought you'd never ask, of course?" He sat up slightly grabbed his phone, and rang someone.

"Did you get it?   Good, now, then go home, I'm staying here overnight, so pick me up at 7.00am on Wednesday morning, and thanks again, as you said she's worth it." He put his phone down, and smiled at me. Get dressed into your pajamas, he put his underwear and jeans back on, quickly.

"Now Nat I don't want any arguing with you, I got you a present." He went to the front door, opening it, there was Barker, with a present, all wrapped in gold wrapping paper, and a small black, suitcase, on rollers.

"Hello again, glad you're back together, he carried the heavy parcel to the kitchen, see you in the morning, boss." He left quietly, putting the suitcase just inside the door.

"Wow, Marcus what is it?"

"Open it." I undid the fancy wrapping, and the gold ribbons, and bows securing it.

"It's a coffee machine, thank you so much Marcus" I felt overwhelmed, as I got all the stuff out to set it up, he'd also put into the box before wrapping, all the coffee beans, 4 cups and saucers, and sweeteners I like.

"This is so thoughtful, I was missing your coffee machine so much today, I found that going back to instant, was just disgusting, thank you so much, I kissed him passionately, taking him in my arm, and holing him as close as I could to my body.

"Pleasure Nat, it is, to see you like this, is worth everything to Me." He kissed me passionately again, and then we got everything ready to have at last a great cup of my favorite brew.

Chapter 17

Last night Andy came back around 10.30pm after work, but he'd been out early, *so perhaps he was meeting Megan?* He saw Marcus and I watching the end of a DVD. It was, funny to see his face, as he realized who was sitting on our sofa.

"Hello Marcus, how are you?"

"Great thanks Andy, had a good day at work?"

"Yes, ok thanks. Is this our coffee machine, Nat?" He surveyed it thoroughly.

"Yes, a present for me from Marcus, but obviously you can use it."

"Cool." The he went off to bed, to leave us alone. After the movie I went to the bathroom, and had another shower, alone this time. The shower I had with Marcus after we had sex this afternoon, was an erotic experience, I won't ever forget, as he, rubbed my back, with my flannel, being gentle around my still slightly sore red area, that was getting smaller. He shaved me, around my vagina, with his shaver that he had in his suitcase. It was such a good one, I trusted him to do it, and so erotic it was, his cock grew as he did. After he finished, he put a condom on, and as he pushed my back gently against the wet shower walls, from behind me He put his arm on the shower wall to stabilize himself. Kissing the back of my neck, rhea my back, then I felt him inside me, he was so gentle, holding the orgasm started to pulse through my body, he came, and the most orgasmic pleasure, pulsed through my wet body, as the warm water, water, sprinkled over us.   We laughed as we finished showering, then he dried my body gently, and put body cream on to me, and massaged it all over my body, it was so erotic.

 As we, lay there, enfolded in each other's arms, it felt as if we were going to make it this time.   My alarm clock goes off, its 6.00am.

"Nat, good morning,." He kissed me passionately after, he rolled me over.

"You're worth all the press following me, you know that." I grinned at him early morning stubble, and just slept in hair.

"Could we miss out on the canes, Marcus?"

"Already thrown them away Nat, yesterday morning, in fact they are in very small pieces. I'll only use what you want to use, and gently, you still want to use the playroom?" I thought about it.

"Yes, but I keep seeing Kelly in there, could we get new bed, and everything, even change to one of the other rooms, and can I choose the décor, and bed?"

"Yes that sounds good, I just want you to feel good in there, and we can do all that, tonight If you like, I'll get some brochures, for you to choose from, and it can all be done immediately."

"Great yes ok, I've got the Dr's appointment at lunch time, but won't be safe for seven days, after I start taking it."

"Great" He got up and went to have a shower; I put the coffee machine on, while he did. I put some pieces of bread in our old toaster. Andy was up, I showed him how to work the machine, and then he took his drink back to give us privacy. Marcus came out of the bathroom, with his black suit jacket on his arm, black trousers, and white shirt, with his open neck; *he looked so scrum to me.*

"I can see you looking, but you'll have to wait until tonight for that." I handed him toast on a plate, and a cup of fresh black coffee, he took it and sat on the sofa. I sat beside him with mine. We turned on the early morning news.

"Yes Natalie and I are in a relationship, you have what you want; now please let us enjoy each other's company." We watched as we kissed passionately.

"Marcus Carrington confirming his relationship with Natalie Hungerford, but who is Natalie, we get all the news, stay tuned." I turned it off. *They are going to find out about my attack, I just know it. I have to tell him first, I think I'm ready.*

"Marcus, I do want to tell you something that happened to me, I haven't been able to talk others about it. I want to tell you, it makes me feel, so bad, but I have to tell you tonight ok in the penthouse?"

"Ok, can't be anything like my past Nat; yes tell me tonight, I'd like to know dinner first?"

"Thanks, you choose."

"Ok," the door buzzer goes, it's Barker.

"Be good at work, I'll talk soon, and see you after work?"

"Great, have an awesome day." I kissed him passionately, a long lingering, erotic wet between my thighs kiss.

"See you later." He went to the lift.

Andy appeared, "He is besotted with you, and you him, it's good to see Nat, but keep the sex down would you, I can't get to sleep." He smiled

"You're joking aren't you? I can't hear you."

"No can't hear you at all Nat, just joking with you." *Thank god.*

"I heard you going to tell him about your attack, that's good, give you someone else to talk to."

"Yes or the press, will put it all over the papers, before I tell him."

"If they do, how will you feel, knowing that everyone, that's millions that are following you are going to know."

"You know, if I didn't love him so much I wouldn't care but I just want him to hear it from me, even though it disgusts me to talk about what happened to me." I get ready for work; I'm feeling so good in my body now. I go to my car, in the garage, I can hear people, outside, talking, so I know what to expect. I put my roof down, and drive slowly through as the entry gate lift, flash, flash.

"Natalie, Marcus Carrington stayed here last night, didn't he?" The same blonde who; I ignore as I drive in the beautiful warm sunny day towards work. I park in the car park, out of sight, walking to the office, more flashes as I go up the steps. *I'm proud of myself, I'm getting used to this. I know I'm just a popular story right now, but they will run out of things to say about me surely?*

"Morning Nat." Megan greets me as I fly through reception.

"Morning Megan great day isn't it?" She smiled, as I went up the stairs, I put my bag on my chair, Donna on the phone, and Trish looked at me.

"You ok Nat? Yesterday off sick I mean?"

"Yes fine now thanks Trish." I smile.

"It's Donnas turn for coffee, but I said I'd get it, just want to use it, and want to chat in the kitchen?" I nodded and tagged along. When we got to the kitchen the kettle had been put in the storage cupboard. I smiled knowing it was getting well used. Even just hot water for tea, I thought of Marcus, when I looked at, grinning like a Cheshire cat.

"We all love this tell Marcus won't you. Are you seeing him tonight?"

"Yes after work."

"What about the press Nat, I can't believe it all; the news has you both in it. Do you mind?"

"I'm getting used to it. I suppose. He's worth it; He came to see me, yesterday as I really wasn't feeling that good, and we got to know each other bit more." *I will just give bare details for her.*

"I thought you, were staying with him for the day, pulling a sick day, instead of a holiday"

"No I wasn't feeling good, but I'm good now." She gets s the drinks.

"I've got an appointment at the Dr's at lunchtime, so I won't be around, just so you know,"

"You back on the pill again?"

"I will be today." I smiled. We walked back to our office, Donna off the phone now.

"Hi Nat you better?"

"Yes thanks Donna, much." I got my computer started and into my morning, catching up with all yesterdays things, as much as I could. *I wonder what Marcus is doing right now; my thoughts went to the sex in the shower, just few hours ago. It made me wet as I thought of his lean, slightly tanned body, pushing me harder against the shower wall, as I orgasmed.* My iphone rang, *Marcus.*

"Hello," I said as quietly as I could.

"Do you want Barker to come and get you for your appointment at the Dr's? I can send him to you, if you want?"

"Oh I'll be fine; it's just a short walk away, Marcus, but thanks for thinking of me."

"Are you sure?"

"Yes I'll be fine, have a good day, and see you later."

"Ok see you." He ended the call. I got back to work again, the morning went quickly, And soon, it got to 10 minutes, before lunch. *I know I can walk to the Dr's literarily just past "The Deli" I'll get lunch on the way back at "The Deli." sorted.* I got my bag ready to take, and walked to reception to see how many press were there.

"Hello sweetheart. How are you?" *Mum. I stared at her happy face.*

"Mum, Al good to see you, but I wished you'd called to tell me first."

"It was your mum's idea, she wanted to surprise you." Al hugged me. It was good seeing them, *but just not today.*

"We didn't realize there would be so much press outside your office Nat, we've come to take you to lunch." *What to do now I; wish I had Barker to whisk us all away now, never mind, first the Dr.* Picking up my phone, I speed dialed the Dr's number.

"Long Beach Medical Centre, can I help." I turned away to make my call as private as I could.

"I have an appointment with a Dr now, that can I change to anytime this afternoon before 4.30pm, I'm Natalie Hungerford?"

"Oh ok let me see, we just had an appointment cancelled for 3.30pm, is that ok?"

"Yes that's fine thanks, see you then." I ended the call

"Nat did you have an appointment? Have we come at the right time?" *She was getting a little stressed over it.*

"No all good mum, where would you like to go? You will have the press follow us you know that, can you think of anywhere more private than on the street?"

"Yes I can, do you know where The Plaza Hotel is Al?"

"Yes, revolving restaurant at the top, always wanted to go there."

"It's pricey, though just so you know."

"It's all good, Nat." He wanders to his Audi A7, and got in, the presses were furiously snapping the cameras and asking questions, there were about 30 different presses, I worked out from around the world, just to take my photos. He drove to the front and parked under the cover, just leave it there, Al I'll make sure it's ok. I walked to Carlton.

"Miss Hungerford, so nice to see you again"

"Hello Carlton, I want to take my parents up to the Seaview for lunch, can we just leave their car there?" I pointed to the newish car.

"I'll have the valet take it to the private car park for you, and bring it round for you when you leave, if that's ok?" Al smiled and gave him his keys.

"Wow what service Natalie, how does he know you,?"

"Marcus and I come here quite a lot." We walk to the normal lift, as we ascend quickly I remember the private lift, is much smaller than this, taking 20, people. Coming out of the lift, we walk into the restaurant; it's full of people, this time, mainly business people at lunch, from their dress.

"Good afternoon Miss Hungerford and these are your parents I understand, I will find the best spot for you, " We follow him to our table, almost exact same spot, Marcus and I love so much. We sit down, and the drinks waiter comes, with our menus.

"What would you like to drink Nat?"

"A sweet red wine, you know the one." I look at the waiter, as he acknowledges me. They order their drinks, which come in super quick time.

"Nat the service is excellent here, the place is full, they found a great spot for us, and I know for a fact that you have to book here. How come?"

"Well Al, Marcus's family own the place, its part of their business, they have more than just 200 stores worldwide." *I was on a run, don't mention the penthouse, I don't want them to know about it, it's my space with him.*.Our lunch menus came..

"Do you have a time to be back by Miss Hungerford?"

"Yes I do, by 2.00pm,"

"How thoughtful, that was of them" my mum said. We chose our food, and it came within 10 minutes. My mum was looking good; she had a dark blue knee length shirt on, with a cotton t-shirt style top on with blue buttons down the top of it.

"You're looking good mum, haven't seen you for ages."

"I know that's why we're here just wanted to see you, especially as you're getting so much press coverage, just wanted check you're ok."

"Yes I am, I am so happy with Marcus in my life,"

"I can see that, now we're here, it's obvious you're in love with him."

"Yes I am mum; I didn't know who he was when I fell for him, not a clue. And yes I'd do it all again, I really would."

"I know, and from what I saw of you kissing he's in love with you too."

"Yes he is, but we are taking it mega slow, at my request. He already asked me to move in with him, but I told him I'll let him know when."

"Good for you Nat. I wish you both the very best. The manager approached,

"Complements of Mr. Carrington," He gave us a large ice bucket on a stand with a Bottle of Bollinger in it. *I wondered how long it would take for him to be notified.*

"Thanks for that." We had champagne glasses, all round, I called him.

"Hi did you get diverted from the Dr's?"

"Yes mum and Al turned up unexpectedly; I thought here would be more private, than the High Street, they've been so good to us, when did you find out?"

"Carlton, of course, he sets things in motion. "

"Thanks for the Bollinger, Marcus, it's amazing."

"Pleasure, your whole dining experience is on me Nat, as I think you already guessed."

"Thank you; see you around 5.00pm ok, I blew him a kiss."

"Looking forward to it, more than you can possibly know, Nat, he blew me a kiss," *my first one.*

"Marcus has already arranged to pay for whole meal and drinks, before we even got up to "The Skyview" so get used to it Al and mum, I am slowly getting used to it."

"Thank him so much, that meal, cost hundreds, Nat let me put something towards it?"

"No it's the way he is, so get used to it Al" He shook his head. We drink our champers and finished our meal; I was a bit stuffed to fit in a dessert anyway. Mum and Al each had a lemon meringue pie , on recommendation. It came within one minute of ordering. I felt very special, at that moment, it wasn't the money he'd just paid out, it was my Marcus, thinking of this whole situation, and I felt proud of him .I looked at my iphone it was only 1.40pm, so we sat a looked at the view, whilst they ate there, delicious sweets. As they finished, we were wished a happy day by the manager, and down in the lift, to find of course, the Audi was parked just outside, with its keys in it. I thanked Carlton, as we went past, he smiled at me. Driving back to the office, my mum looked at me.

"He sounds perfect for you Nat, even if he had no money or celebrity status." Taking my hand she squeezed it,

"Just wanted to make sure you were ok, now I know you are in safe hands, look forward to meeting him at some point, when you're ready ok?"

"Thanks mum I'll keep you posted." I squeezed here hand.

"We won't come in because of the throng still outside, Nat; it was good to catch up, even if a lunch hour is a little limiting." Al moved the car across to the sidewalk. I kissed them both and got out the car, not going to run, just going with the flow. Mum smiled at me as they drove away, I winked at her, I *love my Mum so much, and I'm glad they came here, must remember my new appointment.*

Ii got into the office, and Megan wasn't back from lunch yet. *What a wonderful lunch with my mum and Al, a lovely surprise, I feel so spoilt by Marcus in a good way, though. I told him I wasn't ready for the cars, or full on lifestyle of his, he bought coffee machines, and meals. One day maybe, I'll be ready for us to be together all the time, right now happy to get there gradually, with a lovely bit of practical spoiling on the way.* I had a huge grin as I bounded up the stairs into our office. I re-laid all the lunchtime changes to Trish right through to the end. Trish had been out to the mall and came back with some new clothes. I got myself a coffee, from the kitchen, popping to tell the boss, I had a Dr's appointment at 3.30pm and would be out for a little while. He was fine about it. Went back to my room, and got on with the work on my desk.

The time quickly came to 3.30pm; in fact I'd have to run, to make the appointment now, I grabbed my bag, and flew, out past Megan, who'd returned.

"Back soon, I hope." I ran to the sidewalk, being photographed as I went, and hundreds of questions being fired at me. I went into the medical centre, with flashes going off as I did. I went to the counter.

"I have an appointment at 3.30pm,"

"Oh, we thought you weren't coming as its now 3.40pm, so you'll have to wait until they have gone ok?"

"Ok" *I just have the most fantastic lunch where everything flowed smoothly, why if I was Mary Carrington sitting in here, would have almost certainly got in straight away. They probably have a private Dr anyway. If I marry him at some point, I'll never go to these places; they are like cattle stations anyway. I pick up a magazine, And right on the front is the picture of me and Marcus running up the hill, fuck I want some privacy, I want to be treated as an individual at the Dr's or anywhere else, everyone deserves that.*

"Look it's her, that Natalie, that's going out with Marcus Carrington, lucky bitch, bet she's just after his money.' *I cannot do this here.* I sent a text to Marcus.

"Can I go to your Dr; instead, please I can't bear this anymore?" My iphone rings.

"Yes, not sure why I didn't suggest it before, I couldn't sit where you are now. Come out, and I'll get an appointment tonight, about 7.00pm at the penthouse ok?"

"You're my savior, thanks Marcus." I made sure they heard as I walked through the door onto the sidewalk, I ran to the office door and went to my office getting some more work done. As it edged towards 5.00pm, I was ready for them. Marcus rang just before, to check I was ready. Then he came to the office. Cameras flashed as he went n. He grabbed my hand and gave me the most passionate kiss I've had from hem so far.

"I've missed you." He held me tightly around my waist as we walked to the Limo.

"And me too," I cuddled up to him, knowing that no one could see in. Barker moved off slowly, and to where we were going for dinner tonight.

I was so glad it was Friday, two days with Marcus is what I was craving for.

"You are staying with me, the whole weekend right?" He kissed my lips, his softness, went straight through me.

"Yes, it's all I want, to be with just you, away from the throng of photographers if it's possible."

"Oh it is, I don't get the flashes that you are getting Nat, it's only when I come here, that I really see what you're going through every day, I want to sort it all out for you."

"The Dr can only get here, from L.A. at 5.30pm, so we'll go to the penthouse first, then, go out? If that s ok with you?" I nod; Barker drives us under the car park depositing us by the lift. We walk and exit the lobby; *I felt a little odd being back at the place I'd run from, before.* Walking in to the apartment, he turned security off. He walked towards me, taking me softly by the hand into the master suite; he laid me on the bed

"I'm sorry I hurt you. It will never happen again." And lay next to me, breathing me in, cuddling my back, we lay there until his Dr rang up from reception. Marcus goes to great her at the lift. She's in her late 50's, with long grey hair tied up in a bun.

"Nat this is Dr Striker. My Dr" She holds her hand out to shake, she has a firm grip.

"This is Natalie, Dr Stricker. I'll leave you to it, in one of the bedrooms, he leads me to. As we go in I kiss his cheek. Sitting on the bed, Dr Stricker speaks.

"Why am I here Natalie?"

"I want to go on the pill, please."

Have you been on it before?"

"Yes, unto about a couple of years ago, when I came off it, as I wasn't dating anyone, I came off it."

"Do you remember what it was called?"

"No, I can't sorry."

"That's ok; everything was ok for you on it though?"

"Yes fine"

"Ok I'll give you some Mriogynon 30, to take every day; it has to be taken roughly the same time every day, and within 12 hours of the last, so take one as soon as you finish your period ok? I want you to just fill the form so I can know a bit more about you, then I'll give you the packets." I filled out all the information in the forms, which was medical. She took the form and showed me how to take the tablets, having sugar pills for the period days, which is just a reminder to take a pill every day. l needed to give them seven days before you stop using protection.

"Are you and Marcus already having sex?"

"Yes, what protection are you using?"

"Condoms, "

"Good, those will last you for 6 months, Natalie, just let me know when you want more, ok?"

"Yes, thanks you for coming."

"It was a pleasure to see you." *Wow no internal exam or going to the pharmacy with a private Dr, how cool.* She unlocked the door, and went to see Marcus, he paid her, then she left, he went outside to thank .her and see her into the lift. When he came back he held me in his arms, on the sofa, just sitting there cuddling each other.

"So I can't take these until my period ends, then it'll work out fine, thank you Marcus

"I couldn't bear to go back to that Medical Centre ever again. They got photos of me going in and out though. And I was recognized, in there, being talked about, was awful." He cuddles me

"You won't have to now ever."

"Thank you. I do forgive you Marcus, it's all forgotten about as far as I was concerned, after our being together yesterday,." But obviously being in this place, right now, was bringing him back to where was when I left.

"Let's go out for dinner somewhere, anywhere away from here right now, and then we can go through any furniture changes, later. Ok?" He didn't feel good in there that was certain.

We went out, in the Bentley for dinner at a place neither of us had been to. Actually recommended by Barker, not takeaway, it had good food, it was out of the way a bit which we both liked the idea of. When we approached the country restaurant called "Oliver's" after the man who owned it we went in through the main entrance; it was like a big bar with tables at the side, less 5 star, than we were used to but has it was early still, hardly anyone in it yet.

"Evening, can I help you?" The barman was short and tubby.

"Nat?" Marcus looked at me.

"Bacardi and coke, please" I spied a very old but comfortable sofa, that we could chill out in, with a small table next to it. I pointed to where I was going to Marcus, who ordered his drink, whilst he watched me, sit down. He picked up a menu for us, and bought it on to the table.

"That looks comfy?" He sat down nest to me with his glass of Bourbon, and put my Bacardi on the table, and he put his arm round me.

"I am sorry Nat, I feel so awful when you're with me, in the penthouse, so fucking guilty, and so we'll go to my home tomorrow, ok?"

"Sound's perfect to me." I kissed him gently on his soft lips.

"I really am over it though, it's only in your head of what happened, I truly forgive you Marcus, we'll sort out how to deal with your birth mother, when's she's released, we have a little while, so just please chill.'

"You'll help me, deal with her?" He sounded surprised.

"We're in this relationship together Marcus." He sat with his side on the sofa, taking his shoes off, and me alongside him, the sofa was huge, we cuddled up there for a while until he was hungry, I'd already eaten at lunch, so I was quite full, apparently he'd not had much since the toast, this morning.. He went to the bar and ordered his beef lasagna with salad, and my prawn salad. He came back, with more drinks too. He sat down.

"You wanted to tell me something that happened to you, I'm all ears.' He put his arm around my shoulders. *I was ready now.*

"Nearly two years ago, I was out having a walk, with an old boyfriend of mine, who said he wanted to get back together, so I agreed to meet him at a forest out in the hill near here, so we could go for a walk. Basically he never turned up, he said he changed his mind. I went to go for a walk anyway. (Which I will never do again, as long as I live) I was taken away, and bundled into a car boot, 5 men held me captive, in the woods; I was not heard of by my friends, family or police for 8 weeks. Every hour, I was put on display, with a blindfold on, and they gang raped me. I knew I had to get away, but had no idea where they had me. There was always one of them around to abuse me. One day after the 8th week, I managed to untie my hands enough to be able get out of the place, they had me, I just kept on going, until I was worn out, I had to keep going eventually found a clearing in the woods, then I found a house, where the couple let me use their phone. They told me I was in Canada, which is why I didn't recognize anything I came to. I called mum and Al who were hysterical, and thought I'd been killed weeks ago. I couldn't identify anything; I'd got no idea of what they looked like, as I'd been blindfolded. Nor what they sounded like, they plugged my ears with I don't know what, but I was without sight and sound for all that time. The police never got any further, because, they couldn't prove anything. My ex was taken to the police station, but he knows absolutely nothing even on a lie detector test." I begin to cry, *which I've not done since, it happened.*

"FUCK! Nat Shit, that's unbelievable I don't want that to have happened to you, You are so lovely not you please," He kisses my head, and tears start to come in his so sad eyes.

"It's something I hope that the press doesn't find out about, for your sake."

"Fuck me, what about your sake Nat." He was so angry and then sad again. Our food was put on the table, and he carried on stoking my head, to take away my pain. He kissed me on my forehead, trying to kiss it better.

"What about you being tied up and blindfolded in the playroom, that must remind you of it, so much, fuck Nat fuck them."

"It's odd but I thought about it, before I did it, I'm in love with you, it's what we both, like to do, as consenting adults, I find it erotic with you, I said to Trish and Rosie, separately that you'd actually helped me move on, from all that, it's something I and my good friends and family only know about. The police in Canada will probably have some records, but maybe not, as they couldn't take it any further. I just want to forget it Marcus, forget it ever happened"

"Fuck them" He was clearly annoyed with them. I put some food on his fork.

"Please eat Marcus there's nothing you can do about it." He started eating a forkful, and I ate some of the prawns on my salad. I sipped my glass, and he his bourbon. He looked at me with such sadness, for me, I could feel it oozing from him.

"Marcus it's something I have to live with, just like you do. When you told me about your birth Mum, I felt a kind of affinity with you, someone in your past made you do things, you didn't want to do, it made me lose my self confidence, thinking something was wrong with me. I haven't been able to have a relationship, with a man, because I felt like shit, and didn't trust anyone. It could have been them, playing games with me, and I wouldn't know, Marcus but until now I haven't been able to share it with you, now I have I'm glad." I kiss him passionately, my tongue entwining his for about 5 minutes, we are held in a pleasant moment of bliss, escaping everything from our pasts. We are just focused on the enjoyment of right now, together

Chapter 18

As we fly out of the Long Beach Airport, Marcus winks at me, taking control of his baby and flying home so we can both finally chill out in the privacy, of his acreage home. He flies towards L.A. I *feel better for telling him, but I can't say he does, because he doesn't. He wants me to let him find out who did, it with, so many contacts, but at the moment I just want to leave it, maybe, I'll let him pay to have the records taken away, I haven't decided yet. Time will tell.* I gaze at his adorable face, which I love so much, the thought of just spending the next two days alone with him, is sending me into a sexual frenzy, my hot Marcus. When we got back from the restaurant, last night, Marcus put the key in his desk drawer, in his office then locked it. He thinks by just not going in there is going to help both of us, I'm not so sure. I do like it in there with him, would like to have the option of keeping my hands free just so I can hold him, that's what I really miss about it that's all. He wants to think about it another time, but I'm not convinced he will, he wants' me safe so do I, but when I'm with him I do feel safe. I don't think he believes that. He had got brochures and

locked them in with the keys, I'm happy to just put different things into a different room, choosing things together, so the thought of Kelly is long gone, that's all. As we fly over the acreages, we're getting closer now; he confirms the landing with L.A. Airport, he gets confirmation, and starts to descend, to the H in his garden. *I swear his flying gets better, or perhaps he just wants me safe,.* As he lands, he turns the controls off and does his post flight check. Smith is coming out, he opens the door for me, and now the rotors have stopped.

"Thanks Smith?" He helps me out. Marcus gets out the other side and comes to take my hand, as he walks me to our home for the weekend. *I do love this place, as I see it again memories, of happy times, flood to me. Although if I did eventually choose to live here, it would get a change of décor, perhaps to something even Marcus and I like.* Walking toward the house, *we are truly blessed to find such solace here. We got here early; it's only 9.00am now, so we can chill without the penthouse or the presses anywhere close. Marcus has a 10 foot double brick wall around the house, going on for all around his acres, with an electric fence on top of that, so I'm feeling so safe here, especially when he takes my hand like this, and we just go for a walk.* Arriving at the house, He tells Claire to tell Smith to get my suitcase out of the back, if he forgets. I hug Claire, as she welcomes me again.

"I have a full buffet, breakfast if you're hungry?"

"Maybe, in a little while when I've chilled a little, we didn't get any breakfast, this morning, because we wanted to get here." I took Marcus's hand again and we go upstairs to the master suite, and lie on our bed, he cuddles me around my back, as we lay yet again breathing in each other's aroma. He holds my hand, and kisses it, and stoking it gently like he's trying to brush the hurt away. I'm in awe of his Marcus smell, coming through he has no aftershave on, and he's going with my love of his stubble for the weekend, to see how he likes it.

"We've got plenty of time, I'm really hungry now, let's eat" he leads the way, I'm glad he's finally hungry; he didn't get much to eat much last night. We go downstairs, passing Smith with my suitcase as we do. We go into the dining room, and there is indeed a feast set out between us.

"This will all get eaten, by Barker, Smith and Claire, if we don't finish it, so only eat what you want," His leg wrapped around mine, he looked at me adoringly at me, he left a warm feeling of love, flowing between us. I put some, strawberries, and blueberries on top of some vanilla yoghurt, I spooned into my bowl. It tasted delicious of course. Then I got some just made mini pancakes, from the warmer, drizzling maple syrup over it, again Claire had excelled herself, yet again, no wonder the men eat what's left. In

the corner of the dining room, voila, a coffee machine,

"Did you get another one for here, I pointed at the machine, or has it moved from the kitchen?"

"New one, always' new when required, there's also a new one in the boathouse, if you hadn't guessed. I'm a man of my word, always Nat." He blew me a kiss. I made us both a coffee, it was of course, warm and ready to go.

"Do you always organize everything here so perfectly, or is that Claire?"

"I believe its Claire; she likes to know when we are coming here exactly, so she can work wonders like this gorgeous feast." He waves his hand over the food. I put his then my coffee on the matching mats, on the table.

"Thanks." He sips it. I have had enough to eat now, sipping my coffee, I think I'm now addicted to real coffee, as I can't see myself ever buying instant. Marcus finishes his mushrooms, bacon and eggs; he pushed his plate away, and sipped the rest of his drink.

"You want to come for a walk around the garden; I haven't shown you it all yet?"

"I'd really like that Marcus please"I got up and went to grab his outstretched hand, tingles went through me, *I hope that feeling is always there.* He has a very casual look today, with his stubble and uncombed hair, with his denim jeans and a dark blue t-shirt. He looks hot as usual, but just so much more casual, which I like. *Even though his business suits are a huge turn on, I prefer him casual, like this.* I was already dressed in denim jeans, and a black cotton camisole top, that he bought for me the other day. Walking out of the dining room, into the hall, he stopped to kiss me, passionately Claire walked past quickly not meaning to be there, at all.

"Sorry" she rushed as she moved out of the way.

We moved out into the garden, and started walking, down the driveway, on to the footpath, that seemed to go forever. We stopped at some brick outbuildings near the house that had driveway access. The first building he unlocked the door; it had his toys in it.

"This is where I keep my boys toys, after you Nat." He moved into the building, he had 2 two motorbikes; cycles, Jet Ski, Porsche 911, Quad bike, horse saddles hanging, and in proactive glass covers he has so many guitars, electric and acoustic ones, some signed.

"Wow this is a great room." I walk around to the guitars, and looked at them. They were all in a pristine condition.

"Yes, I keep everything I want to keep in good condition."

"These are signed by the people it says on the cards next to them, that's cool, did you do that?"

"Claire does things like that, she was my woman's touch, I suppose, until you walked into my life." We wander round.

"So you have a horse?" I gaze at all the equipment.

"Not any more, bit boring going on my own, I had it for a couple of years, and then wanted it to go to someone that would use it. It was worth a small fortune, so I donated it to the charity Mum is involved with, so they could either , sell it or get abused kids to be able to ride, doing something different for them, they kept it, and have great fun using it." I kissed him on the lips, pulling him towards me. *He is so generous to others.* We walk out to the path; he grabs my hand as we walk to the next brick building, which is huge.

"This is the staff quarters, where Barker, Smith and Claire all have their own separate, home; they each have a single garage around the other side too." He walks me round.

"I won't go in, it's their space, but it is huge."

"Yes they have their own 2 bedroom complete home in each one." I saw that it was like a terrace of 4 homes.

"Why 4?"

"Because I can." He grinned. We walked to the end of the footpath that had another, more modern building, right near to the river.

"What's this?" He opened the side door.

"An undercover pool, so I can keep it warm all year. It's also got electric, sides that all go up, al fresco style. It's got a bedroom, too so I can enjoy it, and then relax. Sometimes I work so hard, it is a great retreat for me."

"Can I see the bedroom?"

"Sure." He opened the door. There was a king size bed, with black silk sheets, and quilt on it. Then an en suite, which was huge with a double shower, like the penthouse.

"Have you bought anyone else here to use the shower?" I quizzed.

"Why?"

"Just wondered why you put it in?"

"I just went with what I had already at the penthouse, and here. Why do you want to be the first to use it?"

"Come for a swim now?"

"Ok but you have no togs?" He looked at me.

"There are no cameras pointing here are there?" I smiled and led him inside.

"No, oh naked." He caught on. We took off our shoes and clothes leaving them in the bedroom. He stood looking at me, as I stood there, and I gaped with joy at his erection.

"Swim first Marcus."

"Oh" We got in, the warm pool, swimming to the edge; it was beautifully warm, just perfect. He swan up to me, kissed me passionately, his erection, was hard and ready for me. I swam away to the end of the pool, where it was about six foot deep. I was an excellent swimmer, so I wanted to get away from him, and he was fast too, diving under the water, trying catch me before I got where I was going.. Finally I let him catch me, because I was so hot for him. He came up next to me in the shallow end, pinning my arms to the side of the pool. He pulled me out onto the wide shallow steps. Obviously wanting more comfort for me, he held my hand and took me to the bed. Putting me gently down he moved his tongue so hard on to my clit. Back and forth, he was so much harder than usual, he wanted me desperately, I could see. He gave me a condom, to put slowly on his wet cock, after, licking the tip of his chlorine tasting, cock as he moaned loudly. He moved behind me, and then he put the hard erection into me, filling me with his deliciousness. We spooned like that for a while as he pumped slowly then getting harder, back and forth, kissing my shoulders, lovingly as he did. I could feel my arousal climbing; he came quickly, standing still as he did, and moaning again. I heard him come, sending my erotically charged body into spasms of orgasmic pleasure, I pulsed at least twice; he snuggled up to me, kissing my neck as he did. We lay there in each other arms, whilst he was in me, until he came out, removing his condom, into the bin.

"Thanks for christening the bed?" He looked at me with such adoration.

"Pleasure," that's *all I wanted to know, that he'd been alone here before.* We got in the shower together, too exhausted for more play, he kissed me under the water, passionately, and then we soaped each other, and used his shaver to shave me and his balls, and cock area, which I liked on him, I'd decided. I was careful, but it was a much closer shave than the safety razors, I'd used before. We got our hair, washed by each other too, he tenderly massaged the shampoo in to my head, I had a wonderful massage, as I closed my eyes.

"You like?"

"Yes very much." He massaged my head longer, as I stood holding the shower wall in front of him. I was so very relaxed now. He got dressed, and so did I, leaving my hair to dry au natural. I sat on the bed, looking at him as he; just put his comb through his hair, I messed it up, trying to dry it, he looked so sexy, I could go again, but I knew, I would have to wait. He gazed at me, as he moved his body alongside me on the bed.

"Move in with me, right now?" His eyes were so pleading.

"Oh Marcus, I have to sort all this out, I don't know what to do, if I'm honest. My life has changed so much, over such a short period of time. If I move in there are other things I have to sort out too, work, friends my apartment etc, I know I can't stand the press at my every move, but I have to work this out myself, do you see that?"

"Yes, sort of, but you do want to move in, at some point don't you?"

"Yes I do, it just has to be, once I can think clearly?"

"Ok, I do get it, I love you Nat, and I want to be with you all the time." *That's the first time he's said it* I smiled, and kiss him gently on the lips.

"I love you too, Marcus, I really do. I want this as much as you do, believe me; just give me a chance to work it all out." He took my hand kissing it, and walking to the door of the bedroom.

"Want to out to lunch, I'll drive the Ferrari?"

"Have you got somewhere in mind, because I'm happy to stay here if you want."

"Yes a place up in the hills again that I go to quite often, just want to show you."

"Great, if we walk to the house, I can get my make up back on." We come out of the pool house, and walk hand in hand, to the house.

As we go up upstairs and into the master suite, I put my make up on, he hands me a hairdryer, and once my hairs dried I stand and look at him gazing at me from the door.

"You are beautiful, Nat you know that don't you?"

"To you maybe, I think I have to work on myself, still." He comes over and kisses the top of my head.'

"Ready?"

"Yes, let's go." Walking down the stairs, hand in hand, Claire comes out.

"You are eating out boss?"

"Yes just up the road, at "The Plantation." alright, see you later." He grabbed his car keys, as we walked outside to another garage, I hadn't seen, the door went up, and his Ferrari, was there.

"Who moves your cars around, like when we leave things at the airport?"

"Either Smith or Barker, or I just pay someone to get it here." We got in and he moved us down the driveway, through the solid electric gates, that move elegantly sideways for us, and down the road.

As we twist and turns round the mountain road, Marcus is clearly in his element, he is a phenomenal driver, of a very powerful car. He's happy even as we go the, few mile's distance to "The Plantation", which he tells me is so called because, it used to be a plantation for coffee. It's very big and new, red brick building, with a few cars outside. He parks out the front. He kisses my on the lips, gently as he takes my hand, and we walk in through the big wide red wooden doors. Inside it's very modern, with a bar down the whole of the one side, and a restaurant out the back, with some fantastic views, as far as I could see. We walked to the bar, at sat on the bright red bar stools, that were fixed to the floor. It had live music, I think, but couldn't be sure, as I didn't see anyone playing.

"Nat drink?"

"Yes, a Pepsi max please."

"Two large Pepsi Max with ice please." We took our drinks, to the restaurant area, and Marcus pointed to where he wanted to go, so I could then see the acoustic guitar singer now.

"He's good, isn't he?" We sat on a large table, so we see him and the view behind him.

"Yes I've seen him before, I'm glad you got to see him."

"You are as good as he is, you know?"

"You haven't heard me sing? You wouldn't say that then."

"I've heard you in the shower, you sound alright?"

"I didn't know you heard me, only did it because I was happy around you." He took my hand to his lips and kissed it gently. He gave me a menu, which looking through they had lots of choice's I choose, a grilled chicken and avocado Turkish sandwich. He went to order, as I sat there watching the musician. When Marcus returned, I

really wanted to approach the playroom, which I wanted to just change the décor, and room, but he was so happy I left it, we have plenty of time to focus on that, let's just enjoy ourselves today. Within 10 minutes our food arrived.

"Here you are Marcus, good to see you again." The waiter put his crumbed fish and fries down, it was massive. He put my Turkish sandwich down which also had fries on the side of it. I looked at Marcus.

"Sometimes you just wish you got what you ordered, I'll never eat all that?" I had fun trying through, and only 3 very long fries left.

"Well done, I didn't think you would, after you gorging out at breakfast."

"Gorging, I wasn't I had just as much as you." *Cheeky moo.* We were going to have one of their really scummy desserts that looked heavenly, but my tummy was full. As they had been a coffee plantation before, they did have the most blissful sounding coffees, so we each, had one *we* were still listening to the guitar player, whose singing was awesome.

"Wow these are good, aren't they?" He sipped his cold drink.

"They are, perhaps get them on "The Seaview" menu?"

"Right now I just don't want to think about work, but its good idea Nat. Afterwards do you want to for a walk?

"That sounds great, after the music finishes, I think he stops in a few minutes, looking at the board, he has near him.

"Ok" We listened and drank the last of our coffees, I went to the ladies, and put my lipstick back on. Looking in the mirror I realized that I felt like the luckiest, woman in the world today. *He was just the most wonderful man alive, as far as I was concerned. He didn't take what happened to me well, but I know that we'll get over it, together. I want to help him decide when he's ready about his birth mother, but I know he's so stressed over it, so I'll wait just wait for him to approach it.* As I came out, my hot sexy man took my hand, and thrills as always pulsed in me. We walked down the footpath; luckily we both had casual shoes on. It was a spectacular place, the plantation itself was quite barren, but around it was a path, which went through the fields of grass, meadows and through forests. We walked across the top of the plateau, where we stopped and admired the glorious 360 degree, spectacular view.

"How about that for a view?" He put his arms around my body, tightly as we stood gazing at the true beauty of the place.

"It's simply stunning Marcus, thanks for bringing me here, it's so awesome."

"I'm so glad you like things I like, we are such a wonderful match, don't you think?"

"I do."

"Please move in with me?" He turned me round, kissing long and slow, still holding me so tightly."

"We have just been there Marcus."

"Ok what if I buy another place for us to live in, Long Beach, and you can still work, if that's what you want?"

"Not yet."

"Please?" I took his hand, and walked further along the plateau. He stopped me when we got to a seat at the end, sitting down he held me, in his arms, and kissed me so lovingly and passionately. We sat there, at the top of the world it seemed, bathed in such love, as the sun shone down on us. He then stopped asking, but he knew I would, when I was ready. I was glad that he now, appeared to be resigned to that.

"Want to go back home now?"

"Ok, you just want to drive your car don't you?"

"I do love it, it's true, and you love it nearly as much as me I think."

"I do, let's go then." As we start walking slowly, back along the plateau, and along the path, we end up at the Ferrari, looking red and sporty. We get in, and he puts the media player on with the Foo Fighters, playing loudly.

"Awesome, I love the Foo Fighters, too"

"We are a match aren't we?"

"Yes, just drive Marcus." We sang along, slightly off key, looking at each other as he turned the car round, he blew me a kiss, before going out of the car park. We were happy, singing something we both loved, with a hint of sexual innuendo passing between us, for what was to come when we got back home. It was a Ferrari sticking to the ground thrill for both of us, he was a great driver. We went round, and round getting slightly lower on the hill. Then Marcus grabs his chest, and his eyes are closed, the car comes, off the road on the hill, down the lower incline, through the bushes and grass. The airbags go off, I pass out.

Chapter 19

"I'm sure she'll be waking up soon, mum, and going on with her life again." Mum was in tears.

"We only saw her last Friday Rosie, but I'm so glad we did now" She burst into tears again.

"I'm glad too, she was so happy when she spoke to Marcus, wasn't she Al?"

"Yes she was Adele, so happy, what a shame about all this" mum started crying again.

"Sebastian, will be back in soon to see her. Please let her be ok, by then." Rosie starts to cry.

"She'll be ok, Rosie, the Dr thinks she'll wake up anytime, and to keep talking to her, she may recognize your voice, so tell her what went on, in your life, and she will respond, hopefully.

"Nat, it's Rosie your sister, you remember your brother Chris, and he's going to come to see you as soon as he gets back from

England, you remember he went travelling with his friend, well he's coming back to see you soon." She cries.

"Natalie, it's mum, please wake up sweetheart, so I know you are ok? She cries.

"Nat its Al, you remember we had a lovely lunch, at Marcus's restaurant,"

"Don't mention Marcus Al, not until she's awake."

"Oh yea, we had a lovely meal at that revolving restaurant with you on Friday, do you remember? We had a good time and some fabulous food, and champagne, which was so lovely too. Do you remember it all?"

"Al did she just move?"

"No I don't think so Adele, wish she had though."

"This reminds me so much of when Stephen died, in the car accident just the same."

"Adele it's not the same, Nat will wake up from this, and be walking around. Thank goodness she had the Ferrari, which he airbags all round in, otherwise, I don't want to think about it."

"Yes mum, nothing like when dad died, please, I really want her to be safe, please wake up Nat, it's Rosie, your sister, do you remember I'm having a baby? A long time yet, but you are going to be a great, aunt, I promise you. I know you will be."

Rosie sobs,

"Don't fret, Rosie, She'll wake up, focus on that."

"Oh all I know, I'm usually the strong, independent one, now look at me?" She sniffed

a tear back, and held her sisters hand.

"It's ok to be upset Rosie, she's your sister."

"Nat can you hear me, it's mum, we have been here since yesterday afternoon, waiting for you to show some signs of life, please, Nat, please wake up, and talk to me." She sobs.

"Adele can I get you a coffee from the machine, it's a good machine in this place?"

"Yes please Al, you're a love you know that?"

"You tell me enough dear, so I do know yes. Rosie would you like a drink from the machine?"

"Yes please Al, I'll have a can of cold drink please, cool me down a bit, all this stress, probably isn't good for baba." She caressed her tummy.

"You'll both be fine, Rosie. You want anything?" Al kissed Rosie on the cheek and then opened the door to leave.

"Yes please, green tea, if they have it?"

"Ok, see you both in a minute."

"Nat, its mum please wake up soon, just show me your beautiful eyes. You know Rosie after she got back from her kidnap, when I thought she was dead already, this feels like this right now, with, all the not knowing, whether she will open her eyes."

"I suppose a bit, I always wondered if she ever would recover, once the police got her back from Canada. She hasn't told me the full story, so I bet she hasn't told you? "

"Yes she's been through so much, if I knew what fully happened, if she could tell me, I probably wouldn't want to hear it Rosie." She sobs.

"I think you're right mum." She sits on a chair next to the bed, hugging her mum.

"Hi Al, dear thank you." door opens and shuts.

"Thanks Al" he hands drinks to Rosie and Adele. Door opens.

"Ok Natalie its Nurse Webb here is going to give you some more pain relief."

"When she wakes, up which Dr Straicker expects to be anytime now, let me or the nurses know, please, so we can check she's got enough pain relief."

"Thanks Nurse, we will." Door opens and closes.

"Adele did Chris say what time to pick him up today?" He checks his phone.

"He gets in about 3.00pm he wants to get a cab, so we don't have to leave Nat."

"It's probably for the best, he's so independent worldwide traveler that he is, I bet he's grown up, now. Don't you Al?" Looking at her husband.

"Yes almost certainly. It's 2.50pm now, so only a short time to find out."

"It'll be great to have my brother back again, weird but good." door opens.

"Sebastian, love did you sort out what you wanted to do?"

"Yes thanks, Rosie. She looks the same doesn't she; please wake Natalie, there a lot of people are here for you. Its Sunday, you came into here on Saturday, your mum and Al want to catch up with you. This all feels silly doing this Rosie."

"I know, but she is supposed to be able to hear us, aren't you Nat." Door opens, door closes.

"Trish! How good to see you again today, she hasn't changed." Adele sobs gently.

"So I see, come on Nat, its Trish your best friend. Please talk to me, I miss you so much, did you know that Andy, your flat mate, and Megan who works at our work, I think are seeing each other, he swears they're just friends, she on the other hand, is besotted." Door opens and closes.

"Chris," He is wearing denim jeans and blue t-shirt, and a knapsack, on his bag, which he puts by the door, as he comes in.

"Mum, it's good to see you." He hugs her, and she holds him for a while.

"Al how are you?" He shakes his hand.

"Rosie Sebastian congratulations both of you on your baby news." He shakes his hand, and hugs his sister.

"Hi Trish how are you?" He hugs her, for a minute.

"Great thanks Chris, but rather Nat wasn't like this." Door opens

"Sorry too many people in here, could we keep it to just 4, until she wakes up."

"Chris and Trish you stay as you've just got here" Al is polite. Door closes.

"Hey Nat its Chris your favorite brother," He holds her hand, and stands over the bed.

"Your only brother Nat." Trish nudges his arm.

"So did you enjoy yourself, travelling?" She stood opposite, sides of the bed from him.

"Yes it's actually lots more fun when you have a friend to go with, but he fell in love with some girl in London, working in a bar, so now he's staying there, and I didn't know what to do, to be honest. Then I heard about Nat yesterday, and obviously I got on the next flight back." He gazed at his sister.

"Its crap seeing her like this you know, she's my big sister, but she looks so peaceful I couldn't bear it if something awful happened to her, I just couldn't." He looked atTrish.

"It's ok, we all love her, I know her like a sister, as you know" She gazed at him.

"I know, when I had to come back here, I was looking forward to seeing you again Trish isn't that odd, after all this time." He gazed back at her.

"It was 4 years, Chris, I thought Nat and I would be real sister in laws at the time, and you didn't want all that then." He went to, her hold hand, and she pulled it away.

"4 years is a long time Trish, I've changed, What if I did want to see you again?"

"Oh fuck!" *my head.*

"She's awake, Trish she's awake I'll get Mum and everyone" He hugs Trish then door opens, he calls to the others.

"Natalie, its Dr Straicker here, can you hear me?"

"Oh what?" *Fuck where I am?*

"You can hear Natalie, everyone out for a while please, whilst I am checking, her vitals." Door closes.

"Yes" I wipe my eyes, as I open them. *I'm still so tired. There's a nurse I'm in hospital, shit.*

"Good now Natalie, you've been in an accident, yesterday, do you remember?" *Marcus, accident* I open my eyes; I can see flowers all around.

"Marcus?" I shout.

"Yes you were in an accident with Marcus, do you remember?" I nod.

"Are you in any pain Natalie?" I shake my head.

"Ok so I'm going to take you off pain now, you have to let me know if you get any headaches or pain anywhere else ok?" I nod my head.

"Marcus, is he ok?" *I remember him blacking out, as we went down the hill.*

"He's had an operation yesterday, Natalie; we have to wait until he wakes up, which probably won't be until tomorrow. He and you are in one of the best Private hospitals in L.A. He had a minor heart attack, so we have to watch him closely, he may be in here for a while Natalie. This is one of the best for surgery, at Garden Groves Hospital, so he has the best care money can buy. "I *was glad of that.*

"Will he be ok?" I try to sit up.

"I hope so, Natalie, I'm popping in on him every day, so if you want to know anything just ask me." I have a drink of water, from my bed tray in front of me.

"Can I see him?" *Fuck, where are you Marcus, I must find you; fuck it hurts, when I move.*

""I'll take you after your family have all seen you, yes, I'll get you in there, His parents are in with him right now, and since he came in, you've met them Mary said"

"Yes, they are lovely" *I can't believe it, not my Marcus.* Door opens door closes.

"Nat, you're awake, thanks god." Mum cries in relief, and she and Al hug me tightly. *She looks like* shit.

"Hey there, sorry for all the worry, Chris you're back, wow, this is all unreal." He looks relieved and hugs me, on the other side of my bed.

"Did the Dr tell you what happened, and to Marcus?" Rosie, had tears as she spoke.

"Yes, I remember the accident, he will be ok won't he Rosie?" I start to cry.

"We hope so, Nat. they are the best heart surgeon's working with him, so I hope so too Nat." Al is straight to the point. I start getting up,

"I have to see him now, the Dr. said I could, I'll be back later, sorry guys, I just want to see him now." I tell my family I can't *just sit here, when he is somewhere in this hospital, without me.* Al pushes a wheelchair from the side of my room, and I get into it, as he heads, out of the door with such love, of me, I can see.

"Dr Straicker, said can I see him?" I told Al, as we got into the corridor and I see the Dr waiting to take me, she takes my step dad's place.

"You ready?"She asked.

"Yes, will I need this chair, or can I walk now?" We go in a lift.

"This is just temporary, Natalie, just have a rest, you seem fine, but I want to make sure, you are perfect, before you leave here, ok?" The lift door closes, and we go to a different floor.

"This is hopefully just a temporary place until he wakes. Are you ready Nat?" *Shit no*

"Yes" She knocks and leads me into a room where his parents are by his side, there he is, just looking like he's asleep. I walk to his side, glancing at Mary, who has his hand.

"Natalie, I'm so glad you're ok." I hug her so hard. Then go to John, who gets up from his bedside chair, and hugs me too.

"How is he Mary?" I look at Marcus's face which doesn't have a mark on it. *It must have been the airbag's that saved us both. He looks so peaceful, I'd prefer him alive talking to me over this any day.*

"He had exploratory surgery, when he came in. They are doing all they can for him."

"Do they know what caused the mild heart attack?"

"Could be lots of things Nat, I just want him back again, I can't take this any longer."

"I know I do too, we just had such a lovely day too. There was certainly nothing he was stressed about right then, we were singing as he drove down the hill."

"Really, he never ever sung, you certainly changed the way he did things Natalie, in a good way."

"He plays beautiful guitar too, you must have heard him."

"Yes he started playing when we moved out here, as a thirteen year old, and loved it, didn't want any lessons just to choose what to strum away on."

"The Dr's also say he may have inherited this from his bitch mother."

"Mary she gave birth to him, and if she didn't we wouldn't be with him all these wonderful years."

"True I suppose, but how she treated him for 12 years, makes her a bitch."

"I don't doubt that." He sat and read a newspaper. I went to the right side of the bed, stoking his cheek, with my hand, kissing his hand.

Please come back to me Marcus, I want to make love to you, in the pool house, this time you can use handcuffs. Please I love you so much. I looked adoringly at him.

"The nurse says he can hear us, so to talk to him" Mary holds his hand tightly.

"You know Mary it's true, I now remember the people talking before I just woke up, I just heard them, couldn't do anything else. So I know that's true."

"Would you like me to go while you talk to him Natalie just over there, we have a suite attached we can go to, I need to have a little break."

"Thanks Mary", she got up, dragging John with her. I held Marcus's hand, which was attached to a drip, and monitors, ticking in the usual way.

"I love you Marcus, do you remember me and you going down the mountain, you closed your beautiful eyes, Marcus I thought it was forever, fuck you know what if anything happened to you I couldn't go on, do you know just how much you rocked my world Marcus, and I yours too I think, I know. If I had said yes to living with you in the pool house, we'd have never gone out to The Plantation. I should have said yes, to you Marcus, tears well up as I realize this. I love you so much, I think if you didn't have money or celebrity status, I would have yes, from date number 1, It was me having to adjust to your wonderful lifestyle, the press was too much, but if I was living with you when you first asked me, then we'd have been together all that time, and not sitting here. I truly believe that. I want to have my Marcus cuddling around me at night, to hold me, breathing in my smell and yours as we lay together. Please Marcus wake up, I love you, and you said you loved me out loud, please come back to me." I kissed him gently on his lips, making sure not to touch his mouthpiece. Mary walked in, *I hoped she hadn't heard but then really didn't care anymore.*

"None of this is your fault Natalie, he had a heart attack, it's not something you could possibly have foreseen, it could have been anywhere" She *heard me then.*

"You know he asked me move in with him, now then,"

"He was in love with you, why wouldn't he want you to move in with him. I know you wanted to, it was so clear looking at you both, from a distance so to speak" We whispered to each other over Marcus, looking into his sleeping eyes.

"It was just way to soon; I'd never had anyone that made me feel the way he did, ever.

"I had everything moved around because of him, the press just got too much and when he picked me up Friday, he saw how much they were chasing me, he wanted to help,, but the only way to do that is go the next step, it's a big thing after just meeting someone, who you fall for. To being the live in partner of a multibillionaire, moving work friends everything to be with him. But I wasn't ready, but ask me when you wake up, see what I say them Marcus, my love." I kissed his hand. Mary smiled at me.

"What did he like to do, apart from his guitar when he was a teenager?" *Visions of a young frightened Marcus fill my head, I make them go away..*

"Not a lot actually, as I said he didn't talk to me for months."

"That must have been so sad for you?"

"Yes, he spoke to John though; John and I built up the business, getting Marcus to understand it as much as we could. He had been losing out at school, with her so we had him privately tutored, by a man, who was able to get him though the basics, after he was about 15 he was more interested in the business, and he'd got the skills to do it. He is a clever person, must have got it from his grandparents." She smirked.

"So tell me what happened the other day about, his bitch mother getting released, because he gets a bit angry when I try and discuss it."

"Well the English Law at the time was, 20 years for life, no parole. So she's done her time when he is just 33, so the prison contacted me as his legal mother, ask him if she can contact him."

"He doesn't want to, I know that."

"Well who would, perhaps she wants to say sorry? I don't care what she wants; it's all up to him. He said no when I spoke to him, as I knew he would, so that's what I told the prison when they called."

"Good" I kiss his hand.

"I just hope that's the end of it now, for his sake."

"I forgot about my family, that came to see me, I'll just pop back and see if anyone's still here, I'll be back as soon as I can.

"You're in room 33 on the next floor down in case you get lost Nat."

"How did you know that you've been here all the time?"

"I've been down a few times to see if you woke up, met your mum and Al they seem lovely."

"They are lovely, thank you."

The Dr. took me by wheelchair to the lift, and then down to my room, where she leaves me, back on my bed. Chris and Trish are still in there, but everyone else has gone by the looks of it, as I sit on my bed, thinking.

"Nat how's Marcus?" Trish moves her gaze to me.

"Same, have mum and Al gone?"

"No just went for a walk whilst you're with Marcus."

"Oh good," I sit on my bed, feeling exhausted, *I'll sleep well tonight, I wonder if I can be with Marcus tonight?*

"Nat, how's Marcus, any change?" Mum sits next to me, as they come back from their walk. She stokes my cheek.

"Nothing mum, I didn't know you met Mary, Marcus's mum?"

"Yes she knows very well how Marcus is with you; she really wanted you to get through this with him."

'Ah how lovely."

"Rosie said see you tomorrow she'll pop in later in the day."

"That's great. "

"Nat we're going to make a move now too, we have got to get Chris back for a sleep and catch up on his travels. So we'll come down tomorrow too ok?"

"Only if you want to? I'm fine as you can see."

"I'm your mother of course I want to."

"Ok see you all soon," Trish had a cheeky grin on her face, as she waved goodbye. *Wonder what that's about?*

 I looked my iphone which was on my drawer, 6.00pm; I turned on the TV for the local news, to catch up.

"The main story is the same as yesterday. The parents of Marcus Carrington are at the bedside vigil, of their only son and heir. Marcus was with his girlfriend Natalie, when he apparently had a mild heart attack on Saturday after returning from lunch together. We are told by the family that Natalie now fully conscious. John Carrington himself was outside the hospital, a few hours ago, when he gave us this speech." the video of Marcus's dad plays. "I'm so pleased to announce to you all that my sons girlfriend has woken up and appears to be fully well. Both my wife and I are very pound to have Natalie, in our lives, she's a wonderful person. I have prayed for my son Marcus to wake too, so they can move on in their very happy life together. I would like to thank the well wishers, hold a vigil outside the hospital and for all these beautiful flowers" He finishes. I peer outside of my window there are hundreds of people out there, and the flowers all over the garden down to the road.. Some one sees me and points so I wave, I've now got cameras on me, for once I don't mind, these people care about me and Marcus, Look at the love that's coming out down there, I couldn't believe it, what I was running from truly loved me. I wave and then disappeared up to Marcus. As I went back in I held John so tightly, and kissed his cheek.

"I just saw you news video, thank you John, I never thought the press could love anyone more than Marcus and I, did you see those flowers, there are hundreds of people out there, wishing us well, I get it now." We walked to the window, and waved at those loving people, it really wasn't for publicity, the Carrington's aren't like that, and they were as real as the hope on the man's face below us.

Chapter 20

"Ah!!" He pulls at the tube from his mouth, and opens his eyes.

"Marcus, thank god." Mary squeals, waking me.

"Marcus are you ok?" Johns at his side, then gets the Dr. I gaze at him from my bed that had been put next to his, as I wouldn't leave him.

"Marcus, are you alright?" He sits up.

"What happened Nat?" His Dr and John come in; he gives him the checks for hearing, sight etc, all seem fine. He removes his tube.

"Marcus I'm Dr Hinde, your had a heart attack on Saturday afternoon, you've been in surgery when you came in, and asleep since then. I'll let you talk with your family, then if you have any questions let me know." He left.

"Mum what is going on?"

""Do you feel any pain son?"

"No, I'm fine thanks dad,"

"Mary let's give them some space, now he's awake. We'll go to get a breakfast ok?"

"Yes, I'm starving, so glad you're with us Marcus, "I love you, see you soon, ok?" He nods as they go to the café. I go to Marcus and hold him tightly, and kiss him gently on the lips, he feels soft to the touch.

"Nat I remember us going to lunch and then down the hill everything went black as we did, it felt weird, and my chest hurt."

"Does it hurt now still?"

"No, what happened to you, you look ok?"

"I saw you grab your chest and close your eyes, and then I blanked out. That was Saturday afternoon, and it's now Monday morning."

"Wow, I had a long sleep then?"

"Yes, I woke yesterday; I'm fine I just wanted you to wake up."

"I think the airbags in the Ferrari, were what saved both of us, I mean neither of us, has a mark on us."

"I'm so glad you're ok, don't know what I'd have done, if I killed you, by having a heart attack, Nat. You're so special to me, you know that don't you?" He kissed my hand gently

"I couldn't bear the thought of anything happening to you either. I was starting to blame myself for going out, when it happened, but as you're mum said, it would have happened at home or somewhere else, if it was going to happen." He hugged me as he sat up straighter against the soft pillows.

"What happened to my car, I don't remember it rolling or anything?"

"We'll ask your dad when he comes back; I don't know where it is. It saved both of us Marcus, so I love it very much, not as much as you though." I kissed him passionately, as I lay down on the bed next to him. He hugged me back tightly, *god I'd missed his touch.* Mary and John come in, and I get off the bed, holding his hand still. They smile.

"We can give you more time?" I shake my head.

"No come in, I'm going now to get a coffee from the café, in the hospital, John?"

"Yes go down to the ground floor and it's all marked clearly, next to the shop. I can come if you like?"

"I'm alright John, but thanks."

I was able to move around easily now and hated the wheelchair, so I walked in my white hospital gown to the lift, and pressed ground. There were a few nurses and visitors, in there. The lift door opened, and I made my way to the café, which was near the front double glass electric doors. In the café there was a TV, showing the news, I watched as I stood in the queue. "Breaking news, we have just had John and Mary Carrington, here outside the hospital, and have the following report. A video followed;

"We are pleased to tell you that our son Marcus, has just become fully conscious- *cheers* -he is fine, and we hope him to leave as soon as the doctors are happy, in about a week, they tell us. Natalie is with him right now. Tears, thank you for all your support," Mary fades out. *She really is so lovely, so is he.*

"What would you like, cappuccino today I think," checking they had the proper stuff. I sat down, and saw people outside, starting to move away there were heaps of flowers still there for him, which he wouldn't want. I finished off my coffee, and then asked one of the staff to help me. Not wanting to outside in my gown, the attendant, got the flowers, inside on trolleys, then took each one around to each department, there were hundreds, of them so everyone would get some. I left him to it thanking him for his help. He smiled, as he went on his journey. I went into the shop and bought the local Bulletin, which of course had us on it, and a book, for Marcus to read, whilst he was here. I also bought, some toiletries, as my mum had bought some stuff in on Saturday, it wasn't quite what I wanted,. I was getting hungry, and the hospital food was quite nice, despite my discerning tastes now.

By the time I'd walked back to Marcus's room, he was with a nurse, who asked me if I was ready for breakfast now. I nodded, she went and got some food, and Marcus got off his bed to the table to eat it with me, his parents weren't there, I assumed they'd gone.

"Hi I said as I hugged and kissed his beautiful mouth fully, he tasted of just Marcus, au natural, *yum we* ate our bacon and eggs, with whole meal toast, which filled me, I can't remember eating since the Saturday lunch. *I sit gazing at him, he's back, he's actually alive, I had such crap thoughts going through my head, since I woke up. I'm so happy I really am.*

"When did the Dr Say you can go?" I hug him.

"He wants a week, but I'll go mad in here Nat." *Fuck I want you now, you have set my sex drive into action, and all I can think of right now, is you fucking me, anywhere, it's only been a day, since we had sex, I am so fucking horny ,I'm dripping wet right now.* I smooth his raucous, hair around his ear.

"I hope you're out sooner too, I have all sorts of things planned for you." I grinned wickedly at him. *I feel so fucking satisfied, every time he is inside me, and I come. He's the only one; I've been able to do that with ever, and that's the way I want it between us.*

"And for you?" He finished his food and put his water glass on the table.

"I think I'll go tomorrow, I'm perfectly well." *The thought of going back to work, suddenly didn't feel as appealing right then, as I said it.*

"So am I." He pouted.

"I have to go back to work, so I'll come in after to see you ok?"

"You could take some more days, off and stay here, I'm covering the costs. I can support you know that." I nodded.

"I know, and thanks but I think I'd be bored like you, if I take some holiday I can spend some time with you, when you get back home ok?"

"I just want you to stay, here, until I have to go Nat." He kissed my hand.

"I know, but I do have things that I have to get done at work, so when I take holiday we can spend all our days together, able to do whatever, whenever, rather than be monitored by the cameras if I gave you a hand job." I grinned.

"Oh, you say the most erotic things, do you want to try now, I'm getting a hard on?" His erection was huge under the table, as he pulled my hand towards it. His mum and dad walked in.

"We are going to come back tomorrow, give you two sometime together, Marcus, we have put you on leave at the store so you have a few months if you want to, but you don't usually, so just take all the time you want, until you get into work please. We both will be taking over from you, at home and wherever, so all's good ok. Just so you know, we want you to be totally well before you come back ok?" His dad put his hand on his shoulder, as Marcus concealed his erection under the table, along with my hand moving up and down slowly, gently, touching the head, very gently, not to hurt him.

"Yes fine dad, I will take some time off, I don't normally, as you know, but I have Natalie now, and she's told me she's taking some time off, so we can be together, when I come out. So I will take some time off thanks both of you." His dad smiled, and his mum went to kiss his cheek, she looked at me. Marcus winked at me, as I kept him so hard.

"That was a really nice thing you did getting all those flowers, to the other patients Natalie, we found out someone we knew was in here, and went to see them, and the attendant, gave her some flowers, she was stoked , as were all the others I saw. Thank you for doing that."

"It just seemed such a shame to leave them to wilt, and go in the bins. I knew he wouldn't want them, the attendant was very helpful, he did it all really" I lost my concentration with his cock.

"You are a wonderful person; give yourself some credit, Natalie." She kissed my cheek then they left. Marcus had lost his arousal unfortunately, as I had to let him go, to hug Mary.

"That was nice, you are a good person," He pulled me over so I sat astride him on the chair, and his erection grew again he could see my wet pussy, as I opened my gown he parted my slim legs further, so he could kiss my wet fanny and then he kissed me passionately, our tongues entwined, with my pussy juice in both of us, he moaned as I put my hand around his hard cock, under his gown, *no one could see, if they came in I hoped.* Moving my hand up and down, he moaned again, and passionately kissed again, moaning in my mouth, as he came, all over his gown and my hand, I kissed him on his neck, gently and softly, his stubble had really grown by now, he was so fucking hot, so mine. We sat cuddling his arms went tighter round me.

"I love you, so much." He looked satisfied.

"I know, and I love you too Marcus, I never want us to be in any kind of accident ever." I leaned back looking at his wet gown.

"Perhaps you can get changed in to clothes now?" I looked for some, and found a suitcase, packed with underwear, pajamas and 2 pairs of, jeans, black trousers, and 3 t-shirts, and a couple of casual shirts.

"That suitcase is from my home, so Barker must have been here, I think." He has a shower in the en suite, next to us and changes into the clothes. He looked well. He put the wet gown in a bin out of sight, as we giggled, like excited kids. I put my family off that afternoon, because I was perfectly well, and wanted to spend more time with Marcus, before I left.

The nest morning, I kissed him; Barker was waiting for me, outside, the new more spacious room they'd moved him to.

"Please stay?" I shake my head, not really knowing why I was leaving him today, he looked so sad, and hot at the same time.

 "I got you something to read yesterday. "And I pull out "Fifty Shades of Grey." He laughs not knowing what it's about, it's meant for women, but I was hoping we'd get a few ideas?" I grinned at him, walking away.

"Oh well I'd better read it then, now you've got me thinking, thanks, see you later." He opened the book. Barker came to the lift, and we go down together. He is dressed in his dark blue, single breasted suit, with a white collared shirt, with smart black tie today.

"We are all so glad you are both ok, Claire went into shock, and we had to get the Dr out to her, she's fine now, it was so unexpected, I'm glad you both ok now." He was older, than I first thought; now I had a closer look at him.

"Thanks Barker, we are too." I looked at his hard face, knowing he had a heart of gold, not having seen much of him really so far.

"Claire made this packed lunch for me to give you, you know what she's like." He hands it to me. I can see lots of baked goods and a little salad with a separate dressing container.

"Oh that is so thoughtful, thank you, I don't even know your Christian name do I .what is it?"

"Oh that wouldn't be right, I like to be called Barker, anyway." We got in the Limo and he drove me to work. I put the lunch in my bag.

"Thank Claire for me would you?" I said as I got out of the car, into a throng of flashes.

"I will, I'll be here at 5.00pm or just text me on this number, he gave me a card, if you want me any other time like lunch time, ok?"

"That's great thanks see you later Barker." He nodded and moved off. I looked at his card which just said David Barker and his number. *So then I knew David, it suited him.* Walking up the stairs into reception, Megan welcomed me back, and I thanked her.

"Nat how are you, should you be here? Donna sounded so concerned.

"Thanks Donna, I'm well thanks." I looked for Trish and then went to the kitchen, not there. *Odd* so I made a coffee for me and Donna, and went back to my cluttered desk.

"Where's Trish?"

"Must be late, she hasn't called in sick or anything." I carry on with my desk, *I was getting sick of having to catch up all the time, it was constant, perhaps I should change offices or something, I so want change here, I can't see me doing this for the rest of my life, what if I did move in with him, what do I do with this job. Oh I'll work that all out at some future point, he hasn't asked me again, anyway.* Trish walks in all rushed, putting her bike jacket over her chair.

"Oh hi Trish, where have you been?"

"Promise not to scream?"

"Why would I scream?" *Can't think of any reasons, what's she on about?*

"I'm moving in with Chris, we're going to get our own place, I mean rented, but in our names." I screamed happily.

"How did that all happen, I'm so happy for you both."

"When we saw each other at your bedside, we just talked and talked, I'm glad you didn't hear, some of you wouldn't want to hear." *Oh that's why she was smiling yesterday, when they left.*

"So when is this all happening? "

"We want to find somewhere, as soon as possible, Nat; I'm in love with him, always have been I think, I nod, I'm moving out of mum and dad's as soon as I can." She was so excited. *I was too, they were good together.*

"So is he getting a job round here then?"

"Yes, he already saw someone who he used to work for, and they're happy to have him back."

"That's the best news Trish, you've already been together for a couple of years, you'll be fine."

I really am happy for them. I hugged, for a while.

"Yes it is, good for you both, good luck." Donna is happy having seen her go through the break up. The rest of the morning went quickly, having so much to do. Chris, arrives at lunchtime, to take Trish out to lunch, they speed off on his motorbike.

Donna is having lunch with her husband. Meagan is out with Andy, for lunch. I sit alone, and take my picnic lunch from Claire, and put it out on a plate from my hamper, from Marcus, which made me laugh again. I got the last of the wine, into a glass and sat to eat. I felt very lonely, right then; *Trish is going to be meeting up with Chris at lunch now, so I was barely going to see her. I'm so happy for her though, I felt trapped, by the media outside, not being able to just go for a sandwich, without photos all over the place.* I called Marcus, and ate my lunch, and wine.

"Hi how are you feeling?"

"Bored, except for that book you gave me it's given me some ideas." He laughed wickedly.

"Well Trish and my brother, are going to move in together, which is good, but I always have spent my lunches with her. So I'm bored too. That should keep you happy."

"Not really, I am totally well and I could be wining and dining you right now, not being fussed over, by doctors and nurses, I want to leave here early, they can't stop me walking out."

"Are you sure you want to do that?"

"Yes, I am well; he shouts at the room, I can go anytime I want to. So are you with me?"

"Yes I'm all ears." I smile.

"How much holiday can you take?"

"I think about 4 weeks, but it's the timing more than that, they have to get cover for me if I'm off that long."

"There are agencies, they go to?"

"Yes, when did you want to escape Marcus?" *This was sounding much more fun.*

"Today, pick me up now." He screamed.

"Well I can't do today; I'll see what the boss says, ok?"

"Ok just as soon as you can please." I felt the sadness in him; I went to Mr. Smith's office, luckily he was in working.

"Hello Natalie, what is it? You are ok after the accident aren't you?" He put the file, he was holding on his desk.

"Well I could really do with a break if I'm honest, Mr. Smith, is there any way I could take 4 weeks off say tomorrow? My boyfriend is coming out of hospital, after a heart attack as you know; I really want to be there to make sure he's ok?" I put my sad look on.

"As long as you can find a locum Nat, go tomorrow, he'll need you around, when he gets home won't he?" *Sweet!*

"Yes he will, Mr. Smith I'll have to take care of him then."

"Then find a locum and go, I'll see you when you get back." I was excited, I phoned the locum agency, and arranged for the replacement to be there tomorrow. *Sorted* I phoned Marcus back told him the good news, he was so excited. So was I, about to spend a month with the most hot man, I'd ever come across, a big smile crossed my face. When Trish and Donna came back I told the plan

"That's so awesome, have a great time won't you?"

"Of course" knowing Marcus was a fit as fiddle, made me wet. In the afternoon I left the work I had to do, as the locum was coming, I really didn't give a dam instead I had a plan, and had a few phone calls to make, that took up the whole afternoon.

Barker picked me up at 5.00pm I was singing as I left the door. As I got in the flashes went off. I turned to Barker, who had undone the privacy window.

"So you will get someone to pick my car in the car park here and drop it off at my place undercover, ok, that still all ok?"

"Yes that's fine, he'll be there soon, I gave him your spare keys this afternoon. And everything else is sorted, for tonight too. He'll be surprised hopefully."

"Yes I do too, "

Barker dropped me off at the hospital, and stayed outside. I went in to Marcus who had his bags packed ready to go, by the door.

"I told the doctors I'm going, and they gave me all the crap, but I said I'm going to relax at home with you around for the next four beautiful weeks, so they gave me their blessing." Grinning, he flashed his early release form, with visits to his Dr. regularly, their only obligation.

"Good lets go home, Barkers outside, just didn't want you to fly yet."

"They said it's ok to have sex, I checked." He smiled.

"As if that would stop you" He kissed my lips as we, went into the lift for the last time. I held him so tightly.

Barker opened the doors as we got to the car, his face was a picture.

"Well how do you feel, now you have carried out your escape?"

"Better, happier than I've been in a very long time." He kissed me passionately long and slow. He must have run out of jeans, in his suitcase, as he's got his sexy white linen open necked one on, with his smart black trousers. He was so fucking hot sitting there I did think about doing something about it, but I had weeks of him, I got hotter looking ham. As Barker pulled in through the gates, we want down the driveway towards his beautiful home. It was a warm night, we got out and he took my hand, as we walked through the doorway. Cheers came ringing out loud from Claire, Barker and Smith as we walked through to the lounge room, which was full of live music from his favorite guitar player, his mum and dad came and hugged him. My mum and Al met him for the first time, Rosie and Sebastian he'd met, Trish and Chris had come. His face was a picture of happiness; which is all I wanted, he got me a drink of Bollinger for him and me.

And then he went down on one knee in front of me.

Silence as he opened a Tiffany ring box.

"Marry me Nat?"

Fuck!! "Yes."